"I'm sorry. I shouldn't have led you on,"

Carrie whispered, pushing him away with the last of her willpower.

Brock's hands were shaking. He took a deep breath, hoping it would calm him. "You didn't lead me on, and there's nothing to be sorry about. I wanted to kiss you, so I did. Correct me if I'm wrong, but I thought you wanted that, too."

"I did. I mean, no, I didn't." Carrie ran a hand through her hair. "I don't want any part of...of men in general. I have my son to think of and—"

"What a crock!" He took a step back so that he could see her face better. "Half the world's made up of men. Are you writing all of us off because of one mistake?"

Carrie got her breathing under control. "I'm just not interested." She turned on her heel and started walking away.

In two long strides he caught her arm and swung her around. "The hell you're not. You can lie to your son, your friends and yourself, but you can't lie to me. I kissed you just now, lady, and you kissed me back. You can hate it, you can deny it, but you can't change it. You're interested, all right. As interested as I am."

Dear Reader,

Welcome to the Silhouette **Special Edition** experience! With your search for consistently satisfying reading in mind, every month the authors and editors of Silhouette **Special Edition** aim to offer you a stimulating blend of deep emotions and high romance.

The name Silhouette **Special Edition** and the distinctive arch on the cover represent a commitment—a commitment to bring you six sensitive, substantial novels each month. In the pages of a Silhouette **Special Edition**, compelling true-to-life characters face riveting emotional issues—and come out winners. Both celebrated authors and newcomers to the series strive for depth and dimension, vividness and warmth, in writing these stories of living and loving in today's world.

The result, we hope, is romance you can believe in. Deeply emotional, richly romantic, infinitely rewarding—that's the Silhouette **Special Edition** experience. Come share it with us—six times a month!

From all the authors and editors of Silhouette **Special Edition**,

Best wishes,

Leslie Kazanjian,
Senior Editor

PAT WARREN
The Long Road Home

Silhouette Special Edition

Published by Silhouette Books New York

America's Publisher of Contemporary Romance

To Chris Flynn
For commiserating and critiquing,
for laughter and friendship

SILHOUETTE BOOKS
300 East 42nd St., New York, N.Y. 10017

Copyright © 1989 by Pat Warren

ISBN: 0-373-09548-1

First Silhouette Books printing September 1989

Books by Pat Warren

Silhouette Special Edition

With This Ring #375
Final Verdict #410
Look Homeward, Love #442
Summer Shadows #458
The Evolution of Adam #480
Build Me a Dream #514
The Long Road Home #548

Silhouette Romance

Season of the Heart #553

Silhouette Intimate Moments

Perfect Strangers #288

PAT WARREN,

the mother of four, lives in Arizona with her travel-agent husband and a lazy white cat. She's a former newspaper columnist whose lifelong dream was to be a novelist. A strong romantic streak, a sense of humor and a keen interest in developing relationships led her to try romance novels, with which she feels very much at home.

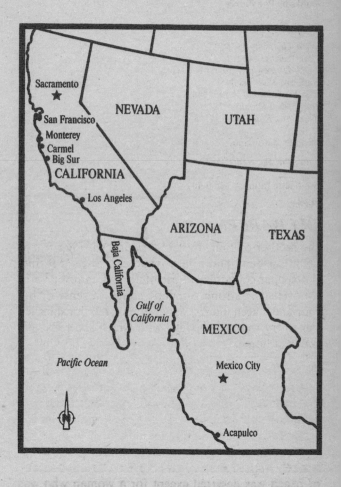

Sacramento
★

San Francisco
Monterey
Carmel
Big Sur

NEVADA

UTAH

CALIFORNIA

Los Angeles

ARIZONA

TEXAS

Baja California

Gulf of
California

MEXICO

Pacific Ocean

Mexico City
★

N

Acapulco

Chapter One

It had to be her. Brock Logan braced one shoe on the bottom board of the weathered fence that separated the scenic overlook from the beach area. He leaned forward to study the painting more carefully as the afternoon sun bounced off it. The canvas propped on the easel wedged into the sand was a seascape in watercolors, subtle shades of blue and green building to stronger hues. Her style was unmistakable, exactly like that of the smaller painting the decorator had shown him only yesterday. And very reminiscent of a photo in a newspaper clipping his friend, employer, and now partner Victor McKamey, still carried neatly folded in his wallet. Yes, he'd found her.

A strong Pacific breeze ruffled his hair, but Brock scarcely noticed as he lifted his eyes. The small stretch of beach was deserted except for a woman who was strolling toward him, the frothy waves swishing around her bare feet. She wore a white oversize shirt, its sleeves rolled up on her slender arms, and dark shorts barely visible below the low hem. He could tell that she thought she was alone by the way she lifted her face to the sun, shaking her head as the ocean breezes swirled her jet-black hair around her shoulders. That, too, fit the picture he'd seen of her. To be certain, he had only to check for the deep violet eyes that Mac had spoken of.

As she stared out to sea, evidently lost in her thoughts, Brock brought his attention back to the still damp painting. Brushes soaked in a jar next to a three-legged stool. She'd captured the sea on a calm day, yet there was a definite electricity, a masked power, a sense of suspended anticipation in the way the waves rushed in against the welcoming sand. A lone cypress clung to nearly bare rock on one side of the canvas, while a red sail, a vivid speck of color, fluttered on a boat near the horizon. He wasn't a student of art, nor a connoisseur by any means, but he recognized talent when he saw it. And so had many others, at least along the west coast, as he'd learned in the past few days.

The signature in the corner read simply Carrie. No last name, no clue as to a further identity. Brock straightened and thrust his hands into his pockets, studying the woman who had bent to dig at something in the wet sand. Most artists he'd run across wanted, or perhaps needed, publicity and recognition. The artist known only as Carrie evidently wanted none and had in fact seen to it that she'd be difficult if not impossible to locate. He couldn't help wondering why.

As legal counsel for McKamey and Associates, a highly respected architectural firm based in Chicago,

Brock Logan had completed many difficult assignments for Mac. But this one was a gift, pure and simple, and one he'd undertaken strictly on his own. Over the years, Mac had told him the story often enough of the daughter he hadn't seen since she was ten. Though Brock didn't approve of the callous way that Carrie, who had to be twenty-eight now, had treated her father, he knew that despite his hurt Mac would give anything to see his daughter.

Adjusting his sunglasses, he watched the woman stoop to wash whatever she'd found in the swirling foam, still oblivious to his presence. He hadn't consciously set out to find her. But, having spent the last month in California finalizing the details of establishing a branch office for Mac's company in Carmel, he'd made a few inquiries, aware that her last known address had been in this area. But he'd come up empty-handed until yesterday when the interior designer working on their new building had brought him a vivid seascape, recommending they purchase paintings by this new artist whose work was suddenly in great demand. Studying the style and the signature, he'd immediately wondered if Carrie could possibly be Mac's daughter, Carolyn McKamey Weston.

The decorator had been able to tell him only that her paintings were available exclusively through the Sonya Nichols Art Gallery in Carmel. The woman at the gallery hadn't been much help. She'd given him the pitch for the paintings, but the minute he'd mentioned trying to locate the artist, the officious redhead had clammed up. He wasn't sure why. Brock watched the waves pound in and smiled, thinking perhaps Sonya had never run into his particular brand of persistence before.

He'd hung around awhile in the small shopping center where the gallery was located and finally had gotten lucky when the delivery boy came out to load a large painting into his truck. A California surfer type, Andy had turned out to be friendly and talkative. He didn't know where Carrie lived, or her full name, but he did tell Brock approximately where she could usually be found painting at this time of day. Brock had driven down toward Big Sur along the coastal highway south and finally spotted the rock formation Andy had mentioned. He'd parked his red Ferrari next to a vintage yellow Volkswagen and climbed out. And now he had only to wait until she came back to pack up her things. Brock watched her rise, stretch her arms toward the sky, then wrap them around her slim frame as she gazed again at the relentless waves, and wondered what she was thinking.

Carrie glanced at her watch and saw she had another fifteen minutes before the bus would arrive. Now that the painting was finished, she'd allow herself a moment longer to enjoy the beauty of the sea, to feel the water splash against her legs, to listen to the rhythm of the waves. It never failed to fascinate her. She was certain there were many beautiful places in the world, but she would choose to live nowhere else.

Closing her eyes, she let the salty spray caress her face as she took a deep breath and hugged herself. This painting, along with the three completed ones in her workroom, would fulfill her obligation to Sonya for the summer. Now she could get started on some larger pieces, and, if Sonya was correct and the demand for her work was still greater than her output, perhaps by the end of the year she'd be able to reduce her bank loan by another sizable amount.

For seven long years she'd been paying on it, with another eight to go. However, if as her reputation grew, her asking price could also increase, then perhaps she could whittle off a couple of years and be indebted only another five. Carrie sighed, realizing that that still was a very long stretch. But worth it. Yes, worth every moment of it, because she had her independence and she had Shane.

Carrie pocketed the delicate ivory shell she'd found and rinsed off for Shane, smiling at how pleased he'd be to add it to his collection. He was what made it all worthwhile, the long struggle to learn, the sacrifices until her work had at last caught on, the occasional lonely moods that always caught her unawares. Shane's smile, his bright laughter, his warm hugs were all she needed, along with her work, to make her happy. Shaking off her momentary melancholy, she turned and started back to her easel. She'd taken only a few steps when she glanced up and, startled, stopped in her tracks.

His forearms propped on the rickety fence, a man leaned forward studying her painting. It was unusual, especially at this time of day, to see anyone on this somewhat forlorn stretch of beach, where treacherous rocks half hidden by the surf made swimming unappealing and dangerous. Carrie frowned as she resumed walking, not pleased to have her solitude invaded or her work inspected without invitation.

Though bent forward, he was obviously quite tall, with broad shoulders beneath a yellow, short-sleeved shirt tucked into tan slacks. Her artist's eye noted an angular face with a square, determined chin and eyes hidden by reflective sunglasses, the kind she hated, the kind one could hide behind. His hair was several shades of blond, thick and curly along his neck. He was tan and fit looking, and, though she couldn't see his eyes, she knew he'd shifted his gaze and was watching her approach. Her eyes flicked to the expensive red convertible parked next to her car, then back to him as she stopped near her easel. Shaking back her hair, she waited for him to speak.

Violet eyes. Even through his sunglasses, Brock could see their unusual color. It was her, he was certain. He could see the wariness in her gaze, the suspicion in her stance. He'd have to move carefully or she'd bolt like a frightened doe, he felt sure. Straightening, he put on a friendly smile.

"I like your work," he said.

"Thank you." She bent to reach for a large, leather portfolio and carefully inserted the canvas, zipping it closed. "Just passing by?"

"Not exactly." He liked her voice, husky and deep, but wondered at her challenging tone. Brock took a couple of steps back, giving her a bit more space. She looked like a woman who didn't like to be crowded.

Carrie placed her portable palette and tubes of paint into a satchel. Finishing, she glanced toward the busy highway about five hundred feet beyond their parked cars. Slightly reassured by the nearby traffic, she looked up at him. "Then what are you doing here?" Shane would be along any minute, and she was getting nervous.

"Marsha Chambers told me about your work," he said, mentioning the decorator. "Do you know her?"

Carrie shook sand from her sandals and slipped her feet into them. "I know *of* her." Draining water from her brush jar, she put the brushes and her rags into the satchel, slung the strap over her shoulder and faced him. "How did you find me?"

"Through Sonya Nichols."

Bending, Carrie stepped between two wide-apart slats of the fence and moved to her Volkswagen. Next to it, his red sports car sparkled in the afternoon sunshine. The contrast with her slightly beat-up Bug didn't escape her, most likely an indication of the differences in their life-styles as well. His suit coat and conservatively striped tie were flung across the back of the leather seat on the passenger side. A slim cordovan briefcase with the initials *B.L.* engraved in gold rested on the cushion. She shoved her bag into the backseat of her car, her mind racing.

Sonya would never tell anyone where to find her, of that she was certain. Who was he, how had he tracked her down and why? She walked back to the fence but kept her distance from him.

"Try again."

His lips twitched, and he gave her a crooked smile. "You caught me. I bribed Andy, her delivery boy. He told me where you could be found painting most afternoons." He watched as she thrust one fist on a slim hip and digested that.

"Take off those sunglasses." He did, and Carrie almost wished she hadn't asked. She found his eyes to be deep blue, slightly amused and as arrogant as she'd guessed they would be. It was broad daylight on a sunny afternoon with a steady stream of cars passing mere yards from them. There was nothing for her to fear. Yet she felt a shiver race up her spine as she regarded him. "You went to a lot of trouble to find me. Why?"

She was taller than he'd estimated from afar, her legs long, tan and slender, yet she still came only to his chin. Her skin was the color of fresh honey and the hair that the wind wouldn't leave alone was black and silky. If her mother had looked like this—and Mac had told him she had—it was small wonder his friend had lost his head over her. "I want to buy a painting."

"If you're new to the area, I might tell you that there are easily a hundred artists in and around Carmel. Maybe more."

"It's you I want."

She'd been right, Carrie thought. A determined chin and a very determined man. She stepped back through the fence. "You wasted a trip. I sell only through Sonya's gallery."

"I don't like working through middlemen."

Carrie stopped in the act of folding her easel. There was a hard glint to his eyes, though he was obviously trying to be affable. Only to get her to do his bidding, most likely. He didn't seem the type who usually had to do much persuading to get his way. "No, I don't suppose you would." She carried the leather portfolio carefully to her car.

Brock picked up her easel and stool and followed her. She was going to be stubborn. Instinct told him if he mentioned her father's name, she'd jump into her car and leave him behind in a swirl of dust. Odd, considering that Mac had been the wronged party.

He watched her settle her painting in the backseat of the Volkswagen. The old model was sprinkled with patches of rust and had a deep dent that wasn't recent on one front fender. Though she used expensive sable brushes, her other equipment was ordinary. And her clothes were certainly not from an exclusive boutique. Something didn't add up here, he decided.

Marsha had told him what attractive prices her work was commanding, and he'd seen the price tags on two pieces at the gallery. Then there'd been all the money Mac had sent her through the years. He remembered the wedding picture Mac had shown him, yet she wore no rings. Where was the daredevil fly-boy she'd married? Had she cleaned out that poor sucker, too, and sent him on his way? Why was she looking like someone's poor relative when he knew that wasn't so? Maybe he could appeal to her fondness for big bucks.

He waited for her to open the trunk, then wedged the easel into the compact space. "Are you familiar with San Carlos Street, off Ocean Avenue in Carmel?"

Carrie picked up her stool. "Yes."

He draped his arms over the open door, watching her. "There's a new building that just went up there, across from the inn. Two story, gray stone. I'm authorized to commission a painting for the lobby, a large painting. *Your* painting. I pay very well." Brock watched her shove the stool into the trunk and slowly look up at him. He had her full attention.

His expression gave nothing away, Carrie thought as she searched his face. There wasn't a soft thing about him, including his eyes. Why, she wondered, did she sense a hint of disapproval in him? He didn't know her. Was it simply a disdain for all artists? "*How* well do you pay?"

He mentioned a figure and watched her eyes widen before she carefully masked her reaction. So she was as interested in cash as he'd guessed she was. He should have known from all he'd heard about her.

Carrie was certainly beautiful, but undoubtedly only the sound of money could make those gorgeous eyes light up. Brock felt a twinge of regret.

Buying a little time, Carrie closed the lid of the front-loading trunk and took several moments to find her keys. For years now, she'd steadfastly guarded her privacy, choosing to live in an artists' community that respected that right. She'd worked at home, sold only through Sonya and had never commissioned a custom painting. She had her reasons, and they were valid ones. She'd never been tempted to break her own rules. And now this stranger had popped out of nowhere offering her a chance to cut the debt she owed in half. But how many strings were attached? She dangled her keys and leaned against the front fender.

"That's a great deal of money." She squinted up at him. "What's the catch?"

He allowed himself a small smile as he stepped back away from her car. "No catch. Don't you think you're worth that much? I could cut the figure in half if it would make you feel better."

She ignored his attempt at humor. "What kind of building is this? Offices? Apartments?"

"Offices. Accounting, architecture, attorneys." All under one banner, McKamey and Associates, but he was purposely avoiding mention of that.

"I see. And what's your connection?"

"I'm the attorney representing the owner of the building." Which was the truth, as far as it went. He held out his hand. "Brock Logan."

She hesitated a moment before slipping her small hand into his. Her skin was smooth, Brock noticed, her grip stronger than he'd expected. In a split second, she pulled her fingers free of him. "And you're Carrie Weston?"

She nodded as she twirled her keys, then looked down as they dropped to the ground. As she leaned to pick them up, her hand encountered his, as he bent to retrieve them for her. Together their fingers closed over the ring of keys as they both straightened. He was very near, giving off a warm, pine scent, clean and masculine. For a long moment, she studied his lean, strong hand and waited for him to relinquish his hold, wondering why her pulse was suddenly uneven. His light touch made her long irrationally for more contact.

He held on, forcing her eyes to finally rise to his. "Will you do the painting for me, Carrie?"

She never reacted to men this way, Carrie told herself, never let herself get close enough to allow it. She wished she didn't need the money. She wished she could tell this man with his quiet confidence and probing blue eyes to go away and not upset her world. But she owed it to Shane to do all she could for both of them. She tugged the keys from him. "I'll take a look at your building."

"Great. When?"

Just then, a horn honked twice. Carrie pulled her eyes from Brock's and looked toward the highway. The school bus, driven by a friendly woman named Dory, had pulled off the road. As she yanked the handle to open the door, Dory waved to her, just as she did every day when she dropped Shane off. Carrie had hoped the man would be gone by the time Shane arrived, but it wasn't to be. Carrie waved back, then broke into a big smile as her son came barreling around the front of the bus. He ran toward her, the tail of his green striped shirt half in and half out of his white shorts, his grin displaying a new gap in the front where he'd lost a tooth only last week. As always, her heart turned over at the sight of him.

The bus pulled away as Shane landed in front of her in a cloud of dust and thrust his lunch box into her hands as he held up a slightly wrinkled paper. Still smiling, Carrie took it from him.

"I got a star today, Mom. In spelling. See?" His attention suddenly shifted to the man standing by their car. "Hi." Then he saw the red Ferrari and his eyes grew huge. "Wow! Is that yours?"

Brock had watched the little scene with keen interest. From the moment the bus horn had sounded, Carrie's eyes had changed. The hesitant wariness had been replaced by a bright anticipation. Though she'd shot him a nervous glance, her obvious pleasure at seeing the boy had taken over. So she had a son. Mac's grandson. Hair as black as his mother's curled into his collar, and his eyes were an odd combination of Carrie's and Mac's, a sort of blue-violet. As if a reunion with his daughter weren't enough, now there was a child to introduce to his grandfather. Brock hadn't been certain he'd done the right thing by interfering in Mac's personal life, but now he knew he had. If only he could pull it off. He watched the boy move closer to his car.

"Yeah, it's mine," he said, walking with the boy. "You like convertibles?"

"Yeah. How fast does it go? I bet no one can catch you in this car." His dark eyes danced with the possibilities.

Brock found himself fighting a smile. "Pretty fast, all right, but the police get a little nervous when you race around public streets." Driving west from Chicago, he'd opened it up on a stretch of deserted highway, and the car had responded like a dream. But he didn't think that was the sort of thing to tell a small boy who couldn't be more than seven or eight.

"Can I go for a ride in it?" Shane asked, peering over the door at the dash.

"No!" Carrie came closer and slipped her arm around his slim shoulders. "We have to go, Shane."

"Aw, Mom, just a little ride?"

"You could come, too," Brock offered, looking amused at her quick protective instincts. He was, after all, a stranger to her and her son, so he'd expected the refusal. What he hadn't expected was to find soft vulnerability in the face of a woman he thought to be cold, insensitive and unfeeling toward the man who'd done everything he could to be a good father.

"I think not," Carrie said, turning her son and heading him toward the Volkswagen. "I'm all packed up, ready to go. Aren't you hungry?" Perhaps an appeal to his appetite would divert him from the Ferrari.

Brock watched the boy look longingly over his shoulder, weighing the thought of riding in a red convertible against a probable snack of cookies and milk.

Shane nodded as his mother's tone more than his stomach won the battle. "Yeah, but maybe later we could go, right, Mom?"

"Perhaps," Carrie said noncommitally as she opened the passenger door.

"Anytime your mom says it's okay, I'll be glad to take you both." If he couldn't win over the mother, maybe he could capture the son. He held out his hand to the boy. "My name's Brock Logan."

A little taken aback by the man-to-man gesture, Shane nevertheless rallied quickly and reached to give Brock's hand a quick shake. "I'm Shane Weston. I'm almost in third grade." He shot his mother a hesitant glance and caught her frown.

Carrie didn't bother to hide her annoyance as she shut Shane's door and circled the car. She didn't know what exactly Brock Logan's game was, but she did know she didn't like him trying to entice her son. She climbed in behind the wheel just as he came alongside.

"Here's my card. Would tomorrow about one be good for you to come see the building?"

The card bore only his name and a Chicago address. She raised questioning eyes to his.

"I'm overseeing the completion of the California building project, but I work out of our midwest office." As a full partner, Brock also had cards with the company name, but the one he'd given her was deliberately vague. He seldom resorted to subterfuge, yet something told him that if Carrie Weston knew of his connection to Victor McKamey, she'd never show up tomorrow. He waited for her reaction.

Shane had evidently run out of patience with adult delays. He leaned toward the window, intent on capturing Brock's attention again. "Jonathan's going to have kittens."

This time Brock gave in to the smile as he raised an eyebrow. "Jonathan?"

Thoughtfully tapping his card on the steering wheel, Carrie answered almost absently. "We didn't know Jonathan was a female."

Brock braced one hand on the hood of her car. "A vet could probably have told you."

Carrie frowned, as if his suggestion were truly ridiculous. "Why would I take a cat to a vet just to discover what sex it is?"

"So you wouldn't be surprised with kittens."

She turned on the motor, and the sound of electric guitars burst forth from the radio. Carrie turned down the volume. "I like kittens."

"Me, too," Shane added. "And we've got a bird named Zeke. You wanna come see? We don't live far." As his mother turned to him, her frown deepening, his face registered the fact that he knew he'd pushed too far.

Guilt mixed with irritation as Carrie studied her son. This wasn't the first time she'd noticed his ill-disguised interest in sharing the company of a man. She'd deliberately kept their life-style somewhat isolated, thinking his companions at school and his collection of animals would make up for the lack. Evidently it hadn't. However, she wasn't about to invite a strange man to their home to fill that occasional need.

Brock knew when to back off. "Thanks, Shane, but I've got to get back to work." He straightened as Carrie put the car into reverse and turned it around.

Carrie sent him a careless wave as she shifted and started forward.

"Hey!" Brock called. He saw her brake lights go on as she brought the car to a halt, then heard the radio change stations again. He walked over and peered through the window as Anita Baker sang about sweet love. Carrie looked up at him questioningly.

"You will be there tomorrow at one?" he asked. He watched while she searched his eyes as if trying to sort out something that puzzled her. Nervously she worked the brake pedal and again the radio station switched, this time to the twang of country music. He smiled. "Interesting radio."

He had a nice smile, Carrie thought. She'd give him that. But that was all she would give him. "Yes. It's done that ever since I got the car."

"You could get it fixed."

"I kind of like it. Adds variety to my life." She smiled at her own foolishness and gave a quick laugh aimed at herself. But it did little to ease the tension that crackled between them like lightning over a stormy sky.

It wasn't quite the smile she'd given her son, the kind that changed her whole face, but he was still oddly pleased to be on the receiving end. "Do you need more variety in your life?" He saw the quick temper move into her eyes as the smile slipped away.

"No more than I already have."

"Mom, I'm *really* hungry."

"We're going." She glanced up at Brock. "I'll see you tomorrow at one." She stepped on the gas, then stopped at the edge of the highway, pausing for traffic. Gripping the wheel, she wondered if she was making a mistake agreeing to meet Brock Logan, large commission or not.

"He's pretty nice," Shane said, looking out the back window.

"We mustn't invite strangers to our house, Shane. You need to get to know someone before you let them into your home."

"How we gonna get to know him if he doesn't come over?" Shane asked with the peculiar, honest logic of a child. "He sure has a neat car."

Carrie watched a touring bus whiz by. "His having a nice car isn't enough to want to get to know someone."

Shane settled back with a sigh. "Bet he'd like one of Jonathan's kittens. You said we probably couldn't keep all of them."

Stubborn and unwilling to let go of a subject, she thought, just like his father had been. "We'll see." Spotting a break in the traffic, Carrie eased the car across the highway and turned onto the winding road leading up the hillside toward their house. Maybe she could distract him with thoughts of food. "I've got chocolate chip cookies, freshly made this morning."

"Great." He turned his face to her. "Do you think maybe Brock could find us, just in case he wanted to?"

Carrie swung the car around the first bend and glanced out the side window. Far below, on the other side of the highway, she could see him standing alongside his red car, his hands in his pockets, his head turned up toward the road they were following. She remembered how he'd tracked her down, even bribed Andy. She let out a deep breath as she shifted into second gear. "I have no doubt he could find us if he wanted to."

Brock opened his car door and slid behind the wheel. Instead of inserting the key, he continued staring at the narrow road that had swallowed the yellow Volkswagen. She was not at all what he'd been expecting to find. She was a paradox—all soft curves and fiery eyes, undisputed talent coupled with a preference for privacy that bordered on the obsessive, and a smile she was most reluctant to share. Or was it just him?

Perhaps she had a sixth sense that made her uneasy about him, a protective device that shielded her from making hasty decisions. Brock could relate to that, having employed an air of indifference many times in his early years to keep from feeling the pain of rejection. It had served him well, and even now there were times when he had to force himself to open up to someone, to share his thoughts and feelings after all the years of guarding them. Maybe that was why he got along so well with Francine. She demanded so little of him. He'd be willing to bet Carrie Weston wasn't undemanding.

He started the engine and listened to the soft purr as he thought of the dark fire behind the violet beauty of her eyes, the hint of temper he'd seen flare, the self-deprecating humor when she spoke of kittens and temperamental cars. She was a woman to get excited over, if not for one small thing: She was a liar.

If the impression she'd given him today wasn't a lie, or a carefully structured role she'd invented for herself, then Mac had lied. And that thought was inconceivable, for he knew Mac to be the finest man he'd ever met. Besides, why would a man tell another that his wife had walked out on him nearly twenty years before, that he'd sent money and gifts and paid the girl's tuition to art school though he'd never once received so much as a card from the child, if it weren't true?

Mac's disappointment and heartbreak had been clear every time he'd spoken to Carolyn, his devotion evident in the yellowed clippings he still carried, two pitiful newspaper pictures his ex-wife had sent him. The first had shown a teenage Carrie standing shyly beside her winning seascape in an art contest, and the second had revealed a starry-eyed young bride standing next to a somewhat cocky but handsome groom. Lost years, at least lost to a father who couldn't stop wondering what had happened to her. Brock now had the opportunity to find out, and he meant to do just that.

His life was better, richer, fuller because of Mac. Maybe he could return the favor. Brock slipped into gear and felt the smooth response of the powerful motor as he moved to the highway that would take him to his rented house on Scenic Drive. It was time to pack it in for the day, though the late-afternoon June sun was still bright in the sky.

He seldom worked less than ten hours a day, more often twelve, but today was an exception. He needed time to think, to chart the course he would follow in getting Carrie to trust him. A methodical man, he knew that planning was a large part of success. And at thirty-four, Brock Logan felt himself to be a success, though not as completely as he would one day be.

As he swung out into highway traffic, he was disturbingly aware of a mental image—a woman's dark violet eyes that had searched his with intensity and a small boy's hopeful face as he'd asked him to come see his cat named Jonathan. Why couldn't she be as genuine as she looked, for Mac's sake? he thought with a rush of irritation. Though he might possibly be able to deliver her to Mac, he couldn't explain away the past. As he stepped down on the gas pedal, he hoped to hell Carrie Weston could.

Chapter Two

She wanted a cigarette badly, which was not a good sign. Carrie searched through first one kitchen drawer, then the next, but came up empty-handed. Sighing, she went back into her bedroom. It was probably a good thing she hadn't found an old pack hidden somewhere. She'd given up smoking five months before and had been fairly disciplined about it . . . except when she allowed stress to get to her. And this morning, as she dressed to go meet Brock Logan, she recognized the stress that made her so restless.

Standing in front of her closet in her bra and half slip, she contemplated the less than impressive contents. Her life-style didn't call for many meetings with yuppie bigwigs with large checkbooks. She usually let Sonya deal with the moneyed buyers. Reaching in, she brought out a peach-colored cotton skirt with matching shell and long, loose jacket. That would have to do. After all, artists weren't expected to make a fashion statement. She placed the outfit on the bed and went into the bathroom. After unwrapping the towel from around her head, she began to blow-dry her hair.

She should have asked him to write a local phone number on his card. Then she could have called to cancel. As she moved the brush through her hair, she decided that would only have been a postponement. Brock Logan would have seen through whatever excuse she'd given and come to her, which she definitely did not want. He was not a man who gave up easily. Of that she was certain. Carrie turned off the dryer.

A sudden thought had her walking to her nightstand. She rummaged through the drawer and smiled triumphantly as she pulled out a rumpled pack of cigarettes. The matches were on her dresser, and in another moment she inhaled deeply and blew out smoke while she swallowed the accompanying guilt.

"Hot damn!" Zeke said from his perch on the drapery rod above the bedroom window.

"Oh, hush," Carrie told the nosy mynah bird. Just what she needed was a bird who sounded like her conscience, she thought as she studied her face in the mirror of her dresser. A little pale perhaps. She reached for her blush, though she seldom wore makeup at all. Still, she didn't want Brock Logan to think of her as colorless and . . . she threw down the brush.

She took another pull on her cigarette and then carefully placed it on the rim of the ashtray. What was she doing, dressing and applying makeup to please a man? Carrie asked herself. She'd done that once before, years ago, deliberately trying to interest another attractive, charismatic man she'd met. And to her shock and surprise, Rusty Weston had seemed attracted to her as well. The wedding that had followed shortly after had been like a dream come true. The nightmare of the next two years had been something she couldn't have anticipated with her limited experience. When she'd recovered, she'd decided never again. She'd do well to keep that decision in mind, she told her mirror image.

What kind of man was Brock Logan? There was no question that he was attractive, though in a much different way from how her husband had been. Rusty had exuded charm. He had loved excitement and living on the edge of danger, needing applause and the approval of others. Brock, she was certain, didn't need anyone's approval of what he was or what he did. He had a calm self-assurance about him, yet there was that hint of danger in his eyes that probably drew women to him like a magnet. Not this woman, Carrie assured herself.

Taking a last puff, she put out her cigarette and picked up her hairbrush. She needed Brock Logan for only one thing: the money he could pay her for a commissioned painting. And she wished she didn't need him for that. However, as the sole support of herself, her young son and their pet menagerie for over seven years now, she couldn't afford to pass up a lucrative opportunity. But she'd be damned if she'd let him see just how much she did need him, she decided as she pulled the brush through her thick hair.

She'd just finished fastening a gold hair clip at the nape of her neck when she heard the doorbell. Frowning, she grabbed a light cotton robe and tied the sash as she walked to the front of the house. Unexpected callers to her hillside home were as scarce as hens' teeth, she thought as she peered through the peephole. Recognizing her visitor, she quickly opened the door.

Sonya Nichols didn't enter a room. She burst into it like a lioness who'd been caged too long. "Carrie! I'm glad I caught you before you hit the beach with your paints. How are you, honey?"

Carrie smiled. Sonya had that wonderful brand of unpretentiousness that can't be faked, purchased or cultivated. As usual, she was dressed somewhat flamboyantly, today wearing a summer dress in a rainbow of colors, with a wide-brimmed straw hat and impossibly high-heeled pink, strappy shoes. Almost daily Carrie thanked her lucky stars that the gregarious woman had come into her life. In her early fifties, Sonya had short red hair liberally sprinkled with the gray she couldn't be bothered to color out, and the sharpest blue eyes Carrie had ever seen. She'd never married, was bright, funny and outspoken, a woman who answered to no one. She'd become a fixture around Carmel, a city known for eccentric characters. Their business alliance went back a long way, and their friendship had deepened through the years. Quite simply, Sonya was the one person Carrie trusted above all others.

"I'm just fine," she answered, accepting Sonya's quick hug. "And how are you?"

"Never better." Sonya pulled a cigarette from her huge handbag and flicked on her lighter as she eased into the corner of the couch. A very pregnant cat ambled over and rubbed up against her legs. Absently she patted the soft head. "I won't keep you but a minute. I hope I didn't interrupt anything important."

Carrie sat down in the opposite corner and turned toward her friend. "No, I was just getting dressed. What's up?"

"Yesterday a man came into the gallery asking all kinds of questions about you. I thought you'd like to know. Tall, good-looking, well-dressed. There was something about him that made me uneasy. He was damn determined to find you, and I was just as determined he wouldn't. His name is—"

"Brock Logan. Yes, I know."

"He found you. Damn!" Sonya blew out smoke in a noisy whoosh. "How'd that happen?"

Carrie wasn't about to get Andy in trouble. "It doesn't matter. He represents that new building on San Carlos off Ocean Avenue. They want to commission me to do a large painting for the lobby. For megabucks. What do you think?"

Sonya narrowed her eyes. "How much?"

Ever the business woman, Carrie thought with a smile. Of course, Sonya hadn't gotten to be a very wealthy woman by accident. When she told her the amount Brock had offered, the gallery owner let out a long, low whistle.

"I knew your work was catching on, honey, but frankly I didn't know just how well. I hear some hotshot architect from the midwest designed that building. I certainly think they have the money. Are you going to do it?"

"I'm considering it. I'm going over this afternoon to look at his building. If I can do most of the work from home, since Shane will be out of school for the summer next week, I'll probably take it. That's too much money to walk away from."

"That it is." Sonya hesitated a long moment as she tapped the ash from her cigarette. "Honey, you know I think you're the most talented artist for miles around, don't you?"

Carrie smiled. Sonya was so transparent. She felt closer to her than she had to her own mother. Much closer, for Natalie McKamey had been immature and more concerned about her own happiness than that of her daughter. "Never mind the buildup. You have some reservations. Tell me."

"Nothing I can put my finger on. Just a gut feeling."

Carrie considered going to the bedroom for another cigarette, then resolutely put the thought from her mind. "Have you been consulting with Greta again?" she asked. If Sonya had a weakness, it was that she believed her astrologer friend, Greta Godwin, could foretell the future.

Sonya's smile was unapologetic. "Matter of fact, I did have her chart both of us. Laugh if you will, but she tells me there's a planetary shift occurring in your sign heralding a big change in your life."

Carrie laughed out loud. How an intelligent woman like Sonya could fall for that garbage was a mystery to her. "I know, love, money and power will be mine momentarily. I've heard it all before, Sonya. I think I'll stick to things more concrete, like working for a living and paying off my debts. As for power, you can have my share."

Sonya exhaled, watching Carrie carefully through the smoke. "What about love, honey? I hear tell it makes the world go round."

Carrie shook her head. "No, thanks. I've been that route, and I'm relieved to be off that merry-go-round.

I get all the love I need from Shane. And you. *You're* the one who should be thinking about a love match.''

Sonya's laugh was husky like her voice, deepened by years of chain-smoking. ''If I haven't given in to the lure of orange blossoms in fifty-two years, it's not likely I ever will.''

Carrie glanced over her shoulder through the picture window and watched the late morning sun shimmer on the sea in the distance. She knew exactly what Sonya wanted to hear and could give it to her honestly. ''That makes two of us, in case you were testing me.''

''I just don't want to see you hurt again.''

Sonya had been the one who'd warned her about Rusty. She'd also been the one who'd helped her pick up her life after he'd nearly torn her in two. ''Relax, little mother hen. This chick only has to fall on her face once to learn her lessons.''

''Glad to hear it.'' Sonya put out her cigarette and rose. ''I've got to run. Call me later, will you? After blue eyes shows you his building.''

So she'd noticed Brock's eyes, too. It was hard not to. ''All right, I will.'' Carrie walked to the door with her. ''I've finished the last of the paintings you wanted. I'll get them to you by the weekend.''

''Great.'' Sonya nodded toward a picture on the end table, Shane smiling self-consciously around his missing teeth. ''How's my little guy?''

''Counting the days till school's out for the summer. He's talked me into a weekend camping trip that I may regret.''

Sonya made a face. ''Better you than me. When they build a Hilton in the woods, I'll consider camping.'' She opened the door, then turned back. ''Keep your guard up. That Logan fellow looks like he's used to getting his way."

"Not to worry. All he's going to get from me is a big fat painting in exchange for a big fat check."

"Okay, honey. See you later."

Carrie watched Sonya climb into her pink Cadillac, her expression pensive. It had been some time since her friend had felt the need to warn her about a man, and in person, yet. After Rusty, Sonya had protected Carrie almost zealously, despite her efforts to convince her friend that the last thing she wanted was to get entangled with someone again. Finally, Sonya had believed her. And now, out of the blue, came another warning.

With a final wave, Carrie closed the door and walked to her bedroom. What was there about Brock Logan that made Sonya uneasy? she wondered as she picked up her shirt. She dropped the material over her head, pulled the skirt into place and fastened the side button. With a sigh, she glanced over at her nightstand. To hell with it, she thought, and lit another cigarette.

Blowing smoke thoughtfully, she stood looking out the window. Blue eyes. Yes, they certainly were blue.

"Play it again, Sam," Zeke chirped as he cocked his head at her.

Wordlessly Carrie glared at him.

The phone hadn't stopped ringing all morning. Brock put the receiver in the cradle and hit the intercom button. "Rhoda, hold the rest of my calls until further notice, will you?" he asked.

His secretary's voice came back to him. "Will do, boss."

He flicked the switch and leaned back, swiveling his chair to gaze out the expanse of windows in his make-shift office. Wispy clouds wove in and out of distant green hills, and beyond that, the blue ocean stretched as far as the eye could see. There simply wasn't a bad view to be had in this lovely town, Brock thought. No wonder the city fathers were so exacting in their building restrictions. Their reservations, their need for reassurance that a large midwest firm wasn't going to ruin their town, had taken up a big part of his morning, putting him behind in his calls.

That's what he got for taking off yesterday afternoon. He'd arrived home after his encounter with Carrie Weston and had gone for a vigorous swim in the huge pool in the backyard. Mac had designed the oceanfront house he was staying in for a television executive friend who'd recently divorced and was spending several months out of the country on a filming project. After some twenty laps, he'd sat on a lawn chair in the twilight of evening, sipping iced tea and thinking until night set in. After all that time, he was annoyed to realize he hadn't come up with a good strategy for handling Mac's daughter.

She was going to be furious when she discovered he'd duped her. He hoped he could convince her to do the painting. If he could interest her in the project before she learned the truth, she might be challenged enough artistically and interested enough monetarily not to back out. She obviously smelled money. He'd seen enough women like her before and knew that money talked. Too bad, for Mac's sake, that she was more interested in big bucks than in a loving father. But Mac certainly must have suspected that about her, given their past. Perhaps getting to know his grandson would be worth having to dish out more money to Carrie.

Where, he wondered, was her mother, Natalie McKamey, the woman who according to Mac hadn't been mature enough to be a good wife while he'd still been struggling to make it in the tough, competitive world of architects? She hadn't cared enough through the lean years, impatient with his workaholic ways. So she hadn't been around to reap the benefits when he'd hit it big and neither had the daughter Mac adored.

Would that daughter now try to gouge him for more money if Brock reunited them? Remembering her wariness yesterday, her hesitancy, it wouldn't appear that she would. Somehow his impression of her didn't coincide with all he'd heard of her past behavior. But he knew from firsthand experience that women weren't always the warm, altruistic creatures depicted in books and movies. Money could put a big smile on their faces, while the lack of it could make them cold, mean and indifferent.

Brock watched the regal fronds of a royal palm sway in a light breeze. And then there was the child, Shane Weston. Happy, energetic, friendly. The boy had invited him to their home with an almost wistful eagerness. He could picture Mac's face at the first sight of a grandson he didn't know he had. That alone would be worth...

The intercom buzzed, interrupting his musings. Brock knew Rhoda wouldn't be bothering him unless it was important. He swung about in his chair and flipped the switch. "Yes, Rhoda."

"I know you told me to hold your calls, Brock, but Mac's on line one."

"Thank you," Brock punched the first button. "Mac, how are you?"

"Terrific, but anxious to finish up here so I can join you. How's it going?" Mac's voice was rich and strong, the voice of a man who seldom had to speak loudly in order for people to listen.

"Coming along fine, though we've run into a little problem with the zoning board. Those guys on the commission are really putting us through our paces. The latest hassle is over our sign. They're fighting us tooth and nail on the dimensions, the location, even the color."

"Sounds like nit-picking. Why, do you suppose?"

Brock leaned back in his chair. "This is a quaint little town, as you know, and a lot of the residents want to keep it that way. They're simply not eager to have unknowns come in, put up a new building and fill it with newcomers."

"Did you tell them we'll be hiring some locals as well?"

"Yes, and that helped. They're having a meeting this afternoon. Hopefully we'll get the sign approved soon. Are you about finished on the Whitney project?" The shopping center complex designed for the outskirts of St. Louis had occupied a great deal of Mac's time and energy for the past six months.

"Yes, and I'll be glad when it's over and done with. Francine and I should be ready to fly out in a week or ten days. How's that sound?"

"Great. When I know the exact date, I'll set up some press coverage for the building's opening." Brock paused a moment, wondering if he should throw out a feeler, then plunged in. "I think I've got someone lined up to do a large painting for the lobby like we discussed earlier. A local artist, quite popular on the west coast.''

''I'll trust your judgment on that,'' Mac said without a moment's hesitation. ''Are you getting any relaxing in, son?''

Brock realized Mac hadn't connected the thought of a west coast artist to his daughter. He took a moment to absorb the affection in the older man's voice. Nobody had ever exhibited concern for him the way Mac had, not his pitiful father, nor his browbeaten Uncle Joe and certainly not his Aunt Emma. He put a smile in his voice before answering.

''Sure. I knocked off early yesterday, went for a long swim, walked on the beach awhile.''

''Alone?''

Brock laughed. ''Yeah, alone.''

''Since you didn't run into a gorgeous mermaid on the beach, I'll tell Francine to stop worrying.''

Mac had privately voiced his view that Francine Thomas, his executive assistant, was the right woman for Brock, yet he hadn't interfered. Blond and beautiful, cool under fire and efficient beyond belief, Francine had been Mac's right hand for ten years. It had been only during the past year that Brock had seen her occasionally outside of work. He'd discovered that they shared many of the same interests and goals, but he was not about to jump into anything and thought he'd let Mac know that.

''I don't think Francine's sitting around worrying about how I'm spending my evenings, nor do I wonder what she's doing. We're just good friends, Mac, so you can relax.''

"I'm always relaxed, Brock. I'll call back in a couple days. And you take some time off, you hear? You haven't had a vacation in two years."

Vacations were for people who had some place they wanted to see and someone in mind to see it with. He was perfectly content with his work, in his daily routine, and felt no need to get away from it all. But he knew better than to argue with Mac. "I just might. See you soon."

Brock was staring at the phone he'd hung up, lost in thought, when Rhoda buzzed to inform him that Carrie Weston had arrived. "Send her in, please, Rhoda," Brock said, automatically adjusting the knot of his tie. Not that he cared what she thought of him personally, Brock decided as he stood and slipped on his suit coat. It was just that he needed her cooperation for Mac's sake. That was all.

There was a brief knock at his door, then it opened and Carrie stepped inside. She took a quick inventory of the room, before her eyes came to rest on his.

"I hope I'm not too early." She closed the door behind her.

"Right on time." He indicated a comfortable leather chair facing his desk. "Please sit down." An artist worked in color and design, so, naturally, she'd know the ones that complemented her. The muted shade of her outfit contrasted wonderfully with the dark beauty of her hair. As she came closer and sat down, he caught the lingering scent of something floral. But when he moved nearer, leaning back against his desk, the airy fragrance seemed to defy description. Brock cleared his throat.

"Thank you for coming." He indicated the lack of drapes and carpeting, the temporary furniture. "I hope you'll forgive our unfinished state." He placed his hands on the edge of the desk as she lifted her deep violet eyes to his. "I'm interested in knowing what you think of our building so far. Strictly from an artist's viewpoint."

Carrie took her time answering. "It blends well with our community, yet seems to have a personality all its own. The pale gray stone, with the softer shadings of pink rock for trim, is very different for this area. Did you have a hand in the choice or in the design?"

He wished her words hadn't pleased him. "I have no architectural training, so no design input. But I did pick out the stone and trim. The entire Southwest seems to be hung up on beige stucco with red roofs. I thought this would stand out without offending any of the traditionalists."

She gave him a small smile. "I think you're absolutely right. Perhaps you're more artistic than you think." His shirt today was a subtle stripe, his suit blue gabardine, his tie an indigo paisley blend. He wasn't conventionally handsome, nor movie-star attractive. His face was deeply tanned, suggesting more a rugged outdoor life-style than that of a city-bred attorney. But it was his body, the carelessly assertive way he held himself, the casual way he wore clothes so beautifully that set him apart. She tried to hold the look but found her own gaze wavering.

"No, I just know what I like when I see it."

Was she reading more into his words than was there already? Carrie asked herself. She crossed her legs and looked up. "Are you ready to show me around?"

"Yes." Brock held out his hand. "Let's go."

She glanced at his hand. "Is that a prerequisite to the tour?"

He held firm. "Humor me."

Though she felt a flutter of reluctance, Carrie placed her hand in his and went with him. For the next twenty minutes, he took her all over the seven thousand square feet of the building, which was in various stages of completion. The lobby was the first stop. He showed her the spot where her painting would hang, and she found herself admiring the color scheme of blues, ivory and pale gray. Continuing, he introduced her to a skeletal crew of secretarial personnel setting things up. She noticed he had a friendly word for many they passed—painters, decorators, furnace men and a carpenter or two. Carrie couldn't help but be impressed that all the people she met seemed to know Brock by name, and have a ready smile for him. And he was from out of town, a relative stranger, one locals would usually be standoffish with.

"You seem to have fit in with our California ways rather quickly," she commented as they wandered farther along. "You're a little more to this company than just its attorney, aren't you?"

"You could say that. I became a full partner last year." Glancing up, he took her elbow and guided her around a bend in the hallway, where a painter was lettering a name on a glass door. "Let me show you the executive wing."

But something stopped Carrie, a fleeting glimpse that touched a core of remembrance. "Wait." Turning, she walked back to where the workman knelt. When she read the name on the door she sucked in a deep breath, her hand flying to her mouth. "No!"

Damn! He never should have taken her this way, Brock thought belatedly. How could he have known this would be the day the names were going on the doors? He'd wanted to explain things to her in his own way, in his own time. Slowly, he walked back to where she stood in stunned silence staring at the gold letters: Victor McKamey, President.

"Please, let me explain." Brock touched her arm.

Coming alive, she whirled on him, eyes flashing fire. "What's going on here? What's your game?"

Wearily Brock let his shoulders droop. "I have no game." He noticed the workman had stopped painting and was listening with avid interest. Giving him a quick nod, he touched her arm and led her along the hallway and into the first vacant office. Opening the door, he ushered her in and turned to face her as he leaned against the frame. "I'd appreciate it if you'd hear me out."

Carrie took a deep breath, trying to calm herself. Emotions tumbled around inside her like a kaleidoscope gone berserk. She clutched her hands together behind her back, fighting for control. "This better be good."

"I haven't been totally honest with you."

"Well, at least we agree on one thing."

"I told you the truth, that the decorator recommended your paintings, that I went to the Nichols Gallery to find you. I even admitted that I bribed the delivery boy. I honestly believe your work is perfect for our lobby. I had a suspicion that you might be Victor McKamey's daughter, from things he's told me, but I wasn't certain. One really doesn't have anything to do with the other. If I'd have told you all this yesterday, would you have come today?"

In control again, Carrie wasn't pleased at having been tricked, but she was more puzzled than angry at why he'd gone to so much trouble. She found Brock to be oddly honest in his deception. "No, I wouldn't have." She walked to the wide windows and stood looking out at the beauty of the distant sea. Damn him for dredging up her past and the feelings she'd thought she'd buried.

His mind racing, Brock watched her. He was handling this badly, which was unlike him. He wanted something from this woman, something only she could give. Not just the painting, but the reunion with her father. Undoubtedly, for her kind, he'd have to sweeten the pot. He put on his most sincere smile.

"You think I have ulterior motives," he began. He watched as she turned to face him, never realizing before how cool a color violet could be.

"Don't you?"

"The most important thing I want is your painting. I won't deny that I'd be pleased if you'd agreed to meet with your father but..."

"No!"

Despite the hint of reluctant curiosity that he saw in her eyes, she swung back to the window. He could afford to be patient. "All right. Just the painting, then."

"I don't know. The rules have suddenly changed."

Brock walked a few steps closer, but didn't touch her. "I'm prepared to double your fee."

There was no way she could not respond to that. Carrie turned. "Why? As I told you, there are hundreds of artists around Carmel and..." But he was already shaking his head.

She took a deep breath. That much money would put her nearly out of debt. Yet, this man obviously wasn't to be trusted. And what role did her father, whom she hadn't heard from in eighteen years, have in all this? Her head began to ache with the possibilities. But she owed it to Shane and their future to put pride aside. Besides, wasn't it almost poetic justice, in a way, to do a painting for her father's building, to have him pay her an incredible amount of money after all the years of ignoring her? Was this his way of easing his conscience? she wondered.

"Why does my father want me to do this painting?"

"He doesn't even know you're here."

"I don't believe you."

He shrugged matter-of-factly. "Can't say I blame you. I've lost credibility with you." Suddenly he moved closer and touched her arm, feeling the tension through her sleeve. "Now hear the truth and believe it or not. Your father's one of the finest men I know. He wouldn't have done this—I did. And I'm not going to apologize for it. For years, he's told me about the daughter he'd give anything to see again, so I thought I'd track you down, bring about a reunion. However, after seeing your anger, I'm not sure I'd be doing him a favor."

"Well, thanks a lot. I . . ."

The door flew open, and Rhoda stood with her hand on the knob, looking relieved. "Oh, I'm glad I found you, Brock. Alan Cramer's at the zoning board meeting in town, and he just called. He's in trouble and needs your help right away."

Brock took his hand from Carrie's arm and swore under his breath. He really didn't need this right now. But he couldn't let their CPA face the board alone. "Thanks, Rhoda." He waited until the secretary withdrew, then turned back to Carrie, trying to look agreeable. He seldom had trouble getting people to do his bidding. Why was this one obstinate female being so difficult?

"I've probably gone about this all wrong." He saw her eyes reflect an affirmation and felt ready to clobber her. He cleared his throat. "I need to get to this meeting, but I badly want to straighten this out. Please, let me take you to dinner tonight and explain. I didn't want to trick you into looking at the building. I simply couldn't think of another way to get you here."

Carrie crossed her arms and let her gaze wander thoughtfully. There was much left unsaid between them. Her father hadn't been a part of her life except in occasional memories for many years. Why had he suddenly made another appearance, or did he really not know of Brock's shenanigans? If so, what was Brock to him that he'd go to such lengths? She hated the curiosity that had her ready to agree to a dinner that would, at best, be uncomfortable. Yet she'd already half made up her mind to hear him out.

Brock watched her expressive face as she considered his invitation. Double lashes, he thought. She actually had a double row of thick, black eyelashes. In combination with the unusual color of her eyes, it was truly unsettling. He could just drop all this, tell Mac of her whereabouts and let it go at that. Or he could find out more. Like where was her flyboy husband, and her unfaithful mother, and what had happened to turn her against the father who still longed for her? He wasn't simply nosy, Brock justified to himself. He needed to know more so he could give an honest evaluation to Mac.

Growing tired of waiting for her answer and aware he had another appointment to hurry to, he jammed an impatient hand in his pants pocket. "Look, take a chance. What the hell have you got to lose?"

What, indeed? She met his eyes for a long moment, then slowly nodded. "All right."

Surprised at her acquiescence, he shot her a quick smile. "I'll pick you up about seven."

"No, I'll meet you. Where?"

He ground his teeth. Damn but she was stubborn. His mind searched for a quiet, secluded place. "The Old Bath House Restaurant. You know where it is?"

She raised a brow at him, but held her ground. "On Lovers' Point. Yes, I know where it is."

"Seven o'clock?"

"Fine." Carrie adjusted her wheat-colored canvas purse more comfortably onto her shoulder and walked through the doorway without so much as a glance in his direction, though she could feel his eyes on her back. As soon as she was away from his probing gaze, she released a deep breath.

Her father. Good God, after all these years. And who was Brock Logan to be dragging them together? And why?

She reached her Volkswagen and groped for her keys. She'd been unused to turmoil for years now, since Rusty's death and then her mother's. And now, here it was again, and the thought didn't please her. She liked her peaceful, uneventful existence. She liked harmony and hated discord. Somehow, she'd known from the moment she'd looked into those deep blue eyes that Brock Logan carried with him a fair amount of trouble.

She slid behind the wheel and started the car. Shifting, she maneuvered into traffic. Victor McKamey was a formidable man. And Brock Logan would be by his side. Squinting up into the sun, Carrie wondered if she really was ready to face the two of them.

Chapter Three

It had been some time since Carrie had felt awkward entering a restaurant alone, as a single female without a companion. She occasionally met Sonya for dinner and her realtor friend, Phil Hebert, for lunch, as well as a few friends she'd kept in touch with from art school. Yet tonight she felt a shade uncomfortable as she strolled into the large foyer of the restaurant tucked into a secluded seaside cove. And her apprehension had nothing to do with feeling out of place and everything to do with the man she was meeting.

The very pretty blond hostess wearing a very short black cocktail dress informed her that Mr. Logan was waiting for her. Smiling prettily, the woman told Carrie that she'd take her to him as soon as she returned from seating the couple she was leading into the dining room.

Carrie stood by the desk waiting, still not sure she'd been wise in agreeing to meet him. Mainly, she'd come out of curiosity. Despite the years of neglect, she'd never quite been able to turn off her feelings for her father. And, though Brock made her a shade uneasy, she was curious about him, too. Why would a man with a law degree choose instead to work for an architectural firm? How had he come to have so much authority that he could, without checking with anyone, double her already outrageous fee? And why would he take it upon himself to try to reunite two people supposedly without the consent of either? Somehow, he didn't strike her as the altruistic type.

And last, but certainly not least, why after nearly eight years of discouraging any man who tried to get close to her did she suddenly find herself trembling under Brock Logan's touch? Carrie eased a strand of hair from her cheek. She moved toward the alcove and waited impatiently for the hostess to return. She was about to discover the answers to some of her questions. At least she hoped so.

At a corner table by the window, Brock set down the wine list. He had no idea what Carrie drank, if anything. Truth be known, he knew very little about her. On a whim, after his meeting with the zoning board, he'd driven along the coastal highway toward Big Sur, but she hadn't been at the beach spot where he'd first found her.

Undaunted, he'd taken the winding road up the hillside where he'd watched her Volkswagen disappear. Nearly to the top, he'd come upon a rambling rustic house with a big wraparound porch perched on a shallow cliff that overlooked the sea. There was a black-topped parking area, and the fenced yard was roomy. It had to be her place, Brock decided, since the only other home in the vicinity was considerably farther up and very small, with an elaborate Japanese garden facing the road.

So she had one neighbor and a remote one at that. Why would a beautiful, talented woman in the prime of life live in such a secluded hillside home with a small son and a pregnant cat? He wondered. Did her ringless finger mean that her husband was no longer with them? That question, and a few others, bothered him. What did she do for fun in this quiet, laid-back community? If Rusty Weston was gone, were there other men in her life? Her son was a cute chatterbox, but he was in school all day, and her work was solitary. Surely by evening or on weekends she longed for some adult male companionship. None of that was really any of his business, Brock admitted, yet he found himself wondering nonetheless.

Her quick refusal to his suggestion that she meet with her father seemed to indicate she wanted nothing to do with Mac. Brock had never known Mac to hurt anyone, and he hoped she wasn't coming tonight to try to convince him otherwise. If Carrie Weston thought she could easily sway his opinions, she was in for a surprise. Narrowing his eyes, he took a long swallow of his ice water.

Just then, he turned his head and saw her standing near the arched entrance to the dining room. The dim foyer lighting cast a soft glow on the rich darkness of her hair, worn loose and free, the same as the first time he'd seen her. She ran a hand through its thickness, unaware of his scrutiny. She wore a long black jacket open over a slim white dress, the combination making her look slender, almost fragile.

Had she dressed deliberately to give him that impression? he wondered as a rush of arousal made him keenly aware of her impact on him. Was she giving him a false image of herself as the concerned mother and reclusive painter? Was she crafty, playing hard to get to drive up her prices? As he saw her follow the hostess around the tables toward him, Brock decided he'd prolong dinner long enough to discover the real Carrie Weston.

He stood, greeting her as she slid into the chair opposite him. It was seven in the evening, yet he looked shower fresh in the same outfit he'd worn earlier, while Carrie could feel a tiny bead of moisture slide down between her breasts. Nerves, she thought as she flashed him a small smile.

"Thank you for coming," Brock said, trying to put her at ease. He'd watched her march toward him as if someone held a gun at her back.

With a brief nod, Carrie accepted the menu from the hostess. "Have you been here before? I understand their fish is fresh."

"No. I stay in most evenings. I like to cook."

She looked up, surprised. He didn't seem in the least domestic. "Where are you staying?"

"I'm renting a house on Scenic Drive." The wine steward arrived and stood silently by. "What kind of wine do you like?"

"Whatever you choose will be fine."

Quickly, Brock made his choice and sent the man on his way. He watched Carrie idly finger a gold heart dangling on a fine chain around her neck. She skimmed the large menu, though he would bet her mind was no more on food than his was. She was truly lovely, her skin the delicate shade of a fresh peach, and she was very nervous. He saw her fingers tremble as she turned the page. This was silly. He reached over and touched her hand.

"I feel like I'm sixteen and on a first date. How about you?" He saw her shoulders loosen a little and her smile warm.

"Yes, kind of." Only she hadn't had much time for dating at sixteen what with school and her job. And she'd married young. "I've never dated much."

Didn't date much, with those knockout looks? Somehow, Brock doubted that. He held her left hand, turned it over and noted again the absence of a wedding ring. "Your husband is..."

"Dead." His fingers were lean and strong, his thumb making lazy circles on her palm. She felt a little jolt inside and took her hand back.

"I saw your wedding picture, and I remember reading about Rusty Weston's aerial shows. But I didn't realize he'd died."

"Yes, killed in an air crash some time ago. Where did you see my picture?"

"Mac had a newspaper clipping of your wedding photo." The wine arrived, and Brock let the steward go through the opening, tasting and pouring ceremony while he watched Carrie absorb what he'd just said. She seemed genuinely surprised to learn of the picture. Or was she just a superb actress?

The waiter left, and he held up his glass. "Here's to your painting." That seemed safe enough.

Carrie clinked her glass to his before taking a small sip. Tart and cool on her tongue, she let the liquid slide down her throat. She raised her eyes and found him leaning forward and studying her. "Where did he get the newspaper clipping, do you know?"

"From your mother."

She wrinkled her brow. "She always spoke so disparagingly of him that I'm surprised she sent him my picture."

"Maybe your wedding made her mellow, and she wanted to share that feeling with your father."

Carrie ran her finger along the rim of her glass. More likely Natalie had been drinking and sent it during one of her sentimental crying jags.

"He has another one, too, taken when you won an art contest as a teenager. That's how I recognized your style. Mac carries both clippings in his wallet."

She found that hard to believe. Her father had sent them away. She'd have to remember that and not let this man turn the facts around. He looked capable of that and much more.

The waiter arrived and they placed their orders. Carrie watched Brock sip his wine, wondering how much she could learn from him. He seemed a very careful, guarded man. "Tell me about my father."

Was it simply curiosity or was he getting through to her? Brock wondered. "Well, he's very successful. The main office of McKamey and Associates is in Chicago and employs over a hundred people. We're opening this California branch, and Mac's considering expanding overseas, possibly London for starters."

Yes, she could believe that. She remembered many evenings when he'd been at work at his drafting table while she sketched at the little easel he'd made for her. Even then, he'd spoken to her of his dreams of one day owning a big company, of having the freedom to do his designs his way. Natalie would go out and leave the two of them alone, and they'd been content in each other's company. At least that's how her childhood memory went. But she wanted to know more about the man, not his work.

"What's he like?"

She saw Brock's face soften. "He's the kindest man I've ever met. He's intelligent, fair-minded, innovative, generous."

Carrie dropped her eyes as the hurt she'd thought a thing of the past surfaced briefly before she pushed it away. Why had her father turned his back on his daughter and yet shown such kindness to Brock? When she was certain she had herself under control, she looked up again.

"And where do you fit into his life?"

The waiter brought their food just then and served it with a flourish before leaving them. Brock tasted his scallops, buying a little time before answering. Both as an attorney and as a businessman, he prided himself in being able to read people. He'd expected to find her defensive and a shade brittle. Instead she seemed to be floundering in a sea of new information, all of which was leaving her more vulnerable than she liked.

"Where do I fit in?" he repeated. "Quite simply, Mac threw me a lifeline, and I gratefully grabbed it. I grew up south of the Chicago area in a small town I could hardly wait to get away from. I managed to get a scholarship and went to work for Mac's company after classes. Later, he subsidized law school for me, and, though I've paid him back, I know I couldn't have done it without him."

Brock cut into his broccoli, acknowledging that he was leaving a lot out. But he'd given her the main thrust. He'd caught a quick flash of pain in her eyes, but she'd covered it quickly. Was she upset that her father had spent money helping him? If she only knew of the several others Mac had helped. Hell, Mac had paid her way through art school, so what was her problem? He studied her face as she pushed the food around on her plate, but her expression gave nothing away.

Carrie was having trouble swallowing. Jealousy was a self-defeating emotion, she knew. Still, she wondered why her father had been so generous to a man who'd begun as a part-time employee, while his own daughter had had to work long years to put herself through art school, even with the small scholarship she'd won. She shouldn't have come tonight, she thought, setting down her fork and taking a sip of wine. Despite the money, perhaps agreeing to do the painting was a mistake.

"Are you all right?" Brock asked. She seemed paler than when she'd arrived.

It wasn't his fault, Carrie told herself. Brock hadn't flaunted the things he'd told her, had in fact mentioned them matter-of-factly only after she'd asked. She squared her shoulders, unwilling to let him see how learning about her father had hurt her, for the second time. She gave him a tight smile. "I'm fine. This fish is wonderful."

She'd put on her cool look again, which he preferred over her phony hurt look. Maybe she thought he'd run to Mac and tell him that his daughter got tears in her eyes when she'd heard about the years since he'd seen her. Maybe she had another think coming.

He finished the last of his dinner and sat back. "How's your mother doing? Does she live around here?" Natalie McKamey was the one he should go see. For whatever reasons, she was the one who'd probably brainwashed her daughter into ignoring her father. And Carrie had learned her lesson well.

"My mother died five years ago." She saw by his face he hadn't expected that.

"I'm sorry. You were close, I imagine, just the two of you here in California."

She'd loved Natalie simply because she'd been her mother. But close? Carrie couldn't think of a soul who'd been close to Natalie. "No, not particularly."

So she'd turned her back on her father and hadn't particularly cared for her mother. She was a sweetheart, all right. Brock drained his wineglass and signaled the waiter for coffee.

Carrie wished she had a cigarette. They seemed to have run out of conversation, and perhaps that was just as well. She'd get her coffee down somehow and then leave. But first, she had to know something. She waited until their coffee had been served before she looked across at Brock. "Was that a firm figure you offered for my painting this afternoon?"

He'd been waiting. Of course, the money. That was the real reason she'd agreed to come, not because she wanted to know about her father. He took a taste of the slightly bitter brew, welcoming the heat that spread down his throat. He should have known her fee was of primary interest to her, so why was he oddly disappointed? From Aunt Emma on down, he'd learned that money talked loudest with women, and still he occasionally let himself hope. His mistake. He nodded grimly.

"Yes, I stand behind my offer. Will you do the painting?"

The sea outside the window was no less cool than the sudden bleak look in his eyes, and Carrie wondered at the cause. He had sought her out, not the other way around, and yet now he seemed to give off that hint of disapproval she'd noticed at their first meeting. What a strange man he was, and a somewhat secretive one. She wasn't at all surprised to realize she'd learned very little about him tonight.

If only she didn't need the money. If only she could tell him to go to hell with his constant questions and his bold eyes. If only she could afford to get up and walk away without a backward thought to either Brock or her father. Carrie rubbed a spot above her left eye. She was tired and ready to go home. Unused to this guarded fencing, she wanted to be seated on her porch high above the sea, with Shane sleeping peacefully in his room, and Jonathan purring on her lap. And she wanted to be smoking a cigarette.

"Yes, I'll do the painting," she said in a soft, resigned voice. "What did you have in mind?"

She listened while he outlined his ideas, which were general and quite vague, leaving her lots of room to do as she pleased. At least he wasn't going to make it artistically difficult for her. She nodded in agreement as he called for the check. In moments they were in the foyer, then strolling out into the warm evening air.

"I'll see you home," Brock said, taking her elbow.

"I've got my car, remember?"

"I'll see you to your car, and then I'll follow you home—to make sure you're all right."

Carrie stopped in midstride on the wide walkway. "Whatever for? This is a perfectly safe community. I wander around here all the time, and I never have someone escort me to my door."

"Never?" His eyes challenged her.

She held the look a long moment. "Rarely."

"Well, you are tonight." With a nudge, he moved her along to the graveled parking area.

"This is ridiculous and quite unnecessary. I...oh!"

She slipped. Unused to walking in the high heels she'd worn, she turned her ankle on the uneven gravel. Her arm shot out and she grabbed a handful of his jacket to steady herself. Close beside her, Brock slid his arm around her waist and kept her upright.

"See what I mean?" he asked, smiling down at her. "You obviously need someone to watch over you." Then suddenly, the smile faded as he saw the look of awareness move into her eyes. In the glow of the street lamp, he could see she was flushed, could feel her shallow breathing as he tightened his hold on her.

He was so very tall and so very close, the strong masculine scent of him reaching out to her. Carrie felt his hand touch her hair almost shyly then burrow under, his fingers brushing against the nape of her neck. Her heart beat wildly, and she felt his solid strength and let herself lean into him, for just a moment. Fleetingly, she acknowledged a buried wish, to share with someone, someone who'd help her carry the load, who'd be there for her always. But life had taught her that there was no such someone, most especially not Brock Logan.

She stood a breath away from him, her eyes closed, the hand on his chest trembling. Her full lower lip quivered with her efforts to control herself, and Brock had the insane desire to lower his head and give in to his sudden need to taste her. He took a deep breath. She smelled clean and fresh and full of longing. But what was he thinking of, allowing himself to get trapped by the feel and fragrance of a woman and forgetting the reasons he was with her in the first place? He had to remember she was Mac's daughter and a little schemer who used men. Then why was his hand even now drawing her closer?

Carrie opened her eyes to find him watching her, his gaze filled with purpose. She had given in to her desire for only one other man's touch, and that decision had irrevocably changed her life. She had no intention of making that mistake again. She eased back from him, this time planting her feet firmly in the gravel. "I have to leave."

He dropped his arms. "I'll follow you." He held up a hand before she could protest. "Don't argue."

Grinding her teeth, Carrie made her way to her Volkswagen and climbed behind the wheel. She hadn't taken a relaxed breath since Brock Logan had ambled into her life. She started the engine, trying to keep in mind that the painting would take several weeks, but then he'd be gone. And she'd be much closer to financial freedom. With that thought, she moved out into traffic.

His headlights following close behind annoyed her greatly, but she drove the ten miles or so within the speed limit. She turned onto the winding road that led to her home and hoped he'd wave and pass on by. No such luck, she thought as he swung in right behind her. Persistence was the man's middle name. At last, she parked outside the wrought-iron gate of the fence that circled her yard. Perhaps if she hurried, he'd merely turn around and be on his way. She jumped out to find he was already strolling toward her.

Coming alongside, Brock opened his mouth to say something, then heard a sound he couldn't identify and looked past her into the fenced yard. In the moonlight, he could make out a skinny white goat braying at him, its ears twitching. He brought his questioning gaze back to Carrie who seemed amused at his reaction.

"That's Billie," she said by way of introduction.

"A guard goat?"

"Cheaper than a dog. He eats leftovers, including the cans sometimes. Handy."

Brock dismissed her explanation and searched her face, looking for clues. "I wish I knew what to make of you."

He was too close again. Carrie moved nearer to the gate. "Why do you need to figure me out? Obviously you've checked out my work, I've already agreed to do the painting, and you can rest assured I'll deliver. Beyond that, you don't need to know another thing about me. Do you ask your butcher for his life history before you accept a cut of meat?"

"My butcher's not my good friend's only child."

Carrie frowned. "I wish you'd just forget that part and . . ."

"I can't." He moved closer, finding the anger that he'd tried to bank taking over, uncertain if it was directed at her or himself. He knew it was none of his business, yet his strong feelings for Mac demanded reasons. "Why did you do it, Carrie? Why did you ignore a man like Mac all these years? Why did you take all the money he sent, the gifts from all over the world, without sending him so much as a note or a card?"

He heard her gasp, but he was too incensed to stop now. "Why did you let him pay your way through art school and not even invite him to your graduation? Or to your wedding? Who gave you away to your flying ace, since you didn't see fit to invite Mac? Did you open his letters, take out the money and throw his words away, not even caring what he had to say?''

Her face had drained of all color, but Brock didn't care. He hadn't meant to rip into her tonight, but when he'd realized all she was interested in was her fat fee, when he'd seen where she lived, high atop a scenic hillside on a very expensive piece of California real estate—even if the house wasn't especially grand—he knew he was about to lose it. He watched her struggle to contain her emotions as she sucked in a deep gulp of air.

"You think you know it all, don't you?" Quickly she scooted through the gate and slammed it shut behind her. "You don't know a damn thing!" Trembling, she ran toward the house, up onto the porch and disappeared around the side out of sight.

Brock hit the top edge of the fence hard with the heel of his hand, dissipating the remnants of his anger. She'd sounded odd, more hurt than angry as he'd expected her to be. Her voice had been shaky, her huge violet eyes swimming in tears. Head lowered, the goat brayed at him.

So close. He'd come so close, and now he'd blown it. Disgusted with himself, he walked to his car and got in.

The sun was low on the horizon the next afternoon as Carrie took a break and climbed onto a jutting black rock in the corner of her backyard. With Zeke sitting on her shoulder, she gazed out at the foamy ocean waves. She badly needed the serenity of her sea, her thoughts still churning from the night before.

"Pretty bird," Zeke squawked. She held out a nutty treat, which he quickly devoured, bobbing his black head in thanks. Carrie drew up her knees and hugged them as she let the endless ritual of the waves calm her.

Brock's ugly accusations rang in her ears, and she recalled the way his blue eyes had turned frosty with each new indictment of her past behavior. Now she knew why she'd caught an occasional hint of contempt in his voice or manner. Her father had told him terrible things about her, all lies.

But why? Dim memories of her father drifted to her. His deep laugh, his gentle hands, the wonderful way he'd smiled. As a child, she'd preferred his company over her mother's, for he had made her feel loved and cherished. Her mother had been a fairly selfish person even then, so she'd lavished all the love in her youthful heart on her father.

Young as she was, she'd sensed things weren't perfect between Mac and Natalie, because they'd argued many nights long after she'd gone to bed and they thought her asleep. But nothing like that last terrible fight when she'd been about ten. She'd never seen her father so angry, her mother so frightened. Carrie flinched as she remembered the words he'd flung at them: "Get out, both of you, and never come back." They never had.

Natalie had hustled the two of them, and what little they could cram into two suitcases, on a bus headed for the west coast. California, her mother had said, was the land of opportunity. Not understanding, Carrie had begged Natalie to go back. But she'd clamped her thin lips together and explained that Mac simply didn't love either of them anymore. She'd had no choice but to believe her mother, though God only knew how many tears she'd wept over losing the warmth of Mac's love.

Carrie watched a boat way out near the horizon toss about as the afternoon winds picked up. Zeke spread his wings and did a little two-step on her shoulder as the salty breeze drifted to them. Shane was in the house curled up with his cartoons and his cat, and she was relieved to have a little time alone. She'd spent most of the day framing some of her paintings, an activity that didn't require total concentration. As she'd worked, she'd let her mind float free. And it had unerringly floated back to Brock.

He admired Mac so, looking upon him as a mentor of sorts. So naturally he'd believe the man he knew over the woman he'd just met. Besides, she had no intention of defending herself against his unjust accusations. But she was angry that he'd felt it necessary to rail at her. It showed him to be judgmental, quick to jump to conclusions, and even quicker to condemn. She was oddly disappointed to learn that about him.

Her father must have wanted Brock's approval badly to lie to him about the way he'd treated his daughter. There had been no letters, no money, no tuition. There had been only the one insurance policy, which she'd been stupid enough to hand over to Rusty, and the gold heart and chain Mac had given her for her birthday just before he'd sent her from his house. She wore it always, though she wasn't certain why.

And what about the newspaper clippings he supposedly still carried in his wallet? Why would he lie about her, yet carry those? Was Mac trying to create the image of a devoted but wronged father? And what had happened to the hundreds of letters she'd sent him, right up until her wedding invitation, which he'd also ignored? Carrie sighed, wondering if she even wanted to find out more since a small amount of knowledge about Victor McKamey was already upsetting her.

She recalled again the way Brock had looked at her last night and wished he could know her side of the story. But she wasn't going to be the one to burst his little bubble about his perfect partner. He'd have to discover for himself what...

Billie was braying repeatedly, dragging Carrie from her thoughts. She turned and looked to the far corner of the yard, then almost laughed out loud. Brock Logan was backed against the fence railing by Billie, who was all but breathing fire as he tucked his head under and gave another long, warning bray.

"Hot damn!" Zeke screeched as Carrie scrambled off the rock and slowly walked toward the fence, pleased at the respectfully hesitant look in Brock's blue gaze.

He hadn't meant to come see her today, not at first, Brock acknowledged. But the longer the day had gone on, the more he'd acknowledged that he'd been wrong. Despite what she'd done or not done, his self appointed mission was to bring Carrie and her father together, not to judge one or the other. He'd always disliked judgmental people. So he'd come to see her.

He'd parked in her drive, and though her car was there, he'd seen no sign of her or the boy. He'd slipped off his shirt and gone down the wooden steps anchored into the bluff at the back of her property. After a brisk walk on the sandy beach, he'd felt better able to face her and had climbed back up and spotted her sitting on the rock in her backyard. But the protective goat had cornered him before he could call to her.

She walked toward him with her slow stride, her eyes on his as the impatient animal held him pinned. She had on an oversize blue blouse over tan walking shorts, a very ordinary summer outfit in California. Yet he felt the tug of attraction with every step nearer she took.

Carrie Weston was as different from Francine Thomas and others he'd dated as a woman could get. She wasn't his type, Brock reminded himself. Why then, he wondered, could he still feel the light touch of her fingers on his? One glance around her cluttered yard, complete with a guard goat and a sulky bird perched on her shoulder, and he could tell she was too bohemian for his taste. He'd come for Mac's sake, to make amends. And because he couldn't get the desolate way she'd looked last night out of his mind.

Carrie stopped mere feet from him, her eyes cool and assessing. He must have come up from the beach for he was wearing only Docksiders and white jeans rolled up midway on his muscular calves. The sun highlighted the blond hair on his chest, set off by powerful shoulders. He hadn't bothered to shave. The overall effect was of an appealing beach bum and was a startling contrast to his previous formality—and totally disarming.

She touched the blue collar around Billie's neck and spoke soothingly to the skittish animal. "It's all right, Billie." With her hand still on him, she looked up at Brock. "You shouldn't have come through the fence. He doesn't like uninvited guests. And neither do I."

He took a deep breath. "I came to tell you something. I was way out of line last night, and I'm sorry." He held out his hand. "Friends?"

That was one she hadn't expected. As Carrie considered his offer, she heard a commotion behind her, a screen door slamming and the unmistakable sound of running feet. Over her shoulder, she saw Shane coming toward them.

"Mom, Mom! You gotta come. Jonathan's having kittens right in the middle of the kitchen floor!"

Chapter Four

If you'll call off this silly goat, I'd be happy to assist Jonathan," Brock said as Billie held his ground. "I grew up on a farm."

"That won't be necessary," Carrie said. But the words were barely out of her mouth when she saw Shane pull Billie by his collar, freeing Brock from his pinned position at the fence.

"Come on," Shane said over his shoulder as he ran toward the door. "This way."

She noticed Brock's quick, pleased smile as he scooted around the goat and hurried after her son. And she'd also seen the jubilant look on Shane's face at having the man with the neat car find them. She'd lost this skirmish, Carrie thought as she trailed after them with Zeke balanced on her shoulder, leaving Billie looking cheated. But she'd better make certain she wouldn't lose the next.

Zeke squawked once, then flew to his perch as she let the screen door slam behind her. Jonathan was stretched out in the corner of the kitchen, two tiny bundles already beside her as she struggled to free her body of the third kitten. Shane's eyes were wide with wonder as Carrie moved him aside to get an old towel out of the closet. As she knelt to ease the towel in place in an effort to make the cat more comfortable, she glanced at Brock who had his big hand on Jonathan's head.

"It's all right, old girl," Brock crooned, "another good push and you've got it." He caressed the straining cat whose eyes were glazed with pain. He shot Shane a quick look. "You got any newspapers around here?"

"You want to read the paper now?" Shane asked.

Brock chuckled as he lifted the cat's shoulders onto the towel. "No. We can use them to catch the afterbirth." He saw the boy reluctantly scamper off for the papers as Carrie caught the tiny kitten and laid it next to the mother cat. "Looks like you've done this a time or two," he commented.

"This is Jonathan's third litter," Carrie explained. "I can't seem to keep her from roaming off."

"Must be a tomcat nearby who roams at the same time."

Carrie ran her hand over the cat's hard belly. She wondered how many more were in there. "Yes. Our neighbor up the way, Mr. Takahashi, has a tom named Domino."

"Three litters. Undoubtedly a love match. What do you do with the kittens?"

"Find homes for them." Carrie sighed. "Naturally Shane wants to keep them all, but with Billie and Zeke

and Jonathan and Gerald, I think we have enough."
She saw the head crowning and hoped it was the last
one.

"Gerald?"

"Shane's hamster."

"Is Gerald a female, too?" He couldn't keep the
amusement from his voice. The last thing he'd have
expected, seeing the cool artist that first day, was that
her house was a veritable zoo.

"I don't know, and I'm not taking chances, so he
lives alone." She saw him ease his hand over to help
the kitten squirm free. "You don't have to help, really.
This is kind of messy."

"It's all right. Lots of things in life are kind of
messy, but the results are worth it. You know, things
like exercising or cooking. Or making love." She
turned to face him, raising an eyebrow, her mouth
dropping open. With a straight face, he went on.
"Well, it's not the tidiest thing two people can do. Yet
it seems to be a very popular pastime."

Carrie heard Shane returning and shut her mouth.
She hadn't been able to think of a suitable reply anyhow.

"This is all I could find," Shane said, thrusting a
small stack of papers at Brock.

"They'll do just fine."

"The kittens are all wet," Shane commented as he
crouched beside them.

"He wasn't home during Jonathan's last delivery,"
Carrie explained as she placed the hairless little kitten
near the mother, relieved that it was the last one.

"Jonathan's going to take care of that," Brock said,
as he arranged the paper under the cat. "She's going
to lick them clean and cuddle them close to keep them

warm, because they don't have any fur yet." He shifted into position. "I'll take care of this part, if you like," he told Carrie.

She saw no reason not to let him since he'd invited himself to this birthing. She stood and turned to the sink to wash her hands.

"Did you lick me all over to clean me up after I was born, Mom?" Shane asked, his big eyes watching Jonathan's tongue washing her babies.

She heard Brock swallow a laugh as she reached for the towel. "Most humans have a doctor and a nurse to help them," she told her son. She saw Brock expertly knead the cat's belly in an effort to extricate the afterbirth. In her wildest thoughts she'd not expected the impeccable Mr. Logan to arrive casually bare-chested and then squat on her kitchen floor helping a cat have kittens.

He certainly knew his way around animals, Carrie thought, as, in no time, Brock had everything cleaned up. In a cardboard box Jonathan was cozily curled up on an old piece of blanket with her four kittens asleep beside her. Carrie directed Brock to the bathroom to wash up, as Shane knelt beside the box petting his cat's head.

"Think we should give them some milk, Mom?"

"I think we should let them sleep awhile," Carrie said, coaxing him away from that corner of the kitchen. "Getting born is tiring."

"Maybe after dinner I can play with the kittens," he suggested hopefully.

"Not for a while. For now, they need only their mother and lots of rest." Carrie opened the refrigerator and pulled out the package of hamburger she'd had thawing. "How does chili and a salad sound for dinner?"

"Can we ask Brock?" He moved closer to the sink where Carrie was unwrapping the meat. "Please, Mom. He helped the kittens get born and you always say you should thank people when they do you a favor."

Carrie sighed at her own words coming back at her at a most inconvenient time. "I'm sure Mr. Logan has lots of things he'd rather do on a Saturday night than eat chili with us."

"Matter of fact," Brock said, walking into the kitchen, "Mr. Logan would like nothing better than to spend Saturday night eating chili with you both." He watched the quick frown appear on Carrie's face before she erased it. He wasn't sure why he'd accepted the invitation. Maybe it was to get her goat. No pun intended, he thought smiling at Shane.

Shane gave him a gap-toothed grin. "See, Mom. I told you he was nice." He walked over to check on Jonathan.

So they'd discussed him, and the kid had been his champion against her obvious hesitancy. He wondered if that talk had taken place before he'd ripped into her last night.

Eating dinner with him two nights in a row hadn't exactly been in her plans, Carrie acknowledged, especially after last night's session by the fence. But Shane was obviously very taken with Brock, and she saw no easy way to explain a refusal to her son. Carrie gave him a skeptical look. "It's not much of a dinner, and I'm not much of a cook."

"I'm not fussy." He pulled a blue knit shirt from where the tail had been wedged into his back pocket and slipped it on over his head. "I'll even make the chili, if you want. I told you I really like cooking."

His hair was all tousled from the shirt, and she watched him run long, tan fingers through it. She was glad he'd put on more clothes, though it didn't help much. Somehow this casual man smelling of the outdoors was much more unnerving than the well-dressed attorney in his pleated trousers and Italian leather loafers.

"No, thanks. I'm not crazy about someone else working in my kitchen." She bent to the cupboard and struggled to free a large pot from the cluttered contents.

She hadn't been crazy about uninvited company either, but here he was, Brock thought as he moved to her side. "Let me help you." He crouched and slid his arm in, grazing hers as he went. He could almost hear her grind her teeth as she stood up out of his way. Finding the pot, he pulled it out, got to his feet and handed it to her with an innocent smile. Her violet eyes studied him as she took the pot.

She was standing close, close enough that he could feel the warmth from her body spread to his. She drew in a quick breath as she fought the reaction to his nearness. Brock inhaled the female scent of her as he watched her gaze drop to his mouth, and he waited.

"Are you always this persistent?"

"Oh, usually more." She nodded as if she'd known what his answer would be.

"I suppose I do owe you dinner. You can stay if you keep out of my way."

"Glad to." He glanced over at the boy. "Maybe Shane can show me around while you cook." He saw the indecision in her eyes, but she didn't say anything.

Shane scrambled to his feet. "You want to see Gerald?"

"I sure do." He put one arm around Shane's small shoulders as the boy led him into a big, comfortable room. Two chairs and a large sofa were angled to face a huge stone fireplace. The furniture was mismatched yet oddly suited to the surroundings. Paintings hung on nearly every square inch of wallspace, some Carrie's, he noticed, some by other artists. A huge window afforded a spectacular view of green mountains in the distance. There was an unplanned coziness, a surprising appeal, a clever blending of colors and fabrics and woods that drew him with its warmth. Much like the woman who'd undoubtedly decorated it, Brock thought.

Shane showed off his bedroom and introduced him to fat and furry Gerald in his cage with an exercise wheel and cardboard tunnels. Then the boy showed him Zeke, who sat gazing at him with an unfriendly eye and refused to say a word. Brock strolled out to the glassed-in porch that was obviously Carrie's workroom and took his time looking around as Shane tried to get his bird to talk.

Here the smell of linseed oil mingled with turpentine. Brock stopped to study an oil painting propped against the wall. This one elicited a different mood than the one he'd seen her working on a few days before at the beach. She'd caught the turbulence of a storm at sea, the violent waves crashing against the jagged rocks, the gray sky filled with angry, threatening clouds. Rugged pine trees clung to a deserted shoreline, barely visible in a misty rainfall. And one pure-white bird defied the ferocity and dipped low near a cresting wave. You could almost smell the salt spray, almost feel the reverberating thunder. There was no denying her talent, Brock thought as he straightened.

A fresh white canvas was propped on an easel, which stood alongside a high stool. Next to it was a rolling cart holding a clutter of art supplies. An assortment of brushes, from quite large to very fine, were stuck haphazardly into two glass jars. There was a worktable with several sections of frames and various sheets of glass. Two wide bookshelves overflowed with art books. Only one item hung on the wall, a framed document. Brock walked over for a closer look.

She'd won a citation, something called the Hanover Award, a scholarship recognition of superior promise in the field of art. Brock frowned. A scholarship? But Mac had said he'd paid her way through art school. Had she taken that money for herself and used the scholarship to get through school? Was she that greedy, that capable of deception? Something didn't add up right.

His gaze took in the room again. Nice, like the rest of the house, but nothing special, nothing overtly expensive. He knew her paintings were selling well and commanding the high dollar. Though the property was worth a great deal, the house she lived in wasn't. She lived in chaos and confusion with her son and an animal menagerie, drove a battered car and seemed to be avoiding the trappings of success. Why? he wondered. Yet she'd definitely brightened when he'd mentioned how much money he was willing to pay her. Where was it all going?

She was a puzzle, and he'd always been fascinated by puzzles.

"I just can't get him to talk, Brock," Shane said as he joined him in his mother's studio.

"That's all right. Some other day." He followed the boy back into the living area.

"Where'd you leave your neat car?"

"Next to your mom's in the driveway. I went for a walk on the beach before coming to see you."

"Could I go see it?"

The keys were in his pocket, the emergency brake on. "Can I trust you not to touch any of the buttons or pull any of the knobs?"

"Sure. Mom says if you can't be trusted, you're not worth a plugged nickel."

"She does, eh?" So Carrie placed a high value on trust, even lectured her seven-year-old on it. Was that normal mother to son conversation for his age, or did she have a particular ax to grind about trusting people? he wondered.

Shane squinted as he looked up at Brock. "Do you know what a plugged nickel is?"

He smiled as he clapped the boy on the shoulder. "I know I wouldn't want to be one."

"It's a fake and a phony," the boy explained, anxious to share his knowledge. "Like with people, it's someone who pretends to be real good in front of you but he's real bad when you can't see him. Mom says those guys are lower than a snake's belly." He giggled. "Do you know what's lower than a snake's belly?"

"No, what?"

"Nothing." Shane grinned, pleased that he'd fooled Brock. "I'm going to check out your car." He headed for the door.

"Remember what I said." Brock saw him wave and run out front where he'd parked the Ferrari. Cute kid. He'd never spent much time around kids, but Shane was okay. Mac would be nuts about him. And the boy was brimming over with information on his mother, if one took the time to sort out his chatter.

Hands in his pockets, he stood looking out the window. A plugged nickel and a snake's belly. Wouldn't Carrie be surprised if she knew what he'd learned about her today?

Carrie put the salad in the refrigerator, then went to check on the chili. Stirring, she saw that it was coming along just fine. She'd thrown the ingredients together with one ear tuned to the other rooms, wondering what her talkative son was telling Brock about her, about their life. She wouldn't put it past him to pump the boy for information, and Shane was so taken with him that he'd tell him anything. Not that she had anything to hide, she thought as she angled the lid on the pot.

She'd heard them laughing together several times, the deep male sound coupled with the childish twitter. Shane was in seventh heaven, she knew, having a man around. She sighed as she set three place mats on the table. This was the one thing she'd denied her son: adult male companionship. Obviously, he'd missed that special relationship. Still, she'd done the right thing, she decided. Better not to have someone than to get used to him only to have him abruptly change and move out of your life. It had happened to her, and she'd promised herself she'd try to keep her son from being hurt that way.

Having finished setting the table, Carrie went to check on Jonathan and the kittens.

Brock stood in the arched doorway and saw the tenderness in Carrie's smile as she touched the cat's sleek coat. She was barefoot, her face was free of makeup, and a simple rubber band held her thick hair at her nape. He decided her beauty was all the more striking because she seemed totally oblivious to it.

The past several days, he'd seen many of her faces: contemplative, angry, tender, hurt, cautious. He'd seen her dressed to impress and not giving a damn. And still he wanted to know more. For Mac, he told himself.

He wanted to know about her past, her husband, her mother. He wanted to know what made her tick, what lay beneath the hesitant facade, the distrust in her eyes. He could and would control his attraction to her. He'd learned to channel his emotions over the years, discarding the ones harmful to his well-being and to his future plans. What he couldn't quite control was the way his heartbeat picked up at the sight of her smile, as it did now.

He stepped into the kitchen, moved closer and saw that two of the kittens were nursing, while two still slept. Carrie continued to stroke the mother reassuringly. "You really do like kittens, don't you?"

She looked up at him. "Mmm. I like all animals. They're easier to live with than most people."

"And they're seldom bad tempered, never leave the top off the toothpaste tube or embarrass you by drinking too much wine."

Carrie nodded as she stood. "That's right. Speaking of wine, would you like a glass? I think I've got some around here somewhere."

"Sure." He watched her search the cupboards and finally pull out a bottle.

"Someone brought this over a long time ago," she commented as she held it up for his inspection.

A dark red Bordeaux. Brock nodded as he took it and a corkscrew from her. He wondered who'd brought the wine, a man she'd asked to dinner or a female friend. A man, he'd guess. He ripped off the foil and swallowed a strange, unexpected mixture of curiosity and jealousy.

Carrie held the glasses while he poured the rich wine. He seemed so at ease in her house, as if this were his tenth visit and not his first. She admired adaptability. Raising her glass, she met his eyes. "A toast?"

"Yes. To all those smart people who aren't lower than a snake's belly."

She smiled. "You've been talking with my son."

"He's full of homey little observations."

And she'd give her best new sable brush to know which ones Shane had shared with Brock. "Isn't he? Where did you leave him, by the way?"

"In front, checking out my car." He waited for the explosion, but saw her eyes hold steady. "That doesn't worry you?"

"Should it? Shane won't hurt your car. He's very trustworthy."

"I thought you might worry about him hurting himself."

"I trust him around home. He knows the limits I've set and usually listens." Well, most of the time, she amended to herself.

Brock touched his glass to hers. "Here's to trust, then." He sipped, watching her. The wine rushed through his blood, warming him. "Isn't Shane a little young to be taking part in philosophical discussions on trust?"

She leaned back against the counter. "What age would you have me start him, ten? Fifteen?" She shook her head, the ponytail shifting with the movement. "You can't just let a child drift, then one day start filling his head full of correct behavior and proper morals. You have to start early and keep at it until it's second nature to him. And trust is certainly one of the most important lessons. He has to learn who he can trust and who isn't worth his trust. People who can't be trusted—"

"Aren't worth a plugged nickel, I know." He smiled to let her know he wasn't making fun of her.

"That's right, they aren't." He looked at her with intensity, despite the smile, as if he was trying to take apart her words, analyze her thoughts. Just then she heard the front door slam and almost let out an audible sigh of relief. She wanted to get this meal over with and Brock Logan off her property. She turned to the stove.

"Mom, that car's really super," Shane said as he arrived in the kitchen at a near gallop. "Some day, I'm going to have a car like that."

"You certainly can if you work toward it," Carrie told him as she stirred the chili. "Go wash up now, Shane. We're ready to eat."

"Okay. Want to come wash up with me, Brock?"

"It's Mr. Logan," Carrie corrected.

"I'd really prefer Brock, if you have no objection." He smiled at the boy. "I've already washed up, but thanks." He watched the boy scoot off. "He's really quite a kid."

Carrie spooned steaming chili into bowls. "I think so."

"You've done a great job with him, especially raising him all alone. How old was he when your husband died?"

"Shane was born three months after his father was killed." Carrie placed the bowls on the table, then went for the salad.

"That must have been rough, mourning a husband, going through childbirth alone."

Mourning a husband? She'd mourned Rusty long before he'd died. But she didn't want to get into that.

She needed a lot of nudging to open up. "Ah, but your mother was with you." He saw a flicker of disappointment pass over her face, and she didn't look up. "She must have been a big help."

"Can I have a soda instead of milk?" Shane asked as he came tearing in, seating himself at the table with a noisy scrape of chair sliding over tile.

Carrie could have kissed him for his timing and decided to reward him. "Yes, you may, but only for tonight." She turned to the refrigerator, wishing Brock would back off with the questions. She could, of course, refuse to answer and send him away with a cool look. But he wouldn't give up, she knew.

Her mother a big help at Shane's birth? Natalie had been off on an impromptu trip to Mexico with one of her men friends and hadn't returned until her boyfriend had run out of money. By then, Carrie had been released from the hospital, and Shane had been three weeks old. But her mother had been filled with remorse and had splurged by spending half of her welfare check on gifts for the baby. Despite her mother's unthinking behavior, Carrie had always found it difficult to stay angry with Natalie for long.

There were four captain's chairs around the maple table, Brock noticed. Shane was already in one and Carrie had set her wineglass next to her son's place, indicating her place, which meant the chair on the other side of Shane was to be his. So she wanted to play it safe and keep the child between them, did she? Carefully he slid his place mat around so he'd be seated next to Carrie instead. Pleased with himself, he looked up to see her dark eyes watching him. He gave her an innocent grin as he motioned toward the large window facing the backyard and to the sea beyond. "I like to look out."

Carrie nodded, her face telling him she'd seen through his lame explanation. He held her chair out for her, then seated himself. "It's starting to rain." He stared out, seemingly engrossed in the graying twilight sky and the huge raindrops pelting the covered porch. It'd been a while since he'd resorted to discussing the weather to keep the conversation going, Brock thought. There was something about the quiet way Carrie looked at him that made him feel like a small boy trying to put one over.

"Maybe we can go for a walk after we eat," Shane suggested through a mouthful of buttered roll. "Mom and I like to walk in the rain, don't we, Mom?"

"Funny, so do I," Brock interjected.

Carrie stabbed her fork into her salad. The man was pretending to enjoy everything they did and inviting himself along to boot. If she told him they liked to hang glide over Pike's Peak on weekends, he'd undoubtedly say it was his favorite pastime, too. Why was he doing this? "It'll be too dark by the time we finish, Shane. Perhaps another day."

"This is quite a house," Brock said, his eyes circling the cozy kitchen. "Did you have it built?"

"No."

"It's Aunt Sonya's house," Shane told him. "She lets us stay here. She owns Mr. Takahashi's house, too."

The boy was a jewel, Brock thought as he ate his chili. Sonya must be Sonya Nichols. He wondered what the house rented for. "Who's Mr. Takahashi?" he asked, directing his question to Shane.

"Our neighbor up the hill. He's a gardener. You should see his place. He made an elephant out of one bush and a big bird out of one in his backyard. What kind of bird, Mom? I forget."

"A peacock."

"Yeah, a peacock. Could I take Brock up and show him, Mom?"

"Not tonight, Shane. Eat your dinner."

"Next time you come, okay?" Shane's eyes, so like his mother's, implored Brock, wanting to be sure he'd return. "You'd like him. He's real nice. He works on our yard, too, and I help him. He's Japanese, right, Mom?"

Carrie stood and took her half-finished dish to the sink. If she didn't get Brock out of her kitchen soon, Shane would tell him every large and small fact about their lives, a thought that didn't sit well with her.

She spooned food into a metal bowl. "I'll have Billie's dinner ready in a minute," she told Shane.

The boy finished the last of his chili and gulped down his soft drink, leaving his salad untouched, then scooted off his chair. "I'll take it out to him."

"Be careful and don't get too wet." She handed him the goat's dinner and glanced over at Brock. He was scooping out the last morsel with his roll. "Would you like more?" she asked him.

"No, thanks. That was wonderful. I thought you said you weren't much of a cook."

Carrie plugged in the coffeepot and sat down across from him in the chair Shane had vacated. She felt more comfortable with a little distance between them. "Oh, I can cook. I just get in a rut making mostly the things a seven-year-old boy likes to eat. Quick and easy. Our menus would leave most men unsatisfied."

"Do you invite a lot of men up here to share meals with you and Shane?"

No, and I didn't invite you, either. Carrie got up to get the cups. "You ask too many questions. I agreed to do a painting for your building, not to be interviewed on my life, past and present." She sat down again and raised her eyes to his. "And I especially resent your interrogating Shane."

Brock shoved his chair back and crossed his legs as he leaned forward. "I haven't asked him a single question, in front of you or behind your back, that you would have trouble with. Your son is friendly and outgoing. He volunteers information. We were getting acquainted. Is that so wrong? What are you afraid that I'll find out, Carrie?"

"Nothing." She said it too quickly, too defensively. "My son doesn't need your friendship."

"I think you're wrong. I don't know much about children, but I'd guess that boy's dying for some male company. Don't you date? Don't you ever bring someone around, some guy who'd take him fishing, or hiking, or camping?"

She got up to pour the coffee, holding the pot with two hands so he wouldn't notice them trembling. "*I* take him fishing and hiking and camping. I would never bring men around, as you so charmingly put it, and have Shane grow fond of them and then be hurt when they moved on. Besides, I don't want him exposed to that kind of thing. I'm enough company for him, along with his teachers and schoolmates." Sitting down, she sipped her coffee. Why was she bothering to explain herself to this man? she wondered.

He was beginning to see. Mac had hinted that Natalie had been unfaithful. Had Carrie grown up watching her mother bring home an assortment of men who'd eventually moved on? Is that why she was somewhat bitter and defensive, why she'd chosen to live a secluded life? Or did her attitude have more to do with her dead husband?

"Did Rusty like this house?" he asked, his eyes in his coffee cup as he drank.

She frowned at him. "You're doing it again, asking questions that are none of your business. Are you building a file on us back in your rented house, marking down everything you learn, so you can present it to my father and earn yourself a big bonus for bringing about a family reunion? If you are, you can forget it, because that's not going to happen."

Brock searched her face as he drummed his fingers on the table. He couldn't blame her for the way she felt, but she was dead wrong. "I talked with your father on the phone yesterday. I didn't mention meeting you, nor will I unless you give the go-ahead. You can trust me on this."

She gave a short laugh. "Trust? Aren't you the man who bribed someone to find me, then omitted a few facts to get me to your building?"

Frustrated, Brock ran a hand through his hair. "I've admitted all that, and I also explained why I did it. I really do want you to do the painting. The reconciliation, I felt, would please Mac, but there's no strings attached to the contract on your painting. Honest."

Honest. Carrie stared into blue eyes that seemed sincere. Yet her experience had been that most men weren't honest. "I've agreed to do the painting. So why are you here?"

"I told you. I came to apologize for my harsh words last night. I was out of line. And because I'd like to get to know you."

"Why?"

Brock scratched his unshaven chin. "Damned if I know. I'm not usually masochistic." He thought he saw a small twitch of her mouth. He held out his hand. "I asked you before. Can't we be friends?"

"I don't want any more friends."

"I do. I need all the friends I can scrounge up." He reached his outstretched palm closer to her. "How about it?"

This is a mistake, she told herself, even as she cautiously slid her hand into his. A big mistake. He was too persistent, too charming, too male. Hadn't she been down this road once already, and found it to be full of potholes?

His fingers closed around hers, warm and strong. His eyes crinkled at the corners as he smiled at her, and she struggled not to let him see how her heart was suddenly pounding. Rusty had overwhelmed her with his vigorous pursuit. Brock wore her down with his infinite patience. Of the two, she thought the latter more dangerous.

"Mom!"

She heard her son's voice before she heard his footsteps and guiltily jerked her hand from Brock's. Jumping up, she went out onto the enclosed back porch and moaned aloud at the sight before her. Shane stood by the door, dripping mud from his hair to his soaked tennis shoes.

"I had an accident."

"I guess you did."

He dragged a slithery gob from his arm. "I was playing with Billie, chasing him, and I slipped and fell into the mud pile by the fence." White teeth gleamed through a muddy grin. "You're not mad, are you?"

"I should be," Carrie said, fighting a smile. "That mud pile's for Billie to roll in, not you." She reached to pull his shirt off over his head.

"Billie ran past and didn't even get splashed."

"Pretty smart goat," Brock said as he joined them. He took the T-shirt from Carrie and placed it on the floor by the door. "Why don't you run his bath, and I'll finish undressing him?"

"Thanks, but I can manage."

"Sure you can," he said as he unfastened the snap of Shane's shorts. "But it's easier if two of us do it. Come on, sport. Push out of your shoes."

Carrie stepped back. He simply had to be a part of everything. She'd never met a man like him. Was he faking? She tried one more time. "You'll get all dirty."

"I've been dirty before."

"I like being dirty, but Mom's not crazy about it."

Shaking her head at the two of them, Carrie went to run the bath. Though Shane hated bubble bath, she poured in a generous amount, thinking he'd need it this time. Sitting on the edge of the tub, she turned off the water as Brock came through the doorway carrying Shane. Gingerly he set the boy into the foamy water.

Carrie handed her son the shampoo.

"You want to help?" Shane asked, looking up at Brock, avoiding his mother's eyes.

"Sure." Pleased, Brock knelt by the tub.

"Really, I can bathe him," Carrie interjected, sounding a bit exasperated with her son. "Actually, Shane's perfectly capable of doing it himself."

"Probably is," Brock said as he tipped the boy's head back and poured water on his hair, rinsing out the worst of the mud. "I kind of like this though. Brings back memories. I lived with my aunt and uncle in this big old farmhouse, and they had three boys, all younger than me. Every night it was my job to bathe them."

Carrie crossed her legs and leaned an elbow on her knee. "How old were you?"

Brock worked up a rich lather. "Dad and I moved in with them when I was four, after my mother died. Aunt Emma gave me chores to do right from day one. Farm chores, kitchen chores, and later on, babysitting chores. Hard work builds character, she used to say." He tipped Shane back in the water again to rinse his head and shot Carrie a wry glance. "By the time I was sixteen, I had enough character for two kids."

"Bet you missed your mom," Shane added, his eyes tightly shut against the sluicing water.

"Well, there were days I could have used someone in my corner, and she probably would have been. Moms are like that."

Carrie couldn't tell if he sounded bitter or sad. "What about your father? Why did he let your aunt work you so hard?"

Brock shrugged as he applied soap to the washcloth. "Dad told me we should be grateful we had a room over our heads and to do as Aunt Emma said. He worked the farm with my Uncle Joe—hard, back-breaking work—and every night after dinner the two of them would sit drinking cheap whiskey till they fell asleep. Aunt Emma was filled with disgust for them, and she wasn't any too crazy about little boys, either—not her own and certainly not me. She liked to go to church and sing hymns." And later, after his father had died quietly in his sleep, she'd liked the money Social Security sent her for Brock's care.

Carrie watched the gentle way he ran the cloth over Shane's bony legs, tickling his toes and making him laugh. He'd told her a lot, yet not in a self-pitying way. More like a factual recital. Still, she was certain such a hard childhood had left a mark on him. He was much more complex than she'd originally thought. "No wonder you were anxious to get away from there."

Brock rinsed the suds from the boy. "Yeah and I never want to go back. Not to that town and not to that life." He pulled the plug from the drain and turned to look at her. "I guess we all have something in our childhood that we don't like to remember." He lifted Shane from the tub, stood him on the rug and handed him a towel. "Can you take it from here, sport?"

Shane dabbed at his wet arms with the towel. "Yeah, thanks." A sudden thought struck him. "You're not leaving yet, are you?"

Drying his hands, Brock smiled down at him. "Oh, I think your mom's about ready to throw me out. Mustn't overstay my welcome, or I won't be asked back." She'd probably been ready for him to leave an hour ago.

"*I'll* ask you back." He turned to his mother. "You're not going to throw him out, are you, Mom?"

Licked again, and she knew it. Carrie dragged the end of the towel up to help dry her son's hair. "Not quite yet. He hasn't finished his coffee. I'll get your pajamas."

Brock followed her out of the bathroom and went on into the kitchen. She'd been maneuvered into letting him stay by her son and her good manners, yet she wasn't as unhappy about it as she'd been when he'd first arrived. Maybe she was getting used to him, possibly even enjoying his company. For the life of him, Brock couldn't figure why that had become important to him.

He settled into a kitchen chair and gazed out at the dark sky, wondering at his strange reaction to Carrie Weston. Last night, he'd said things to her he shouldn't have, and said them cruelly. Now he knew exactly why he'd done it. She was getting under his skin, and he didn't want that.

It would be best, for both of them to end abruptly what they never should have begun. He was certain she felt the undercurrent of attraction, too. She was all wrong for him. He'd escaped from his hellish beginnings and made something of himself by careful planning, by mapping out his future and following the charted course.

He needed smooth sophistication in a woman, not bohemian playfulness. He needed an efficient, complacent, predictable partner, not a strong-willed, distrustful and independent one. He needed a woman who dressed stylishly, who'd be an asset to his career, someone undemanding and uncomplicated. He didn't need someone who padded around barefoot in a yard full of animals, looked at him with large, vulnerable eyes and had a mouth that beckoned him to taste her.

The sound of bare feet hitting the bare wooden floor brought him out of his reverie. Shane came barreling into the kitchen and stopped in front of Brock. He cocked his head and studied him a long minute.

"I have to go to bed now. You can hug me goodnight, if you want to."

The kid was a heartbreaker. Brock scooped him into his arms for a big hug, inhaling the soapy-clean scent of him.

"Mom promised you can come back. Will you?"

"You bet." He gave in to the urge to ruffle the boy's hair. "Sleep tight, sport."

Satisfied, Shane ran to his bedroom.

Brock sat back down. He was rubbing on a mud spot on the knee of his pants when Carrie walked in and moved to the counter.

"Are you ready for a fresh cup of coffee?" she asked. When he didn't answer, she turned to him. He was lost in thought, his fingers working the fabric of his jeans. "Did you hear me?" He looked up and she saw that his eyes were dark and unsure.

"He told me I could hug him if I wanted to." He shook his head. "That's some kid you've got there."

Carrie crossed her arms over her chest and leaned against the counter. She wasn't surprised that Shane had gotten to him. "A child's hug is magic, didn't you know? That's why they're so stingy with them." She watched him a moment longer, but he seemed to be looking at something she couldn't see. "Did you want that coffee now?"

"What?" Slowly he stood. "No, no thanks. It's late and I've got to go." He took a step toward the door. "I want to thank you for tonight. I know you didn't want me here but . . ."

She brushed off his comment and opened the door. "I'd better see you to the gate." Her smile was teasing. "Billie might still be hungry."

He didn't smile back but instead slipped his arm about her waist and inched her close to his side as they walked. He seemed so different from last night that Carrie didn't pull away as her fist instincts told her to do. The rain had all but stopped with only a light drizzle falling and cooling her heated skin. From his pile of straw, Billie gave a low, throaty bray but didn't get up. In the distance an owl gave a hoot that echoed softly through the canyon. By the time they reached the gate, her heart was thudding in her chest at his nearness.

Brock stopped and turned her to face him. Her eyes were huge in the light of a hazy moon. He needed to know something. "Was your marriage a good one, Carrie? Were you happy?"

She wanted to jump in with a standard answer, the one that would stop further questions. But somehow she couldn't. "No," she said softly. "I'd filed for divorce two months before he crashed."

He felt badly about what she'd gone through but oddly pleased at her answer. She was close, warm and fragrant. She'd tried to hide it from him, but several times tonight he'd seen the way she'd watched him, her eyes filled with curiosity, a need she would deny and a hint of desire. It was time to satisfy all three. His lips grazed hers, whisper soft. He felt her hand flutter to his chest.

She turned her head aside. "No. I . . . I don't do this."

He eased back from her. "Do what?"

"Kiss men I don't know. I simply don't."

"Do you kiss men you *do* know?" He raised his hand to cup her chin, ran a thumb over her lips and watched her eyes turn smoky. "Kissing is good for you, Carrie." He let his fingers trail down her throat. "The Institute for Mental Health says everyone needs six hugs a day and at least two kisses." Her face was inches from his as he drew her closer. "I'd wager you're a few kisses behind on that scale, Carrie."

His mouth covered hers, and his arms tightened around her. Though he held her firmly, his mouth was soft, persuasive, seducing her slowly. She hadn't expected gentleness, nor a slow exploration, yet that's what he gave her. She sensed a patience in him, something she'd never experienced in a man's kiss. She parted her lips slightly, and his tongue moved inside. Head spinning, she gripped his shirtsleeves and let herself feel.

He hadn't meant to start anything, hadn't set out to kiss her. Or maybe subconsciously he had, for he wasn't normally an impulsive person. He hadn't expected to find her quite so warm and willing, so responsive. He also hadn't expected to want to taste and touch her everywhere, to have the kiss go on and on.

He smelled the rain in her hair and fought the urge to plunge his hands into the dark thickness and let it fall in waves around her face. He tasted shyness mingling with desire, and he longed to know more. Shifting slightly, he took her deeper and heard her soft murmur.

How could she have known she'd wanted to be touched just like this, to be held this exact way? She'd denied herself so long, forgotten the hunger that could build so quickly, the madness that could flare out of control in moments. Sweet passion—she'd been there before, or had thought that was what it was. She knew the velvet trap that acquiescence could bring. She should have walked away the first time. She would pull away this time.

"Please, Brock." She pushed at him with the last of her willpower and eased back. "I'm sorry. I shouldn't have led you on."

His hands were shaking, and he was shocked to see it. Brock took a deep breath and hoped it would calm him. "You didn't lead me on, and there's nothing to be sorry about. I wanted to kiss you, so I did. Correct me if I'm wrong, but I thought you wanted that, too."

"I did. I mean, no, I didn't." Carrie ran a hand over her damp hair. "You don't understand. I don't want a part of kissing or casual sex or men in general. I have my son to think of and . . ."

"What a bunch of crap!" He took a step back so he could see her face better. "Half the world's made up of the male of the species. Are you writing all of us off because of one mistake?"

Carrie got her breathing under control. "That leaves fifty percent you can go after, and I wish you luck. I'm not interested." She turned on her heel and started toward the house.

He caught her in two long strides, touched her arm and swung her about. "The hell you're not. You can lie to your son, your friends and yourself. But you can't lie to me. I kissed you just now, lady, and you kissed me back. Hungrily. Thoroughly. You can hate it, you can deny it, but you can't change it. You're interested, all right. As interested as I am.'' He dropped his arm. ''You're just not happy about it.''

Before he could change his mind and haul her back into his arms, he hopped the fence and walked to his car. At the door, he turned to see her still standing where he'd left her. ''To tell you the truth, I'm not happy about it, either.'' He got behind the wheel and started the engine.

Trembling, Carrie watched his red taillights disappear down the winding road. No, she was *not* going to let herself get involved with another man, most especially not with a man who was deeply entwined with her father. *She was not.*

Resolutely she turned and walked around the rain puddles to her door.

Chapter Five

I can hold the end of the tape if that'll make it easier for you," Rhoda Hudson suggested.

Tape measure in hand, Carrie turned from the wall she'd been studying and looked at the neat, efficient-looking secretary. She'd come to the McKamey Building unannounced this morning to take some measurements and get a feel for the lobby where her painting was to hang. She needed no assistance in measuring, since her metal tape was the kind that could easily run up a wall and stay in place. But Carrie decided it wouldn't do any harm to befriend Brock Logan's right-hand woman. Before this contract was fulfilled, she might need a friend or two on her side.

She gave Rhoda a smile. "Thanks. That would be a big help." Carrie gave her the end of the tape, and together they measured the ivory-colored wall. Carrie made a few notations on her pad. "Do you have any idea what will be placed along here so I know about how high the painting will have to be hung?''

Rhoda ran a hand through her salt-and-pepper hair. "Just green plants, I believe the decorator said." She pointed to the far wall. "Over there will be a conversational group—a couch and several chairs, a couple of tables, I imagine. But we want the painting to be the focal point, the first thing that someone entering the lobby sees."

She couldn't have asked for more. "Was that the decorator's idea?"

"No. Brock's. He's quite impressed with you." Rhoda's eyes were kind but held an undeniable curiosity. "With your work, that is." She let her words hang in the air, but when Carrie didn't comment, she went on. "Would you like a cup of coffee? I have a pot going in my office."

Carrie stuffed her tape and notepad into her large tote bag. She'd expected to quietly hop in and out without running into anyone, so she'd worn her casual clothes—white jeans and a yellow cotton top. She eyed Rhoda's soft silk blouse and trim skirt and felt a little out of place, but decided she would chance it. "If I'm not holding you up..."

"Not a bit," Rhoda said as she led the way around the bend to her office. "I've also got the color charts the decorator left, which you might be interested in seeing."

"Yes, I would." The click of Rhoda's high heels on the still uncarpeted hallway was overly loud as Carrie followed her down the deserted corridor. From her earlier visit, she knew that Rhoda's office connected to Brock's, and as they neared, she hoped he wasn't in. She wasn't quite ready to see him again, not with the memory of the kiss they'd shared last night so vivid in her mind.

More than eight years had passed since she'd felt the tug of desire he'd forced her to face last evening. She'd been out with a couple of men since then, mostly at Sonya's insistence, for the gallery customers often wanted to meet the artist. The dates were an odd combination of business and supposed pleasure. But she'd been uncomfortable and ill at ease, anxious for the evenings to end. Finally, she'd told Sonya she wanted no part in promoting her own work, that she'd do the paintings and the older woman would have to do the rest. And she'd stuck to that. Until Brock.

Not that any of those casual businesslike dinners had put her in a position of encouraging a good-night kiss. She'd always insisted she drive herself to the restaurant so there'd be no loss of control on her part. Perhaps she'd have taken that step, seen one of those faceless men the second time, if any of them had appealed to her. None had.

She'd let no man touch her, not physically and not emotionally. Not since Rusty. At nineteen, when she'd first met the flying ace, she had let herself go with the tide of feelings. In recent years, she had had her lonely moments. But basically, she'd not missed the contact, the entanglement that clouded her mind and impaired her judgment ... until last night when she'd been reminded of the sensual pull that could be so enervating. And she was determined to resist it this time.

"I hope you'll overlook the disarray," Rhoda said as she walked to a card table set up in the corner of her spacious office. "The carpeting goes in next week, and then the new furniture will be delivered. At least they're finished painting at this end of the building."

She handed a Styrofoam cup to Carrie. "I hate working with makeshift supplies, but we'll have to put up with the mess for another few weeks."

Sipping the coffee, Carrie walked over to the bank of bare windows looking out onto a small sloping yard. Several workmen were planting flowers, a nice splash of color amid the towering palm trees. "You have a lovely view."

"Yes, especially compared to our office in Chicago. There, on a clear day you can see the building across the street."

Carrie turned, wondering if she dared indulge her curiosity with this sharp lady. "Have you been with Brock long?"

Rhoda walked over and sat down on the wide window seat. "From the day he came aboard, I guess you could say. I'd just been through a rough time personally, and Mac knew I needed a diversion. Brock was a sophomore in college, bright and eager to learn, working only part-time, and he was assigned to me."

"So you showed him the ropes?"

"More or less. I'd been the mother bunny in the typing pool up to then, but after a draining and terrible divorce, I wasn't sure I wanted to do that anymore. Mac had had a similar experience and knew how emotionally wrung out I was. He promoted me to a position as sort of a roving assistant, teaching the new kids. And Brock was one of the ones who lasted." She smiled at the memory. "He wanted to know everything. Still does. I love a mind that wants to learn. He made me sharpen up so I could answer his questions. After law school, he joined the firm full-time and asked me to be his secretary."

So her father had been his mentor, and this kind woman had been like the mother he'd never known. After his insensitive aunt and his uncaring father, Brock had been fortunate, after all. "He's lucky to have had you."

Rhoda drained her cup and set it down. "We're all lucky to have had Mac. He's the driving force in this company. Brock doesn't trust women too readily, though occasionally he'll take my advice. But he listens to Mac."

Carrie took her cup to the table and picked up the color charts. She wondered if Rhoda's interest in Mac was more than professional, then decided it was none of her business. She didn't particularly want to get into a discussion of her father's merits at the moment. But it seemed Rhoda was intent on making her point.

"Mac should be here sometime next week so you can meet him. He's truly a wonderful man."

Carrie studied the chart. "So I've heard. Do you think I could borrow this chart? I'd like to match some of the colors."

"Sure." Rhoda stood and walked to her desk. "When do you think you'll have the painting finished? We've got a grand opening scheduled to take place in a couple of weeks."

"We may have to postpone that date," said a soft voice from the doorway.

"Francine!" Rhoda said with a smile. "I didn't know you were arriving today."

Carrie looked at the newcomer and immediately wished she'd taken more care in dressing for this visit. The woman was tall, a good five foot eight, she'd guess, and quite slender with pale blond hair done in an elegant French twist. Her suit was raw silk, a cool-looking mint green that matched her eyes, worn with an ivory blouse. A thin leather briefcase dangled from long red-tipped fingers.

"I'm only here for a couple of hours. I had to take care of some business in Monterey, and I thought I'd surprise Brock."

"You say we may have to postpone the opening?" Rhoda asked.

"Mmm. The Whitney project is taking longer than expected to complete. Mac's there now, and I'm flying to join him later this afternoon. It could possibly delay us a bit." She sauntered into the room, her gaze sliding to Carrie.

Rhoda remembered her manners. "This is Carrie Weston. Francine, the artist who'll be doing the painting for the lobby. Carrie, Francine Thomas, Mac's executive assistant."

"Nice to meet you," Francine said. "I've heard you're very good."

The eyes were friendly enough, Carrie noted, though the woman herself seemed distracted as she reached out for a quick handshake. "Thank you."

Francine turned back toward Rhoda as she checked the time on her slim gold watch. "Is Brock in, Rhoda? I haven't much time."

"I believe so." Rhoda pushed the intercom button.

"Yes, Rhoda?" came the quick inquiry in Brock's deep voice.

"Someone to see you, Brock."

"Who is it?" He sounded impatient.

So, obviously, was Francine. Before Rhoda could reply, she was opening his office door and strolling in. "Hello, darling. I thought I'd drop in for lunch."

From where she stood, Carrie couldn't see into the room, but she could hear. There was a slight hesitancy, then she heard Brock's chair move back on the bare floor.

"Well, this is a surprise," he said as Francine closed the door behind her. To her ear, he hadn't sounded especially pleased, but perhaps that was what she wanted to hear.

Darling. So that's how it was, Carrie thought. She should have known a man as attractive as Brock would have a woman somewhere. Or women. He'd been lonely last night, and Shane's warm hug had mellowed him. The feeling spilled over to the kiss he'd given her. That's all it had been.

Only it hadn't felt like that.

"Francine's been with the firm a long while," Rhoda explained. "She works closely with Mac on his personal projects."

Good for her, Carrie thought as she settled the strap of her bag more comfortably on her shoulder. It was time to leave before this chatty woman told her Francine's life story, which she most definitely did not want to hear. She found a smile as she turned toward the door. "Thanks for the coffee, and the charts. I'll return them in a couple of days."

"No hurry. Can you find your way out?"

"Yes, thanks. Bye." Walking rapidly, hoping Brock and Francine would stay put until she'd safely cleared the building, she headed down the hallway toward the lobby.

She was glad she'd come. For a few crazy hours, she'd let herself slip back into her teens and spend an inordinate amount of time thinking about a man again. Now that she'd seen for herself that Brock was involved with someone, she could cut out the nonsense and get back to work. Which was for the best, since she hadn't wanted an involvement of any sort, anyway.

Getting behind the wheel of her Volkswagen, Carrie sighed as she searched for her keys. Francine was just the kind of lovely accomplished businesswoman she'd have imagined Brock would be attracted to. Someone who dressed beautifully and would be at home in the boardroom as well as hostessing huge cocktail parties. Yes, his kind of woman. Carrie started the car.

She needed to get the paintings in her backseat over to Sonya's gallery, then to get home and get busy. She frowned at the cloudless blue sky. For some reason, even the thought of beginning a new painting didn't excite her. Maybe she was coming down with a cold.

The lunch wasn't going well, and Brock wasn't quite sure why. Maybe it was because he had a lot of paperwork he wanted to finish today and he resented being interrupted. Maybe it was because he didn't much care for surprises. Or maybe it was because he knew Francine had no real reason to show up today, except to see him. Ordinarily that wouldn't bother him, though she didn't make a habit of arriving unannounced. Why her unexpected presence today was annoying him he couldn't have explained.

"You haven't heard a word I've said for the past minute and a half," Francine's quiet voice accused. "Is something the matter, Brock?"

He was looking out the window, watching a sailboat cruise by on the far horizon. Watching and wishing he were on it, a picnic basket on board, and

Carrie Weston seated alongside him as they headed for a secluded inlet. Startled by the direction of his meandering thoughts, he turned back to Francine. "Sorry. I've got a lot of my mind."

She gave him a forgiving smile. "The zoning board still giving you a hard time?"

He grabbed the excuse she'd given him. "They're a hard bunch, unwilling to compromise."

Francine reached for her briefcase and unzipped the outside pocket. "I thought as much, so I looked up a similar case we'd dealt with on that Brentwood project." She extracted a folder and offered it to him. "In case you need it for ammunition."

Usually her quiet efficiency pleased him. Today it irritated him along with the thought that she didn't feel he could handle the problem without her help. Nonetheless, he took the papers from her.

"Have you had a chance to meet any of the locals, to get acquainted with anyone special in the two weeks you've been here?"

He looked at her sharply, but her expression was merely curious. "I've been pretty involved at the office."

"I met that artist you've hired to do the painting for the lobby, Carrie Weston. She's very beautiful. What's she like?"

Brock frowned. "When did you meet her?"

"She was in Rhoda's office when I walked in. There's something familiar about her, but I can't put my finger on it."

What had Carrie been doing in with Rhoda? he wondered. He should have known Francine would spot the similarity. Mac had shown Carolyn's picture to her, too. He was surprised Rhoda hadn't made the connection. He didn't want her identity known throughout the company before Mac arrived and before he could get Carrie used to the idea.

"Oh, you know, these artists are all alike. Listen, I'd rather you didn't mention her to Mac just yet. She's an unknown, and I'd like to introduce them myself later."

Francine gave him a puzzled look, but nodded. "Certainly."

Brock signaled the waiter for their check. "I'd better get you back so you won't miss your plane."

Digging in his wallet for his credit card, he saw from the corner of his eye that Francine had noticed his eagerness to send her on her way, but was choosing to ignore it. Irrationally, he wished she'd get angry and tell him off instead of taking everything so beautifully in stride. He could well imagine, given the same set of circumstances, that Carrie Weston would. He could picture those violet eyes narrowing in indignation, the color moving into her lovely face, the quick reply and...

"Are you certain there's nothing troubling you, Brock?" Francine asked. "You seem more than just distracted."

The waiter arrived, and Brock thrust the card at him before turning to her with a frown. "I don't know what you mean. I'm fine." He was acting like a first-rate heel, and he knew it. She'd come all this way, and he wasn't even pretending he was glad she had. He tried to put warmth in his smile. "I'm really glad you surprised me with this visit. It's always good to see you." He hoped the words didn't sound as false to her ears as they did to his.

Looking somewhat appeased, Francine rose and made her way through the tables to the front of the seaside restaurant as Brock followed. Even when he treated her badly, she reacted with calm acceptance. Wasn't that one of the things he'd admired about her, the fact that she never appeared frazzled or ruffled, rarely showed anger or petulance? She was, by most men's standards, lovely, intelligent and charming and would be an asset to her husband in every way.

Brock had thought at times that perhaps Francine Thomas might be the perfect mate for a man on the rise. The fact that he didn't feel passion for her hadn't really bothered him, for he thought passion too fleeting a thing to build a marriage on. Somehow, during the last week, he'd begun to question that theory.

Outside the restaurant, Brock took Francine's elbow to guide her to his car in the adjacent parking lot. But she stopped and stepped back from him. With a wave of her hand, she indicated a row of taxis waiting in the curved driveway.

"I think I'll take a cab to the Monterey airport. I know you have a million things to do, darling."

Her habit of calling him *darling* was one of the things he'd change about her, Brock thought, but he was too pleased at her letting him off the hook to mention it today. Yet a lingering sense of guilt made him voice at least a token protest. "I'm not *that* busy, really."

Slowly she touched his cheek, then ran her slender fingers around his jaw. Her smile was a little off center. "Yes, I think you are. I only hope by my next visit you'll have your business cleared up and that you'll save a little time for me. A little private time."

Brock signaled the first cab in line and watched it draw alongside. "It's a date. Give my best to Mac." He leaned down for a quick kiss.

But Francine evidently thought to shore up her argument. Tossing her briefcase in through the open cab door, she reached to pull his head down for a thorough, lingering kiss. When she opened her eyes, she studied his a long moment. "Don't work too hard, darling," she whispered, then folded her long legs into the taxi.

Brock loosened his tie as he watched the cab pull into traffic. What, he wondered, had that been all about? Though he'd considered an alliance with Francine, he'd never hinted as much to her. Did this surprise mean she had had the same idea? Walking to his car, he ran a hand through his hair. Kissing him on the sidewalk in public was so unlike Francine. Maybe it was that strange intuition women had that had warned her his attention was waning. She'd obviously wanted to leave him with a reminder. Yet her kiss hadn't moved him, hadn't made him long for more. Not that they'd shared many kisses. Actually, they'd shared very little outside of business and a few casual dinners.

Thoughtfully Brock got into his car. He liked Francine. At thirty-four he knew he ought to be thinking of settling down. He did want a family. Still, he was in no hurry. He slid the key into the ignition. A son would be nice. A bright kid like Shane.

At the driveway, he put on his turn signal and waited for traffic to slow. *You can hug me good-night, if you want to.* Yeah, he was one super kid. Brock headed for the office. He wondered if Carrie had gotten started on the painting yet. He pictured her in her studio, seated on that high stool, concentrating on the canvas in front of her. Probably she'd have her hair in a ponytail to keep it out of the way. She'd have on shorts and one of those baggy shirts and . . .

Braking for a light, he glanced at the store on the corner. There was a big sale going on. A sudden idea hit him, and, grinning, he maneuvered around the corner and pulled up alongside the store. Shane would love it, he thought as he climbed out. He'd be getting off the school bus in another half hour. He shoved his nagging conscience aside and decided his paperwork could wait until morning. He'd hurry on over, surprise the boy.

"You really don't have to feed me every time you see me," Carrie told Sonya as they strolled along Ocean Avenue on their way back to the gallery after lunch.

"Oh, you know I love to eat outside on Flaherty's patio. It's such a beautiful day."

"I know you love to sit out there and have half of Carmel stop by and say hello," Carrie teased her. "A bit like the queen holding court, I thought."

Sonya chuckled as she adjusted the sash of her belted paisley blouse. "It's hell to be popular." She squeezed Carrie's arm. "You've been rather quiet today. Are you already busily planning your new painting for that building?"

In reality, her mind had been more on the man who'd commissioned the painting than on the work itself, Carrie thought, though she wasn't about to tell Sonya that. "You know how it is when I start something new. My mind drifts."

"What's he like?"

"What's who like?"

They stopped at the curb as the light turned red. Sonya turned her head toward Carrie. "The man with the blue, blue eyes. Brock Logan."

"Oh, him."

"Are we going to fence a while, or are you going to tell me?"

She should have known she wouldn't be able to get away with not filling Sonya in on everything, Carrie realized. The older woman had always been able to see through her best masked strategies. She hadn't talked with her since she'd first gone to meet Brock. Perhaps she'd come to Sonya today subconsciously wanting to talk about the situation, though she'd managed to avoid the topic during lunch. Sometimes hearing yourself say things out loud helped clear the cobwebs. And Sonya's insight had an uncanny way of zeroing in on the heart of the matter.

Stepping off the curb as the light changed, Carrie sighed. "The sign will be going up on the building soon. McKamey and Associates. My father's building. And Brock's his protégé."

A sharp intake of breath was the only sign that Sonya had heard her. "Let's go sit over there," she said, indicating a park bench set in a shady alcove outside a busy T-shirt shop catering to tourists. She settled the folds of her wide skirt as she sat down, pulling Carrie down beside her. As people strolled by, eating caramel corn, studying city maps, smelling of suntan lotion, Sonya took her time lighting a cigarette. "There's a certain privacy in crowds. Now, tell me."

And so Carrie did, about the way she'd discovered the truth, their dinner together and Brock's visit to her home to apologize. She told it all, except the way the evening had ended with a kiss. That was a lapse, a momentary interval in her life's plan that she had no intention of repeating.

"It sounds like he's interested in more than just your painting," Sonya concluded. "I don't like his deception, and I don't like him trying to get to you through Shane. Do you think your father put him up to all that?"

"Brock claims my father doesn't know he's found me. And, of course, Mac would have no way of knowing about Shane's existence, except through Brock."

With a freckled hand, Sonya fought a gust of wind for control of her reddish-silver hair. "Hmm, I wonder. If Mac's company is that successful, he must be a very wealthy man. He could have hired private investigators to locate you. Or perhaps offered a reward. Maybe that's what Brock's after."

Carrie shook her head. "He may be many things we're unaware of, but I doubt Brock can be bought. Besides, he drives a Ferrari and dresses right out of GQ."

"Honey, everyone's got their price tag, and it's not always money. Maybe he thinks he'll score a coup in the company if he hands Mac's daughter to him on a silver platter, complete with grandson."

Carrie looked skeptical. "He's already a full partner, and he has a law degree. He talks of Mac in glowing terms, as more like a mentor than an employer. And so does his secretary. Of course, that doesn't surprise me. Mac was always warm, loving and generous to me until . . ."

"Until he ordered you from his home?" Sonya covered Carrie's hand with her own. "I can certainly see, having known your mother, how he might have sent Natalie packing. But his ten-year-old daughter? You might want to keep that in mind, honey. I'd hate to see you get hurt all over again."

Carrie sighed. "Believe me, I don't want to walk back through all those memories, either." She swung troubled eyes to Sonya's concerned face. "Brock told me he wouldn't force a meeting between us, even though my father's going to be here for the grand opening of his building in a week or two. I want to believe Brock, but . . ."

"But it's hard to believe a man who's lied to you before."

"It is, for me—after all the times Rusty lied to me, and, like a fool, I believed him." She rubbed her forehead wearily.

"You weren't a fool. You were young and in love."

"But I'm older now, and certainly not in love, yet I wonder how much wiser I am."

Sonya's perceptive blue eyes narrowed. "Brock wouldn't have to win you over if he plans to tell your father he's found you. All he has to do is give McKarney your address and let him take it from there. It's more likely Brock's interested in you personally. You're a beautiful woman with a great deal to offer. I think he's fallen for you." Sonya took a long pull on her cigarette.

Carrie shook her head. "I met the woman he's involved with this morning, Francine Thomas. She's my father's executive assistant, and she flew in just to see Brock for a couple of hours."

"How do you know they're involved?"

She shrugged. "I could just tell. She's certainly his type—blond, cool, sophisticated. I sure can't see her kneeling on a kitchen floor helping a cat have kittens."

"What?"

"Nothing, just a thought. I'm glad I found out about Francine. It'll be that much easier to keep our relationship strictly business." She stood, shoving her hands into her slacks pockets, wondering why she was a little shaky today. "I've got to get home and get to work. The sooner I finish that painting, the sooner Brock will be out of my life. Once the building opens, he'll be back in Chicago at their main office. And so will my father."

Slowly Sonya rose, still studying Carrie's face. "Yes, that will be best for all concerned."

"Right." She leaned to kiss Sonya's cheek. "Thanks for lunch. I'll call you next week."

"Are you planning to work all weekend?"

"Today's Shane's last day of school, and I promised him I'd take him camping tomorrow and Sunday. But next week, I'm going to hit it heavy."

"Good girl. Call me."

"I will." With a smile, Carrie turned to make her way to her car. Glancing at her watch, she saw she'd better hustle if she wanted to make it home before Shane's bus dropped him off.

He'd gotten a little carried away at the store, Brock decided as he pulled his car alongside Carrie's in her driveway. He hoped she wouldn't be angry with him because the man behind the counter had said he couldn't return any of the sale items he'd purchased.

Getting out of the car, he glanced up at the cloudless afternoon sky. What a beautiful day, he thought as he pulled off his tie and flung it on the seat on top of his suit coat. As he rolled up his shirtsleeves, he wondered what it would be like to live in a climate where the sun shone nearly every day. A native of Chicago's often inclement weather, he envied those who enjoyed California sunshine daily. He'd even told Rhoda to take the rest of the day off when he'd called in to tell her he wasn't returning today. She'd had trouble keeping the surprise from her voice. She wasn't used to his new habit of playing hooky.

Billie came over to the gate, but made only a mild throaty sound, and his stance was nonthreatening. Perhaps the goat recognized him, Brock thought as he opened the trunk and pocketed his keys. Hefting his large purchases into his arms, he glanced about the front and side yard but could see no one. They were undoubtedly inside or out back. Carefully, he maneuvered through the gate with the inquisitive goat trailing close behind as he walked toward the oceanside.

He saw Carrie as he rounded the corner of the house. His heart surprised him by skipping a few beats as he watched the sea breezes lift and swirl her dark hair about her head. She was dressed casually, standing barefoot in the grassy area by the porch talking with a short Oriental man who was sculpting her bushes with artistic strokes of his hedge clippers. It had to be the Japanese neighbor from above.

Zeke, perched on Carrie's shoulder, swiveled his black head and saw him first. "Pretty boy," he squawked and Carrie turned. He saw quick surprise register on her face, then a frown appear as she took in all that he was carrying.

"Hello," he called as he neared. "I came to see Shane." He stopped by the door and saw her violet eyes fill with suspicion.

Slowly she walked over to him as the gardener went back to work. She looked at his bundles, then moved her gaze up to meet his. "Why did you do this?"

Brock shifted the heavy load in his arms. "Because I thought Shane would like..."

"A fish tank!" The screen door slammed as Shane appeared carrying a large laundry basket heaped to the top with folded clothes. He set it down in the grass before rushing over to Brock. "Wow! And fish, too. Who's it for?"

"It might be for you, sport," Brock said, unable to contain a smile at the boy's enthusiasm. "If your mom doesn't object."

"She won't object. She loves animals, even fish. Don't you, Mom?" Shane peered into the glass tank Brock still held and studied the two golden fish and one larger black one that blew bubbles upward in the plastic bag filled with water. "A black one, too. And seaweed and a castle and a filter. Mom, look at this stuff. It's neater than Jeff's."

"Who's Jeff?" Brock asked.

"My friend. He lives near school. I visit him once in a while, but his tank's real small. Wait'll he sees this." He looked up at his mother, excitement lighting up his face. "We can keep it, can't we, Mom?"

Carrie felt like bopping Brock right in the noggin with the fish tank—fish, castle and all. It was hard for her to believe that the immaculate Mr. Logan, wearing a sparkling white shirt, neatly pressed blue slacks and leather shoes with a shine you could brush your teeth in, had suddenly developed a penchant for goldfish. Maybe Sonya was right. He was trying to get to her through Shane. But why? She brushed a lock of hair from her face and looked at her son. How—just how—could she refuse him? And Brock damn well knew it.

"I suppose so, but . . ."

"Great." Delighted, Shane gave her a big smile before skipping back to Brock. "Let's take it to my room."

"Ah, Miss Weston, a moment, please," the Japanese man interrupted. "I'm finished in back. You want the same treatment for your front bushes, just like last time?"

Carrie tore her gaze from the problem at hand and gave him an apologetic smile. "Yes, that will be fine. Mr. Takahashi, this is Brock Logan. Brock, Mr. Takahashi is our neighbor."

The gardener wiped his hand on his overalls and offered it to Brock with a smile that showed a shiny gold crown. "I am pleased to meet you."

Brock maneuvered to free his right hand enough to grasp the small, calloused one for a quick shake. "Likewise." He nodded toward the completed bushes. "You do nice work."

Mr. Takahashi gave a slight bow. "Thank you." He turned back to Carrie. "I shall pick up the clippings when I'm all finished."

"Thanks so much." She bent to move the basket of clothes to the edge of the walk. "And your laundry's all set right here."

Again, he gave a quick bow, another smile, and walked around the corner of the house.

"Come on, Brock," Shane said, holding the door open.

"Laundry?" Brock asked Carrie with a puzzled frown. "You picked up his laundry?"

She shot him an exasperated look. "No, I *do* his laundry. And he does my bushes." She waved toward the open door. "I suppose you might as well take that inside."

She took in laundry? Following an exuberant Shane to his room, Brock had trouble believing that. Why would this well-paid artist resort to taking in laundry, even if only in exchange for yard work? It didn't make sense.

"Think this will hold it?" Shane asked, indicating a three-legged table alongside his bed with a small lamp on it. "That way I'd be close in case something happened at night."

"I don't think so, sport. We need something much sturdier, like a . . ."

"A bookcase," Carrie offered as she came into the room. "Let's take these books off the top here and that should do it."

"Is there a wall outlet behind there?" Brock inquired as he gingerly set the tank atop the bookcase. "We'll need to plug in the filter."

"Yes." Hands on her hips, she watched him remove all the paraphernalia. "No neon lights blinking overhead? I'm surprised."

Brock shot her a look acknowledging her sarcasm. "Matter of fact, there's a top to the tank, with light included, but they were out of them for this particular model. I've got it on order."

"I should have guessed."

"A light, too?" Shane was all but dancing as he held the plastic bag of fish. "I've got to think of some neat names. Did you have goldfish when you were little, Brock?''

"Nope. My aunt wouldn't allow *any* pets in the house."

"Boy, she'd sure hate it here, wouldn't she?"

Carrie slipped her arm around her son's shoulders. "Now, you know you have to learn to take care of these fish, Shane. Pets are a responsibility, they depend on you."

From his back pocket, Brock whipped out a folded booklet. "Here's something that'll teach you all you ever wanted to know about fish, and then some."

"We can read it together, Mom." Then, looking as if he didn't want to slight his new benefactor, he turned to Brock. "You can listen, if you want."

A diplomat, yet, Brock thought. "Why don't we sit down and go through it right now, so we don't set things up all wrong."

Shane jumped on his bed and landed in a sitting position. "I'm ready."

Brock sat down next to him and looked up expectantly at Carrie. He was pleased to see she looked a bit taken aback. He'd seen her swallow down her temper a couple of times because of the boy. If he didn't genuinely like Shane, he'd have felt guilty using the boy to soften the mother. He was beginning to think it wasn't all that easy softening Carrie Weston. Then he remembered the way she'd felt in his arms, her mouth locked to his, her arms going around him. He didn't question his motives. He only knew he wanted to taste her again—and soon. And his gut instincts told him she wanted that, too.

"I've got to start dinner." She handed Brock the book with a resigned sigh. "You'll undoubtedly be joining us?"

He grinned. "So nice of you to ask. I could come back tomorrow if you'd rather..."

"Hey, no," Shane interrupted. "Not tomorrow. We're going camping tomorrow." Suddenly his eyes lit up again as a new thought struck him. "You could come with us, Brock. Do you like to camp out?"

"Of course he doesn't, Shane," Carrie went on hurriedly. This whole afternoon was rapidly running out of control. "Brock's a busy man with much to do and..."

"I *love* camping." He nodded at the boy. "Thanks for asking me." Putting on his best innocent face, he held the look. "That is, if your mom doesn't mind a stranger butting in."

"You're not a stranger anymore. Is he, Mom? Please, can he come?"

Caught again. Carrie almost moaned aloud. If only she knew when Brock would be dropping in, she could warn her son not to...not to what? Not to politely invite a man along he liked, who'd befriended him, helped bathe him and brought him fun gifts? How could she explain that? But two days and one long night alone on a mountain trail with Brock loomed ahead rampant with hidden traps. Maybe she could dissuade him.

"Are you sure you want to do this? I mean we sleep on the hard ground, in bedrolls. We walk for miles, climbing hills. We fish in a stream and cook over a campfire. We..."

"Sounds wonderful," Brock interjected. "A long time ago, I went a couple of times with a friend and his father. We had a lot of fun. I always wished I could have done it more."

Carrie tried to harden her heart to the yearning tone of Brock's voice. One more try. "Won't Francine Thomas be wanting your company this weekend?" she asked, knowing full well the woman had probably taken a plane out of California by now. She hated the jealousy implied in the question, but a lot more than just a weekend was at stake here. Her peace of mind, for one thing.

Well, well, Brock thought. For a moment, he'd thought her violet eyes had turned green. Jealousy in a woman who'd said she wasn't interested? Now that was something to think about.

He crossed his legs at the ankles and looked up at her innocently. "She's no longer in town. Besides, I don't think she'd like to join us. Francine's not the camping type."

"Mom, come on. Don't you think taking Brock camping is a nice way to thank him for bringing us a fish tank."

Carrie ground her teeth. "All right." She glared at Brock as Shane gave her a big grin. "Be here, 6:00 a.m. sharp, ready to roll." She started to leave, then turned back at the doorway. "And get yourself some rugged camping duds and hiking shoes, 'cause we're going to walk your urban legs down to your knee-caps." Turning on her heel, she left the room.

As she stormed down the hallway, she heard Brock's low chuckle and Shane's victory whoop follow her. It would seem some battles were impossible to win, Carrie decided.

Chapter Six

There were advantages to living in a tourist town, Brock thought as he laced up his brand new hiking boots. He'd left Carrie's last night after dinner and had found many of the stores still open. He'd strolled the avenue until he'd located one that sold camping equipment and had purchased boots, a jacket and a sleeping bag, deciding he'd make do for the rest of his needs with what he'd brought from Chicago.

Standing, he flexed his toes and took a few steps in the heavy shoes. They'd never make it on the best-dressed list, but they would serve him well. He glanced out the window of his rented house toward the sea. The sky was only slightly lighted, the clouds a pale gray. At five-thirty in the morning, the sun was still not visible. Grabbing his jacket and sleeping roll, he made for the door. He didn't want to be late and give Carrie ammunition for one of her frosty looks.

Heading into a pinkening sunrise, the hum of the powerful engine the only sound, Brock tried to sort out his feelings. The kid with the big eyes so like his mother's had gotten to him. Funny, because he'd never been especially drawn to kids, never known any on a close basis since he'd been an adult. Shane was bright and eager for life, his curiosity about the world and everything in it contagious. Maybe, if Brock's mother had lived, he'd have been more like that as a boy. All one really needs is one parent who loves him like crazy to have a good chance at happiness. That's all Shane had, and he was pretty terrific. What if he had two parents?

Dangerous questions. He had no intention of volunteering to be a father to Shane or to let Carrie complicate his life. All he wanted from her was her trust, and maybe her friendship. So he could introduce her and her son to Mac and let them take it from there. He wasn't really a man with a mission. He needed to repay Mac, in some way, and this was the only answer he'd come up with.

Then, he could get on with his life. Work awaited him back in Chicago, exciting and challenging work. There were the possibilities of branches opening in London, then perhaps Paris, and he'd be a viable part of it. He'd traveled extensively already for the company, but this would involve being in charge, leadership, the opportunities he'd waited a lifetime for. And there was Francine.

Despite the petty things about her that had annoyed him yesterday, he did like her. She'd fit in, in Chicago, in Paris, wherever they chose to live. They talked the same language, shared the same values. Francine had once mentioned she'd decided children probably weren't part of her future plans, and he'd felt the same way at the time. Children complicated things, stole one's energy, divided one's loyalties.

Brock turned the Ferrari up the winding road leading to Carrie's house, remembering how he and Shane had read the booklet together last night, stretched out side by side on his bed. Then they'd carefully filled the tank with tepid water, put in the artificial ferns Shane insisted on calling seaweed, and the little castle, and then set up the filter. Finally, when the temperature had been just right, they'd slipped in the fish.

That's when he wished he'd had a camera to record that little guy sitting in front of the fish tank watching his fish get used to their new home, as enthralled as if he were watching his favorite television show. And Brock had sat right beside him. Just before dinner, Shane had leapt up and spontaneously hugged him, thanking him for the best present he'd ever had.

When had this all happened to him, this interest in kids and animals and fish? Hell, he'd never in his whole life even owned a dog. From the bedroom doorway, Carrie had watched her son hugging him, her eyes dark and serious. He could almost hear her saying "Don't hurt him, please." He wanted to tell her he had no intention of hurting Shane. But would he, unintentionally, when he left? Nah, he'd be flying back to California on business frequently and could see him anytime.

Another couple of weeks and he'd be gone, and Carrie could relax again. He knew he made her nervous, and he kind of enjoyed her discomfort. He didn't want commitment from her, or to take over her life, or to hurt her child. He just wanted a few more days with her so she'd have faith in his judgment and agree to meet Mac. That's all he wanted, or so he told himself as he parked his car next to her Volkswagen and turned off the motor.

That wasn't quite true, he admitted as he gazed at the sky, closer now here high atop her hill. The truth seemed easier to face when one was nearer the heavens. He wanted her.

Last night, after dinner, they'd sat on the rug in front of the hearth and played checkers, the three of them. Two playing and one kibitzing from the sidelines and challenging the winner. She'd frowned in concentration, she'd feigned a move to try to trick him, she'd laughed at him as he'd lost game after game, and she'd giggled like a schoolgirl when Shane had beaten her twice in a row. The sunset rays had poured in through the window and highlighted her skin. And he'd sat there, watching, churning with unexpected desire for her.

There'd been other women in his life, some closer than others. He recognized physical needs, but he'd managed to put them in perspective and had never knowingly hurt anyone because of them. He'd had a few mutually satisfying relationships, but he knew better than to let transient desires rule his life. So he was all the more stunned to find himself sitting there pretending interest in checkers, while the need to touch her had him all but sitting on his hands.

She wore loose, floppy clothing, layers on layers, which only made him wonder more what he would find if he could strip each layer from her. He wanted to touch more than the bare smoothness of her arm and the soft silk of her cheek. He wanted to feel her skin next to his, her heart beating in time with his.

And the wanting was increased by the knowledge that, despite her words to the contrary, she wanted, too.

Brock got out of the car and grabbed his jacket and bag. Losing it. He was losing it if he sat in a car at sunrise and let sensual thoughts of Carrie Weston tie his stomach into knots. Enough, he told himself as he made his way to the back door past a snoozing billy goat. At this rate, he was going to have one hell of a time getting through the next two days and a night. He pounded softly on the door.

Shane came streaking to the door wearing jeans tucked into his hiking boots and a yellow San Diego Chargers T-shirt.

"Hey, sport," Brock greeted him as he walked through the door the boy held open for him. "I didn't know you liked football. Maybe this fall we can catch a Chargers' game."

"That'd be great."

Brock looked up to see Carrie standing in the porch doorway to the kitchen, a warning in her eyes. He cleared his throat self-consciously. "That is, if I get back this way during one of their games."

Shane's face clouded. "Are you going somewhere, Brock?"

"Not just yet, but one day soon." Time to change the subject before they started out on a glum note. He held up his sleeping bag. "Think this will keep out the bears and coyotes?"

Shane giggled. "There's no bears or coyotes up where we camp."

"I certainly hope not, 'cause if there is, you might just find me crawling into your bag with you."

"Mom takes a big knife along, just in case. Maybe we should both crawl into her sleeping bag."

Over the boy's head, he grinned at Carrie. "Not a bad idea."

She gave him a frosty look then took in his outfit, including the brand new boots. "Just bought those, eh? Boots need to be broken in before hiking. You may have some mighty sore blisters by nightfall."

He walked past her to pick up the cooler she'd obviously just finished packing. "Come on, Carrie. Stop being such a wet blanket. We're going to have fun today."

She looked a shade doubtful, but she stopped frowning.

"What's a wet blanket?" Shane asked.

"It's your mother when she's trying to be bossy."

She wrinkled her nose at him. "Did you bring a change of clothes?"

"Yes, ma'am," he said, giving her a snappy salute. "Rolled up in my bag, per your instructions. You'll find I always follow the camp director's orders."

"I'm counting on that." She turned to Shane. "Is your backpack all ready?" He nodded and handed it to her so she could help him strap it on. "There, that's not too tight, is it?" Shane shook his head. "Okay. The fish have been fed, and there's plenty of cat food in Jonathan's dish. Zeke's in his cage, so is Gerald, and Mr. Takahashi's coming by tonight to feed Billie. I guess we're all set."

As she locked up, Brock tied the tightly rolled sleeping bags on his back and picked up the cooler. When she turned to join them, she frowned again.

"We can't have you carrying everything. You'll drop over from sunstroke or fatigue before lunch. Let me take the cooler."

Brock shook his head. "Nope. Me Tarzan, you Jane. You lead the way." He kept a straight face as Shane giggled.

"Look, Shane and I have done this before, and we split up the load so no one's overburdened. Why are you acting the martyr?"

"I'm not. If it gets heavy, I'll drop it down the cliff and we'll eat wild berries and drink stream water." Again Shane giggled. "Are you going to stand here arguing with me or are we ever going to start out?"

"All right, but don't say I didn't warn you."

"So you did. Let's go."

Carrie swallowed any further retorts. The man was obviously a novice at this and ill prepared with his soft, office hands and his laid-back executive's body to know what he was getting into. Of course, the day he'd arrived wearing only rolled-up dungarees he hadn't looked too out of shape. But she was certain the most strenuous exercise he'd done lately was to slam shut the door of his sports car.

She led the way along a narrow dirt path that stretched out from their property and across to the adjacent mountain, which was much higher and mainly uninhabited, at least on this side. She set an easy pace, not for Brock's sake but because Shane's legs were short. Besides, the object was to look around and enjoy.

The morning fog from the Pacific was still rolling in on the hills, giving the dark green ground cover and the Monterey pine trees a hazy look, but she knew it would burn off by noon, if not sooner. Already the sun was dangling over the horizon, inching its way up. They were still walking on ground parallel to the house, but directly ahead they'd soon hit the steep incline that would separate the men from the boys, she thought, glancing back at Brock. He seemed to be walking effortlessly behind Shane, enjoying the scenery. Well, time would tell.

"Know what that orange flower is?" Shane asked Brock over his shoulder as he pointed.

"Nope, can't say I do."

"It's the California poppy, our state flower." Looking pleased to show off his knowledge of the great outdoors, Shane fell back a step so he was almost alongside Brock on the narrow path. "And you see that butterfly up there on that leaf?" He waited for Brock to gaze up where he was pointing and nod. "That's a monarch butterfly. There's a city not far from us where bunches of those butterflies live, and if someone's caught hurting one he can be tossed in jail. Right, Mom?"

"That's right, in Pacific Grove just north of Pebble Beach."

"Yeah. And they got this great place over near there called Seal Rock where all these seals sun themselves on the rocks in the ocean right alongside the road. Baby seals and mother seals. You ought to go see it, Brock." He looked up at him. "Maybe me and Mom can take you sometime," he added hopefully.

It sounded as if Carrie had used these small trips to educate her son on his surroundings. Brock held a low leafy branch out of the boy's way so he could get past. "Maybe. Where are the daddy seals while the babies and mothers sun themselves?"

Shane had a ready answer. "They're standing guard, making sure no one hurts them. That's a daddy's job, to protect. That's what Ninja turtles do."

"What?"

"Ninja turtles. It's a cartoon where turtles are like pretend people. They have wars and everything."

"Wars, eh? Yeah, that sounds like people, all right. And the daddy Ninja turtles protect the moms and babies?"

"Yeah, from all enemies. You have to come over next Saturday and watch the Ninjas with me."

Carrie had been listening to their chatter, marveling at how such a worldly man as Brock could talk so easily to a child, and not talk *down* to him. She stopped and pointed to a high ridge. "When we get up there, we can take a break, maybe have something to drink if you're getting warm. Are you?"

"Not me," Brock said.

"Me, either," Shane chimed in.

"Well, this poor female Ninja turtle is, so we'll stop soon." She moved on, smiling at her son echoing Brock. By now, if they'd been alone, he'd have been pestering her to stop. But he wanted to show Brock that he was tough. She wished Shane weren't getting so attached to the first man he'd spent any measurable amount of time with, though she could understand her son's need. She'd wanted to keep them apart, but Brock kept showing up, intruding on their lives, and already Shane was hooked. And, quite possibly, he wasn't the only one.

Perhaps tonight, in the quiet of a dark mountain night, when Shane would be asleep, she could talk to Brock about not making promises to her son that he had no intention of keeping. Already, Shane had TV shows in mind to share, trips to Seal Rock and attending Chargers' games together. She knew Brock would be leaving in two weeks or so. He had no right to make the boy care, then leave. He wouldn't like hearing her warning, but she had every right to protect her son from being hurt. She trudged past a gnarled pine, ducking out of the way of the twisted branches, her eye on their first rest spot.

As she'd known, distances were deceptive when one was climbing a mountain on a winding path. By the time they reached the ridge nearly an hour later, the sun was already making her skin damp, and Carrie was the first to drop onto a dark green patch of grass. The two guys followed suit. She passed cold drinks around from the thermos and took a long drink herself.

Shane, who was restless and energetic, was up and exploring the area after resting scarcely five minutes. As she automatically warned him to be careful, she noticed that Brock wasn't the least winded, nor were his feet hurting as she'd predicted.

"You're in better shape than I'd have guessed," she admitted. "Do you work out?"

He lay back on the prickly grass. "Yeah, pretty regularly. Your father's a nut on physical fitness, so he had a gym installed in the basement of our Chicago building. It's free to all employees, so I use it several times a week." He smiled at her. "You won't have to worry about me passing out on you."

She'd noticed that lately in their conversations he referred to Mac as "your father" instead of by name. A subtle change, but he was trying. And he never missed an opportunity to extol Mac's virtues, which appeared to be many. The implied message was, could a man who's so thoughtful and good to his employees be as bad as she thought he was? The question hung in her subconscious.

"I'm surprised you're into this mountain-climbing and camping routine," Brock said as he looked over at her sipping her juice. She had on a loose cotton sweatshirt, and jeans tucked into boots. Her hair was in a ponytail, and she wore not a speck of makeup. She looked barely twenty. Not too many women heading for thirty could get away with looking as fresh and lovely as she did in that outfit without cosmetic help.

"I was dragged into it, I assure you. When Shane started school, he came home with stories about how his friends went camping with their parents. So I had to learn, or let him go with strangers." She shrugged as she gazed out on the panoramic vista spread before them. "Now, I really enjoy the view, the peacefulness, even the exercise. In my work I mostly sit, so it's good for me."

"Aren't you afraid, a small woman and a child camping alone at night, far from help if you needed it?"

"I've scouted out this mountain pretty well by now, and I stay near the trails. We'll run into people here and there all day, so we're never really alone. And I do carry a very large knife, as Shane told you."

"Would you use it?"

"To protect my son? Absolutely."

He believed her. The mother bear protecting her cub—in the absence of papa bear. "Have you ever had to wrestle a bear or anything?"

"There's very little wildlife on this mountain, if you don't count the creepy crawlies, a few squirrels and chipmunks and the fish in the streams." A light plane overhead caught her attention, and she shielded her eyes, watching it pass between the two largest green hills.

Incredible, isn't it? Deal yourself in right now and get 6 fabulous gifts ABSOLUTELY FREE.

1. 4 BRAND NEW SILHOUETTE SPECIAL EDITION® NOVELS—FREE!

Sit back and enjoy the excitement, romance and thrills of four fantastic novels. You'll receive them as part of this winning streak!

2. A LOVELY BRACELET WATCH—FREE!

You'll love your elegant bracelet watch—this classic LCD quartz watch is a perfect expression of your style and good taste—and it's yours free as an added thanks for giving our Reader Service a try!

3. AN EXCITING MYSTERY BONUS—FREE!

And still your luck holds! You'll also receive a special mystery bonus. You'll be thrilled with this surprise gift. It will be the source of many compliments as well as a useful and attractive addition to your home.

PLUS

THERE'S MORE. THE DECK IS STACKED IN YOUR FAVOR. HERE ARE THREE MORE WINNING POINTS. YOU'LL ALSO RECEIVE:

4. FREE HOME DELIVERY

Imagine how you'll enjoy having the chance to preview the romantic adventures of our Silhouette heroines in the convenience of your own home! Here's how it works. Every month we'll deliver 6 new Silhouette Special Edition®novels right to your door. There's no obligation to buy, and if you decide to keep them, they'll be yours for only $2.74* each—that's a savings of 21¢ per book! And there's no charge for postage and handling—there are no hidden extras!

5. A MONTHLY NEWSLETTER—FREE!

It's our special "Silhouette" Newsletter—our members' privileged look at upcoming books and profiles of our most popular authors.

6. MORE GIFTS FROM TIME TO TIME—FREE!

It's easy to see why you have the winning hand. In addition to all the other special deals available only to our home subscribers, when you join the Silhouette Reader Service, you can look forward to additional free gifts throughout the year.

SO DEAL YOURSELF IN—YOU CAN'T HELP BUT WIN!

*In the future, prices and terms may change, but you always have the opportunity to cancel your subscription. Sales taxes applicable in N.Y. and Iowa.

You'll Fall In Love With This Sweetheart Deal From Silhouette!

SILHOUETTE READER SERVICE™
FREE OFFER CARD

PLACE YOUR WINNING CARD HERE!

4 FREE BOOKS • FREE BRACELET WATCH • FREE MYSTERY BONUS • FREE HOME DELIVERY • INSIDER'S NEWSLETTER • MORE SURPRISE GIFTS

YES! Deal me in. Please send me four free Silhouette Special Edition novels, the bracelet watch and my free mystery bonus as explained on the opposite page. If I'm not fully satisfied I can cancel at any time, but if I choose to continue in the Reader Service I'll pay the low members-only price each month.

235 CIS R1X7
(U-S-SE-09/89)

First Name		Last Name
PLEASE PRINT		

Address _____ Apt. _____

City _____ State _____ Zip Code _____

Offer limited to one per household and not valid to current Silhouette Special Edition subscribers. All orders subject to approval.

SILHOUETTE NO RISK GUARANTEE

- There is no obligation to buy—the free books and gifts remain yours to keep.
- You'll receive books before they're available in stores.
- You may end your subscription at any time—by sending us a note or a shipping statement marked "cancel" or by returning any unopened shipment to us by parcel post at our expense.

PRINTED IN U.S.A.

Remember! To win this hand, all you have to do is place your sticker inside and DETACH AND MAIL THE CARD BELOW. You'll get four free books, a free bracelet watch and a mystery bonus.
BUT DON'T DELAY!
MAIL US YOUR LUCKY CARD TODAY!

If card is missing write to:
Silhouette Reader Service, 901 Fuhrmann Blvd., P.O. Box 1867, Buffalo, N.Y. 14269-1867

"Hey, Mom," Shane shouted as he came thundering toward them down the dusty path. "That looks like the kind of plane my dad flew, doesn't it?"

"Yes, it does."

Shane flopped onto the grass next to Brock, scooting on his knees to the edge of the cliff. Automatically his mother's hand pulled him back from sitting too close to the rim. "My dad was a pilot. I've got lots of pictures of him and his planes. He could fly anything and do all these dangerous tricks, upside down and everything. My dad wasn't afraid of anything. I sure wish I could have seen him in action. He was wonderful, right, Mom?"

"Your father was a terrific pilot," Carrie answered carefully, her eyes still on the plane.

Brock watched her face. She'd evidently built up a good mental picture of Rusty Weston in her son's mind. Must have been hard to do, considering she was in the process of divorcing the man at the time of his death.

"Can you fly a plane, Brock?" Shane asked.

Brock saw Carrie lower her gaze to his, her expression unreadable. "No, Shane, I can't." Was that a flicker of pain he saw in her eyes before she looked away?

"I'm going to learn to fly one day." The plane dipped out of sight, and Shane lost interest. He scampered to his feet and ran up the path.

"Don't go far," Carrie told him. "We'll be starting off soon."

Brock sat up and rested his arms on his bent knees, watching her pack away the thermos and cups. "I have to tell you again, I admire the way you're raising that boy."

She closed the lid of the cooler and snapped it shut, then gazed off toward the sea for a few moments. "A long time ago, my father told me a rather complicated tale of this bear. The point of the whole story was that some days you eat the bear, and some days the bear eats you. Meaning, of course, that you win some, and you lose some. In my own life, when I think of Rusty, I believe the bear ate me." She turned to face him. "But when I think of Shane, I know I ate the bear that day."

"That's a good way to look at things. It seems you do have a few good memories of your father."

More than a few, Carrie thought. And Brock's appearance in her life had brought some of them back to her, albeit unwillingly. Maybe it was time to stop fighting her memories. "Yes," she said softly. "I won't argue that he had his good points. But . . ."

"Hey, Mom," Shane's voice yelled for attention. "Look at me. I'm Mighty Mouse."

Carrie turned in the direction of his voice, then looked up into a nearby old tree. Shane stood on a high branch, clutching a thick vine in his hand, grinning at her. Her heart leapt into her throat as she jumped to her feet. "Shane! Get down from there!"

Brock quickly stood but kept his voice calm. "Shane, don't upset your mother. Come on down."

"This'll hold me easy. I already tried it." He pulled twice on the vine to demonstrate its sturdiness. "I'm going to swing down and show you."

"No!" Carrie shouted moving toward the tree. Her world had suddenly tilted.

But Shane was past hearing, caught up in showing off for his new male companion. With another test pull on the vine, he swung off. But he hadn't calculated the length of the vine. His weight was sending him straight for the edge of the precipice. Suddenly he realized his mistake. His eyes widened in fear, and he let out a wail.

Moving strictly by instinct, Brock rushed just alongside the spot where he calculated Shane would be flying out into thin air. He leapt up and tackled the swinging boy as the vine snapped with a crunch. Giving a quick twist to his body, he managed to land on his side on the grassy bank very near the edge, the boy cradled in his arms. He let out a grunt as Carrie rushed over. Brock lay still a moment, breathing hard as Shane edged out of his strangle hold on him.

Carrie pulled her son into her arms, gathering him close in a fierce hug, her face chalk white, her eyes closed. Her hands ran over his small frame, checking for cuts or broken bones, amazed to find him unharmed, as the boy burst into tears.

"Dear God, Shane." She stroked his hair as he hiccuped into her shoulder. At last, she eased back from him. "You could have gotten killed." She wiped the tear streaks from his cheeks with trembling fingertips. Over her shoulder, she glanced down at the rocky embankment.

She'd known they were dangerously high, but she'd forgotten how steep a drop it was. There was a ledge-like outcropping, very narrow, that ran perhaps fifty feet along the bluff, then only endless yawning yards of bushes and small trees and hard stones to the bottom far, far below. Carrie shuddered uncontrollably.

"I'm sorry, Mom," he sobbed out. "I thought it would hold."

Just like his father, Carrie thought, always ready to take a dangerous chance. She'd prayed he wouldn't inherit Rusty's reckless nature, but it seemed he had. "You simply have *got* to be more careful, to stop and think." Hearing Brock sit up with a soft moan, she let go of Shane with a guilty start and turned toward the man who had rescued her son.

She touched Brock's arm. Without a thought to his own safety, he'd saved Shane's life. She felt tears well up as he raised his head to look at her. "How can I thank you?" Despite her best effort, now that the danger was over, her voice was quivery.

"You don't have to thank me. Anyone would have done the same thing." Brock saw the depth of emotion in her expressive eyes and slid his arm around her slender shoulders.

He sounded oddly embarrassed at being thanked, but she couldn't let it go. "Not thank you? He's all I have in this world." She moved closer, laying her cheek against his as her hand caressed his other cheek, hoping he wouldn't see how close to tears she still was. "Thank you, Brock. If something happened to Shane, I don't think I could go on." Her voice was whisper-soft, raw with emotion and fear barely abated.

She felt awfully good in his arms, but this wasn't the time or the place. Brock squeezed her lightly and pulled back from her. "He's none the worse. You can relax now."

Her concern shifted to him. "Are you all right? Here I am, going on about Shane and you took the brunt of the fall."

He held up one scraped elbow. "I think I'll live." He turned to look at Shane sitting alongside them.

The boy glanced at Brock's bleeding elbow, then hung his head. "I'm sorry, Brock. I didn't mean to get you hurt."

"Sometimes, when we pull dangerous stunts, others are injured," Carrie told him. "Promise me you're going to start using your head more?"

Shane wouldn't look up. "I promise."

"I brought some antiseptic and bandages," Carrie said, getting up to retrieve her backpack.

Brock's heart went out to the boy, but he knew Carrie was right in letting him know he'd done wrong. Nonetheless, he touched Shane's shoulder. "I remember once when I was about ten, I pulled something similar. The house we lived in had a low porch roof, you know?" He waited until Shane looked up and nodded. "We had some hay piled up on one side, and I decided I'd jump from the roof and land in the hay."

Carrie returned, seated herself next to Brock, reached for his elbow and began cleaning the scrape.

"So I jumped, and I didn't hurt myself. There was only one problem. I landed on my younger cousin and broke his arm. Not only did my aunt nearly kill me, but she made me do all of my cousin's chores as well as my own until his cast came off." He ran his hand over the boy's soft curls. "That taught me a lesson, sport. Think you learned one today?"

"I guess so."

Carrie spread ointment on the wound and put a Band-Aid over it. Getting to her feet, she eyed her son. "I certainly hope so." She looked up at the sun moving relentlessly toward the noon position. "We'd better get going if we expect to make our campground before dark."

The near tragedy had had a subduing effect on Shane, Brock decided as they marched along, for the boy stayed safely between the two adults the rest of the morning. He didn't wander from them as they ate lunch and he was far less chatty. Even when they'd fished for dinner in the cool mountain stream, he'd resisted showing off his fishing style with the collapsible poles Carrie had tucked into the cooler. Too much, Brock thought. So when the hamper was full of fish, he livened things up by starting a water fight with Shane in the stream.

They'd left Carrie back at the campfire getting the rest of their dinner ready and had waded in in their underwear, leaving their clothes under a tree. Shane was giggling and splashing him with gusto, his usual good humor restored, when his mother showed up on the bank of the stream, hands on her hips and a scowl on her face. Caught playing like a kid, Brock sent her a guilty glance and picked up her squirming son, carrying him to the rocky shore. With a flourish, he set the boy on the grass as his mother quickly wrapped a big towel around him.

"I just can't leave you two alone for a minute, can I?" she asked in a mock scolding voice. She rubbed Shane's hair vigorously as he shivered in the cool night air.

"Guess not, ma'am," Brock said in his best western drawl as he winked at Shane. The boy grinned back as she all but rubbed his ear off.

"And you're worse than he is," Carrie told Brock as she shifted her eyes to him. Then, quite suddenly, she stopped rubbing.

He stood there silhouetted against the sunset, looking strong and lean and very appealing. The water dripped from his hair, down his hard chest and along his muscular legs. His wet briefs outlined a prominent bulge that set her pulse racing. She felt the heat rise as she looked up the length of him and met his dark blue eyes watching her. She hoped the twilight hour prevented him from seeing the effect his near nakedness was having on her. She also hoped her voice would be steady.

"There's another towel under that tree," she told him as she returned to drying a wiggling Shane.

"Thanks." Brock walked past her and grabbed the towel, hiding a smile. So she was a shade more interested than she'd thought herself, was she? Good, because he didn't have to see her stripped down to her underwear to notice her. Walking behind her for miles, seeing her slender, jeans-clad legs climbing hills just ahead of him, inhaling the warm fragrance of her while they'd shared lunch had had his mind busy for hours. Slowly he pulled on his jeans and wondered how he was going to get through the night.

Dry and dressed, Shane jumped up on a rock and called out. "Ready, Brock."

Carrie looked up from folding the towels. "Ready for what?"

Brock walked over to the boy as he eased into his shirt and turned his back to him. Shane climbed on his back and put his arm around his neck. Brock grabbed his legs and wound them around his waist as they both turned and grinned at her.

"You can't ask Brock to carry you, Shane. You're too heavy."

"He didn't ask. I volunteered. Don't forget the fish." Clutching the boy, Brock started toward the campfire about a hundred yards from the stream. He heard Carrie mutter something as she trailed after them. If she was surprised that he was volunteering for silly antics with her son, he was stunned. But there was no question in his mind. He was having the best time that he'd had in a very long while.

Brock cleaned the fish, then panfried them over the open coals while Carrie heated the bread and set out potato chips and a plastic container of fresh tomatoes, cucumbers and olives. He noticed the night closing in fast and the air turning cooler as they sat around the fire in a circle eating, chatting and laughing at everything and at nothing. Shane sat close to him, occasionally reaching out to touch him as he made his point. Or perhaps just to reassure himself that he was still there. Brock found himself looking into that small face and swallowing a lump more than once. He'd have to back off before this three-foot character got a permanent hold on his heart.

Brock buried their trash and gathered a ready supply of wood to keep their fire going while Carrie washed their utensils and put everything away. She helped Shane into his jacket as he stifled a yawn.

"I see someone's sleepy," Brock commented as he spread out the sleeping bags. He pointed to Shane's bright red bag decorated with a smiling Snoopy. "It's ready anytime you are."

"I'm not tired," Shane denied as he hunched closer to the fire. "You know what's the best part of camping?" he asked Brock. He hurried to answer as Brock sat down. "You get to sleep in your clothes. Except Mom makes me change my underwear and shirt and socks in the morning."

Brock crossed his legs as he chewed on a toothpick. "Women. They got this thing about cleanliness. It can be a real pain."

Shane nodded vigorously. "Sure can." He shot his mother a cautious look and was pleased to see her smile as she sat down next to him. "Can we sing?" He turned to Brock. "Mom and me usually sing before we go to sleep. You know any songs, Brock?"

"Not many. What do you sing?"

"'Waltzing Matilda's my favorite. Did you see *Crocodile Dundee*? That Mick's a super guy."

"No, I haven't, but I think I remember 'Waltzing Matilda.' You two start, and I'll jump in."

Brock listened to the two voices, one soft and feminine, one childish and unformed, and after the first chorus, he joined in. They made it through two versions of 'Matilda,' then Shane sang a somewhat squeaky rendition of 'Tie Me Kangaroo Down Sport' interspersed with yawns. At the end of the song, he didn't object when Carrie suggested he snuggle down into his bag.

"I'd like to see Australia, wouldn't you, Brock?" Shane asked as he came over to say good-night.

"Sure would, sport. Maybe one day."

"Yeah. This is the best, the three of us, isn't it?"

The kid asked some hardball questions. He didn't dare look up at Carrie. "The best." He pulled Shane into a fast hug. He was getting awfully used to little-boy hugs. "Sleep tight, Shane."

"You, too." He climbed into his bag and kissed his mother. "And you, too, Mom."

"I will. Sweet dreams, Honeypot," she whispered, using his childhood nickname.

Shane frowned. "Mom, not in front of Brock."

Hiding a smile in his neck, she squeezed him one last time. "You're growing up too fast, kid. Good night."

Slowly she wandered to the other side of the campfire, where Brock sat staring into the fire. Now the hard part, she thought as she stretched, giving the impression that she, too, was sleepy. The truth was she was tired, but too tightly wound to be sleepy. She sat down on her own bag and reached up to undo her hair. "You ready to turn in?" she asked him.

"Pretty soon," he said, watching the fire. "Times like these I wish I had a cigarette."

Carrie had had the same thought. "You quit smoking lately?"

"Quite a while ago. My father died of emphysema." And cheap booze and broken dreams. "I didn't think it was worth it. But every once in a while..."

She rolled onto her stomach and shook out her hair as she settled her chin on her folded hands. "I know what you mean. I still smoke occasionally, though I've been trying to give it up. My mother smoked and drank—a great deal. I really stay away from liquor; I only have a glass of wine now and then. I get worried that it's in the genes."

He glanced over and saw that Shane was already asleep, his mouth open. He turned to look at Carrie. "Like your son being drawn to danger as his father was?"

He didn't miss much. "Yes, that worries me. It's not the first time he's pulled some daredevil stunt. You jumped off the roof. He slid down the drainpipe one day a few months ago. Nearly broke his leg."

Brock lay down on his bedroll, bending his arm and propping his head on his hand, leaving only a small space between them. "It depends on if you put more store in heredity or in environmental influences. Were you drawn to Rusty Weston because of his reckless nature, his celebrity?"

She gazed for a long moment into the fire. Had she been? Perhaps. "Who knows? I was nineteen and..." And naive in that she hadn't even seriously kissed a boy up to that point. Yet she was worldly wise in sex, since she'd been exposed to the sounds and smells of it for years through the thin wall of her mother's bedroom. How could this cosmopolitan man looking at her with his serious eyes ever understand all that, even if she could muster up the courage to tell him?

"Inexperienced?" he finished for her.

She gave a short laugh as she watched her hands play with the zipper of her sleeping bag. "Certainly that. I'd had exactly two dates up until that day. One of my mother's boyfriends got tickets to an air show and took both of us. He was loud and pushy and managed to finagle front-row seats and later an introduction to the star of the show."

"Rusty."

"Yes." He'd been so handsome in his leather flight jacket, the hat that he always wore at an angle, the smile that melted every female heart all the way up to the bleachers. And she'd been no exception. "When we were introduced, he kissed my hand. I thought it was the most romantic thing." She shook her head, blushing slightly at the memory. "So damn young and so damn gullible."

"And it went on like that?"

"Oh, yes. He asked me to dinner that night. My mother, of course, was all for it. She was always telling me to go out more, probably to get me out of her way. Rusty romanced me in grand style for the two days he was in town. When he left to continue his tour, the flowers started arriving, and the phone calls persisted. Money never mattered much to Rusty. Show me the nineteen-year-old naive girl who wouldn't go for all that.''

''He must have fallen hard.''

''I thought so, at the time. He'd fly into town just to take me to dinner, then fly out at midnight so he'd be in time for the next show in the next city. It sounded like an awfully glamorous life to me. Three months later, he had a diamond ring sent to me special delivery. I thought I'd died and gone to heaven.'' She gave a self-deprecating smile. ''Young girls that trusting and stupid ought to be locked up until they come to their senses.''

''So you accepted the proposal.''

''Yes. I'd been dying to get out of my mother's house for years. I give her credit, though. She stayed sober for the wedding. Rusty's folks sent a check and didn't bother to come. We were married only eighteen months before he died. I didn't meet his parents until his funeral.''

He knew he had no business asking, but he badly wanted to know. ''Did you love him, Carrie?''

''Why else do nineteen-year-old girls get married? At least it was what I *thought* love was. I hadn't been exposed to a lot of shining examples. I wasn't pregnant. I was the last of the virgin brides, I think. Maybe that's why Rusty pursued me so. I was a challenge. Heaven knows he didn't have much trouble luring other women into his bed.''

So that was it. Somehow, he'd thought so. ''You made a mistake. No one can blame you. You were only nineteen.''

She gave a quick shake of her head. ''I don't think of my marriage as a mistake. Without Rusty, I wouldn't have Shane.''

She was right, but not having had a child of his own, Brock hadn't looked at it that way.

"Rusty taught me a lot, some of it not so good, but he helped me grow up. Much of it was painful, but necessary. We all have to face life's realities sooner or later."

Carrie slowly stood. "I have to go to the stream to... to wash up." It was dark, very dark, beyond the edge of the trees, but she needed a little space, a little time. She'd revealed too much, and she felt exposed, defenseless. She started to move away.

"Did you file for divorce because Rusty was unfaithful?"

She stopped, then glanced back at him. "No. I filed for divorce because he told me, the last time I saw him alive, that he wasn't coming back to me ever again, that I was too small town for him." Quickly she turned and ran toward the water.

Chapter Seven

Slowly Brock walked to the tree line where Carrie had disappeared beyond the shadowy light spreading from the campfire. He knew she needed to regroup, to scold herself for telling him as much as she had. He wished she didn't regret confiding in him.

He leaned against a tall pine and tore off a piece of bark, shredding it absently as he stared up at the stars winking for attention. Too small town, eh? Chances were, Rusty Weston hadn't been man enough for her. Men like him were a dime a dozen, small-time stars puffed up with their own hype. She was better off without him, but he guessed she already knew that. She was more angry at herself for having believed in Rusty than she was sorry to have lost him. Silently he waited for her to return.

Carrie took off her shoes at the stream's edge and waded in, watching the moonlight shimmer on the flowing water. The cooling liquid dispatched her thoughts. What was there about Brock Logan that had her and her son confessing every secret about their lives? On the one hand, it was nice to have someone who listened so well, who seemed to really care what she thought or felt. On the other hand, she questioned his motives, especially since she knew very little about him, she realized, and he had learned a great deal about her. If only she could be certain he wouldn't use his knowledge against her.

All the talk about Rusty had brought back a flood of memories she'd just as soon not relive. Too late she'd realized they'd had nothing in common, that Rusty wanted the applause and attention of life on the road and she wanted a home, stability, someone who cared deeply and only for her. Growing up, she'd been denied such steadiness and had thought he'd supply it.

But she'd gamely traveled on the circuit with him, trying to keep him happy, to keep him smiling, and finally, just to keep him. Then she'd found out she was pregnant, and her body was no longer her own. She'd had chronic morning sickness and Rusty had had little patience with her. He'd also lost interest in their marriage bed about then, and had begun staying out late after his air shows. He'd return sullen and moody, smelling of cheap whiskey and heavy perfume, and be unable to understand why she wasn't interested in making love with him when he was like that.

Finally, after one particularly humiliating night when he'd told her she was like a fish, cold and unresponsive, she'd had enough. But she couldn't face returning to her mother's house. She'd shown up on Sonya's doorstep with one slightly battered suitcase and one badly shattered dream. Carrie took a ragged breath, remembering the frightened, waiflike creature with the huge, empty eyes who had stared back at her from her mirror in those days. She never wanted to be that low again, to risk that kind of involvement again.

An owl hooted in the distance, and she looked up at the fullness of the moon. It was so peaceful here with the rushing water and the mysterious night sounds. But there was the man waiting by the fire yet to face. She sighed and turned around. She'd better go back before he came plowing after her.

Brock pushed off from the tree as she came through the trees into the clearing, holding her shoes in her hand. She blinked in the firelight as she stopped in front of him, obviously surprised to see him standing there. "I wanted to make sure the coyotes didn't get you," he explained, as she gazed up at him. Her expression was hesitant and vulnerable, but he'd never seen her more beautiful. He took a step closer and ran the backs of his fingers down her silky cheek. He watched her eyes go smoky with unspoken needs.

Moving slowly so as not to frighten her, he dipped his head and touched his lips to hers. Gently he increased the pressure ever so slightly, back and forth, and felt the breath tremble from her.

"What are we doing here?" she whispered.

He kissed the corner of her mouth. "Kissing. We're kissing, Carrie. It's a quaint, old-fashioned custom."

"I don't..."

"Kiss men you don't know. Yes, you've told me, although I'm not sure I fit that description any longer. And I asked if you kissed men you *did* know, and you never answered me. Do you remember?"

She remembered, all right. She remembered their conversation and the kiss that had followed. And the memory had kept her awake more than one night. "This isn't a good idea. I don't know what you want from me, unless it's the obvious, and I've already told you that I don't want that." Carrie shook her head. "I'd better check Shane." She turned and began to run toward the campfire.

"Wait. Let's talk."

"There's nothing to talk about," she called over her shoulder. "We've said enough tonight." As she increased the length of her strides, she could hear him coming after her. She sighed and stood still a moment. Moments later, she heard Brock skid to a stop beside her.

"Why are you running from me?"

"I'm not. I just wanted to make sure Shane was all right." She sighed again and sank down on the soft grass, bracing herself on her arms and gazing across the clearing toward her son.

Brock fell to the ground beside her, his arm circling her waist. "He's fine, still sound asleep. I can see from here." They needed to lighten the mood, he thought, needed to let the hurtful memories she'd been recalling slide back into the past. Gently he tugged her onto her back, saw the wariness in her eyes and gave her a devilish grin. "Are you ticklish, Carrie?" he asked as his fingers moved to her ribs.

"Yes!" She squirmed, then realized he had her pinned, his legs loosely thrown over hers as his hands worked their way up and down her sides. Fighting the giggles, she pummeled his back with her fists. "Stop it!"

Brock laughed as he reached under her jacket to better torture her. He felt her fingers trying to tickle him back. "Sorry, but I'm not ticklish."

She let out a shriek as his one hand hit a particularly sensitive spot. "You're going to make me waken Shane."

"Okay, okay." He let up and sagged onto her, chuckling and breathing hard. She kept fidgeting to get free of him, but his weight on her was too heavy for her to move him. "Hold still. I've stopped."

"Let me up!"

"Not yet." He lifted to look at her as she turned her head toward him. Her dark violet eyes were filled with laughter, and the glow of the nearby fire highlighted her thick cloud of hair. Still she struggled beneath him, her soft body coming into contact with his, rubbing against him, unwittingly arousing him. Brock felt the mood suddenly shift from playful to aware. "Do you know what you're doing?" he asked as she continued to thrust and push.

"No!" she whispered fiercely, striving to break free of him. Lord, but he was heavy, Carrie thought as she shoved her hips up against his. As she did, she saw his eyes darken, felt the hard evidence of his desire. Suddenly the smile slid from her face. Time seemed to stand still, the night sounds to all but disappear as he stared down at her, on his face a look of stunned passion. His question hung between them as she searched his gaze and fought the battle raging within her.

Her traitorous body lifted toward him without her permission, yearning for the hardness that pressed against her as another breath escaped from him. Did she know what she was doing? "Yes," she whispered, "I know exactly what I'm doing." And her arms crept around his neck as she reached for his kiss.

How could a hard mouth be so gentle, so giving? she wondered as she felt the magic begin. He kissed her slowly, dreamily, coaxing her to relax. He was mesmerizing her with lazy, lingering kisses, and her skin flushed in a way that had nothing to do with the proximity of the fire.

She sighed his name and felt his tongue slip between her lips and take possession of her mouth. His arms slid under her, lining her body close up against his, and shamelessly she strained to be even nearer. In moments, he had her edgy and eager, but part of her was still trying desperately not to let things get out of hand.

But, oh, the taste of him, dark and wild and very male, numbing her senses. And, oh, the feel of him, strong and sure, yet tender and sensitive, drawing her to a place she knew she'd never been. And, oh, the scent of him, sharp and distinct, clean and captivating, clearly recognizable as his alone. In moments he'd taken her from drowsy pleasure to desperate longing.

More than anything, her initial uncertainty had touched Brock. He'd felt her hesitancy change to a recognition of her need as he slanted his mouth over hers, changing positions, taking her deeper. Now she was letting instinct guide her as her mouth moved under his, her tongue tangled with his and her body pressed into his.

He moved down to taste her throat and kiss the pulse beating wildly there. His tongue danced into her ear, and he felt a shiver race along her spine where his hands crushed her to him. Unable to stay away, his lips returned to capture hers. When he shifted his lower body into intimate contact, she moaned into his mouth. Her anxiety mingled with her awakening passion.

"It's all right," he murmured and angled slightly away from her. "Nothing's going to happen." And he gentled her with soothing touches and feathery kisses so she would know she had nothing to fear from him.

This was how it should be, how it could be, Carrie thought. From the first kiss at her front gate days ago, she'd somehow known he could take her to this place where she forgot herself, forgot being afraid, forgot everything but him and the way he made her feel. When his hands slipped between them and inched under her jacket and then her sweater, she gasped, then willed herself to calm down. The progress of his long, hard fingers along her skin was slow, almost leisurely, the kind she could stop any moment. She felt his mouth make love to hers while his hands closed over her breasts, and the smoldering heat raced through her body.

Oh, the sweet, hot pleasure of his touch on her bare body, the tender way he stroked her, lighting an answering fire deep inside her. She seemed to grow fuller, her flesh reaching out for his touch. Making love had never felt like this before. Other hands, rough and hurried, had raced over her, taking without giving. She hadn't sampled the sweetness, the sharp beauty, until now.

Like a drug, it was addictive. And frightening. She pulled back from him.

"Don't be angry," she said breathlessly, "but I need to stop. I'm just not ready for all this." Not ready? It had been eight long years. Perhaps she was ready. But she was so damn scared.

Brock kissed her forehead gently and took a deep breath. "I'm not angry." More than anything right now, she needed reassurance, he thought. It would cost him to stop now, but he'd manage somehow. He eased back, got to his feet and offered her a hand up. "Come on. It's getting chilly. Let's zip into our bags and warm up."

Carrie took her cue from him and, eyes averted, allowed him to pull her up. She checked Shane, kissed his cheek as he slept on, then climbed into her sleeping bag as Brock loaded a few large branches on the fire to keep it going. She watched him move his own bag closer to hers and crawl inside, facing her. Stretching, he zipped up, then leaned over to place a light kiss on her nose as his big hand closed around hers.

"Okay now?" he asked.

"Yes. Thank you." If only he knew how close she'd come, how much she still wanted to lie with him, close alongside him, their bodies touching. How much she wanted—perhaps *needed*—his loving. Ah, but he didn't know. She laid her head in the crook of her arm and studied him. Or did he?

"What are you thinking?" he asked softly.

Oh, no. He wasn't going to catch her in that velvet trap. Her mind scampered for a safe thought. "I was hoping Mr. Takahashi remembered to feed Billie," she lied.

Brock wrinkled his forehead. "I've been meaning to ask you, why is it you do his laundry?"

"Because he does my shrubs. An arrangement that works out well for both of us. Sort of the barter system. You may have heard of it."

She sounded defensive, but he didn't care. He had to know. "Why does a well-paid artist like you need to wash someone else's clothes, or to barter, if you want to call it that? You command a high dollar for your work. Where does it all go?"

So that was it, the question that had been haunting him. He'd accused her the night after their first dinner together of taking money, gifts and tuition from her father, then unfeelingly ignoring him. Perhaps it was time he learned at least some of the truth.

"Much of the money I make goes to Southern Pacific Savings, a local bank where I'm paying off a loan. Seven years down, and I have eight more to go."

"But what about all the money Rusty made? I've heard aerial stuntmen do really well."

She gave a short, mirthless laugh. "He did all right, but what he made he spent—on a flashy sports car, expensive clothes, other women and his own plane. He died leaving a huge debt on the plane, which is what I'm still paying off."

"That's what you're paying on for fifteen years?" His voice was incredulous as he half sat up, his attention riveted now on her pale face. "But what about his sponsors? Don't they supply the planes in return for plugs? What about the people who put up the money for his stunt show before he crashed? What about insurance?"

"In his usual irresponsible way, Rusty hadn't bothered to take out life insurance. He'd tired of working for others. He had dreams of making it big on his own, being his own boss. The trouble was, he didn't have the self-discipline." She banked her anger, realizing the futility.

"I had only two things from my father when my mother and I left his home. This gold heart on a chain—" she fingered the necklace she always wore "—and an insurance policy for fifty thousand dollars. Once Rusty discovered I had that policy, he nagged me incessantly. Finally I cashed it in and gave him the money. That's how he got started on his own."

"You can't buy any kind of plane for fifty thousand dollars," Brock said, trying to sort it all out.

"Of course not. He used the fifty thousand as part of the down payment, borrowed from everyone he knew and convinced a bank he was a solid risk for the rest. When he crashed, the bank's lien was insured, but not the personal loans. Sonya helped me get a loan to pay those individual investors back."

"Was your signature on those individual loans with Rusty's?" He saw her shake her head. "You could have walked away from them." She looked surprised he'd even suggest it.

"No, I couldn't have," she answered softly.

Brock clamped his jaw together, his mouth a grim line. "So you were twenty years old, six months pregnant and facing a huge debt. You could have gone to your father. He was already sending you money and..."

She sat up, anger blotching her cheeks pink. "What money? I don't know where you get your information, but I never once received a dollar from my father after my mother and I left his house. I know Natalie wrote to him occasionally, and she may have sent him pictures of me, but I didn't know about that until you'd told me." Wearily Carrie lay back down, the old hurt pushing through, clouding her good sense that would have kept her silent.

"I'd been working on and off for Sonya Nichols at her gallery before my marriage and during the few times we were in town. When Rusty died, I went to her, not to my mother. Sonya took me in, helped me get the loan, helped me get a scholarship to art school, gave me a place to live and even watched my baby while I attended classes." She angled her head toward him and saw his eyes, dark and suddenly uncertain, watching her intently.

"This Mac you speak of so warmly, who helped you through law school and built a gym for his employees—I don't know him. The father I remember never once, with all his wealth and power, contacted me or sent me a penny. You claim I ignored him. *I did not.* I sent letter after letter, for years. An invitation to my graduation and, yes, I did write to ask him to walk me down the aisle. I heard nothing, not one card or note. You can believe that or not." Carrie raised her arm and placed it over her eyes, shutting out the light and the unfriendly world.

She sounded so sincere, Brock thought. But if she was right, then Mac had lied. And why would he have done that? He ran a hand through his hair, wishing for a moment that he'd never jumped into the McKamey family problems. But then he'd never have met Carrie, and, despite his tangled feelings, he knew he wasn't sorry about that.

His heart went out to her. By anyone's standards, life hadn't been easy for Carrie Weston. She'd had a father she believed had abandoned her, a drunken, uncaring mother and an arrogant womanizing husband. Right now, Brock had no intention of arguing with her over whether she or Mac were telling the truth. He certainly didn't need to add to Carrie's problems. He fervently wished she hadn't become one of his.

She looked small and defenseless. She had shouldered heavy burdens basically alone for a lot of years. There was no room in his well-planned, carefully organized life for her. He hadn't consciously sought her, yet here she was. Already she was filling him with dark desires, and the promise of fulfillment was becoming an obsession with him. Yet she was draining him, sapping his strength of purpose, fogging his brain. And his arms ached to hold her.

Brock leaned forward, unzipped his bag and scooted close to her, touching the arm that still covered her eyes.

"No," she said, putting out her hand to him to hold him away. "I don't *want* this."

"Hush," he whispered, the sound of his voice thick in the wild fragrance of her hair. He slid his hands about her and snuggled her to him against her token resistance. "I just want to hold you. No pressures, no demands, Carrie. Just a man and a woman holding each other in the darkness. Sometimes we all need to feel someone's with us against things that go bump in the night."

After a long silence, her arms eased about him, and he felt her gradually relax as she laid her cheek against his chest. Gently he stroked her hair and her back as he held her in the circle of his arms. She felt fragile, a small woman struggling alone for years, yet strong and independent, asking no quarter. Perhaps in the morning she'd hate herself for letting go, but tonight she needed his comfort, and Brock found himself surprisingly pleased to be there for her. Basically a loner, he'd never had someone lean on him. Even if it was against her will when her defenses were down, he found he liked the feeling.

Just when he'd thought she was dozing off, she shifted and looked up at him, her eyes huge in the firelight.

"Don't make me want too much, Brock. I'm not sure I can handle another failure."

"If someone failed, it wasn't you." He eased them both into a more comfortable position, settled her against his body and pulled his sleeping bag over them.

Before he could close his eyes, he felt her reach for his hand and lift it to her lips. Softly she kissed his fingertips, then twined her fingers with his and tucked their joined hands under her chin. In moments her breathing was slow and even.

His chin resting in her hair, Brock drew in a ragged breath. He heard Shane's muffled snore as he glanced over to make sure the boy was sleeping soundly. Finally he sighed and shifted his gaze to the stars overhead, wondering how in just a short week and a half he'd complicated his life so seriously. And wondering what in hell he was going to do about it all.

The next week passed quickly, too quickly, Brock decided on Friday morning. There hadn't been a day when the weekend camping trip hadn't been skittering in and out of his thoughts. He'd deliberately put off calling Carrie, trying to put a little space between them. He'd even been crazy enough to think that out of sight meant out of mind. Wrong!

Even now as he made his way to his nearly completed office, glancing at his mail as he walked, he found his mind returning to last Sunday morning.

Carrie had awakened still wrapped in his arms, and the moment her eyes had popped open, she'd jumped up and away from him, her eyes as large and startled as those of a frightened doe.

"What is it?" Brock had asked as he'd sat up.

"Shane," she'd whispered. "He mustn't see us together." She'd squinted in the early morning sun and seen that her son was still curled in his bag, his back to them.

"Has he never seen his mother in the arms of a man?"

She'd frowned at him as she'd pulled on her boots, her eyes stormy. "No, and he never will."

He'd sat there watching her march off toward the stream, as puzzled then as he was now. Surely it wouldn't compromise the morals of a seven-year-old to see his mother lying fully clothed with a man. Perhaps he still had a lot to learn about kids, Brock thought. The fact that lately he wanted to know more was beginning to worry him.

He'd had the fire rekindled and breakfast started by the time she'd returned. The enticing smells had awakened Shane, and after eating, they'd hiked homeward, reaching sea level on the windward side of the mountain. They'd gone swimming in the warm surf and had arrived back at Carrie's house at dusk. She hadn't asked him in, and he hadn't pushed. Even Shane had been subdued, having picked up on their moody silences. Brock had driven home wondering if Carrie deeply regretted dropping her guard and allowing herself to sleep one night in his arms. Had Rusty Weston hurt her so much that she would deny herself even that small intimacy?

* * *

Brock nodded almost absently to Rhoda who was on the phone and walked past her into his office. Sitting down, he tossed the mail onto his desk and swung his chair toward the window. He had nothing pressing to do. He'd spent many long hours at the office this week and was pretty well caught up. They were almost ready for the grand opening, which was tentatively scheduled for sometime next week. He needed to talk with Mac.

Swinging around, he picked up the phone and asked Rhoda to track Mac down and get him on the line. It was a full twenty minutes before she buzzed him back and informed him that Mac was unavailable but that Francine was in the main office and wanted to talk with him. Frowning, Brock punched the blinking light.

"Hi, Francine. Where's Mac?" A bit brusque, he knew, but he wasn't much in the mood for preliminaries. He wasn't quite sure what he was in the mood for, actually.

There was a slight pause before her smooth, unruffled voice came across the wire. "It's good to hear from you, Brock. I thought you'd forgotten us."

He drummed impatiently on the desktop. "Hardly. I've just been busy. Mac out of town?"

"Yes, he's on his way to London. They've run into a snag on the Haverhill Building, and nothing would do but that Mac go in person to settle things. Britons don't care to deal with underlings."

Brock smiled at the hint of distaste in Francine's voice. He knew her well and guessed that she'd offered to go solve the problem and they'd turned her down, injuring her pride. "So when do you expect him back? We're about ready to open here."

"He said to tell you if you called that he hopes to be back by Monday or Tuesday at the latest, so go ahead and schedule the opening for Wednesday." She hesitated a moment, then went on. "Mac almost called you to go with him to London. There's another project there he's considering bidding on, though there's a lot of opposition from locals. It seems they want us to open a branch there if we're to be allowed to bid on future buildings. I believe Mac has it in the back of his mind to ask you to head that overseas project after the California opening. Wouldn't that be wonderful, darling?" She waited for Brock's reaction.

It was what he'd been wanting, a chance to be the innovator, to prove himself, to make his mark. He could live in London a while, then perhaps move on to Paris to set up an office there. Travel, the challenge of decision-making at the top level, having a hand in company expansion—it was what he'd been working toward. And he could tell that Francine saw herself alongside him, most likely as his wife.

Where was the elation he'd thought would come as he took another step closer to his dream? The poor boy from the other side of the tracks had made it big. Lifetime security, position and prestige were in his grasp. A month ago, hearing this news, he'd have been on top of the world. Why now was he hesitating?

"Brock, are you there?" Francine asked. "Did you hear me?"

"Yes. The London office is a possibility I'll have to discuss with Mac when the time comes." His statement was carefully worded, he knew, and maddeningly evasive, not exactly what she'd wanted to hear.

Her voice was a shade cooler. "Fine. I'll tell Mac you phoned. I'm sorry you missed him."

"Me, too." He'd really wanted to talk with Mac to...to what? Tell him on the phone that he'd found his daughter and she was beautiful and warm and had touched his heart? And, by the way, her story about their past didn't quite match her father's? Perhaps it was best that Mac hadn't been in. It was a conversation that should take place face-to-face.

"We'll see you Wednesday, then?" Francine sounded vaguely annoyed.

He tried to put warmth in his voice. "Yes. I'm looking forward to it. I'll set things in motion here. Stay in touch, will you?"

"Yes. Take care of yourself, darling."

Brock replaced the phone, feeling unaccountably depressed. He got up and went to the window. Another beautiful day, warm and sunny. A good day to...he stared at the cloudless blue sky a long moment. Well, why not? He turned to pick up the phone. He'd been working hard and deserved a little fun. He could picture Shane's eyes when he told him of his newest surprise.

Rhoda came on the line, and he asked her to quickly locate Joe Hanks for him. While he waited, he let his mind drift to Carrie. He'd thought he wanted cool compliance, the familiarity of shared goals and the serenity that Francine offered. Instead, more and more, he found himself yearning for a softly feminine woman who wouldn't be easy and wouldn't be compliant. Carrie was too damn independent, a difficult woman with a hurtful past to overcome, who would fight him all the way. And he could hardly wait to see her again.

When the phone rang, Brock couldn't prevent a smile of anticipation as he picked it up and made his arrangements.

"Wow! This is neat. I can't wait to tell Jeff and the others." Shane's young voice was filled with wonder. He turned to look at his mother strapped into the seat across the aisle. "Isn't flying neat, Mom?"

"Yes, definitely neat." Carrie watched her son press his face almost into the glass of the window as they flew down along the California coast. She glanced up at the man seated next to her whose eyes watched her rather than the view out the window. "All right, so you were right. This was a good idea."

Brock picked up her hand from the wide armrest and threaded his fingers through hers. It had taken him a full two hours to persuade her. "What is this, a woman who admits when she's wrong?" he teased.

Carrie's expression sobered. "It wasn't the ride I was against, you know," she said in a quiet voice. "When you came dashing in to ask us, and I saw Shane's face, I knew he'd never forgive me if I didn't say yes. It's just that..."

He squeezed her hand. "It's just that you're afraid to take any gift at face value, that you think I have ulterior motives and that you don't want me spoiling your son."

Spoiling wasn't what she was afraid of. Disappointing was closer. But she put on a smile and tried not to be the wet blanket he'd accused her of being last weekend. "I just don't want Shane to get used to...to having a private plane standing by at the airfield awaiting his pleasure, being whisked off to Mexico for dinner as if it were down the street or..." She waved her hand to indicate the plush interior. "...to grow fond of all this."

"Every kid deserves a little spoiling now and then, a day playing hooky at the circus, something to thrill and excite, don't you think?"

She lowered her voice even more. "His father lived for thrills and excitement. I'd like a little more for Shane than those shallow goals."

Brock cupped her chin and forced her to face him. "He has a lot more already. He has you." Lighten up, Carrie. One plane ride does not a decadent life-style make. Why are you so afraid to let him—and yourself—just sit back and enjoy now and again?"

Because every time she'd done just that, it had been like a Fourth of July firecracker—beautiful and bright for an instant, but leaving her with just a trail of dark smoke in the end. She looked into the deep blue of his eyes. "For the same reason I hate window-shopping. I don't want to gaze at something shiny and new and desirable, only to find I can't have it. It's too easy to get used to things that give us pleasure and too difficult to give them up."

And people, Carrie thought. Too damn easy to get used to charming people who dazzle you with presents and plane rides, then move on when the mood suits them, move on to cool blondes with perfect manners who are better suited to their lives. She turned her chin from his grasp, wondering why she suddenly felt like crying.

Her eyes had become suspiciously bright, Brock thought, making him wish she'd share her real thoughts with him. He moved his mouth close to her ear. "I have no intention of hurting Shane, Carrie. Please believe me."

She believed he meant it. She also believed the road to hell was paved with good intentions. The opening of the McKamey Building was set for Wednesday, Brock had told them. A few more days and most likely, they'd all be gone. She had only to get through those days. There'd be plenty of time later to ponder and perhaps regret. She turned to him with what she hoped was a bright smile. "I want to believe you."

"Mom!" Shane called. "Look at the lights down there. And you can see roads and tiny cars moving. Wow! Look at that lake."

Brock kissed her lightly on the nose and unfastened his seat belt. "Hey, sport. You want to come up front with me? The pilot's name is Joe, and I'll bet, if you're really good, he'll let you sit next to him and watch him land the plane."

"You mean it, Brock?" Shane's excitement was almost too much for him to contain. "All right!"

Brock helped him unstrap. "Okay, let's go. We're almost ready to set down in Acapulco. And wait until you see the restaurant where we're going to have dinner. It's on a hill higher than the mountain we climbed last weekend."

He winked at Carrie as she watched them head for the cockpit.

"What's so special about the restaurant?" Shane asked.

"You get to watch these boys, some just a little older than you, dive off between jagged rocks far below to the sea."

"Why do they do that?"

"They like to take chances, I guess."

Carrie watched them disappear behind the door and sighed deeply. She wasn't one who often took chances, and yet here she was perhaps taking the largest one of her life. She was letting Brock Logan move into her heart.

Carrie sat in the passenger seat of the Ferrari, Shane sound asleep in her lap, while Brock drove them home from the airfield. She muffled a yawn and saw on the dashboard clock that it was one in the morning. Small wonder she was sleepy. "This is the latest I've been out since . . . since I can't remember when."

Brock glanced over at her, his hand resting on the wheel. "You should do it more often. Between paintings, you need to play a little. We all do."

She cocked her head at him. "Do you?"

"No, not as much as I should. But then I'm pretty particular about my playmates." He sent her a sidelong smile. "I picked wisely tonight. I'll never forget Shane almost hanging over the railing at La Perla watching those boys dive. His eyes were as big as quarters."

"Mmm, now he wants to take up diving. I think you've created a monster."

"He's a good swimmer. Maybe next weekend I could teach him to dive. The place I'm staying at has a pool and..." He caught her look and realized he was doing it again, making future plans that included Shane and therefore his mother. He hadn't the right. By the end of next week, he could very well be gone, back to Chicago or perhaps on to London. He closed his mouth and gripped the wheel as he turned onto the winding road that led up to her house.

Brock held the sleeping boy as Carrie unlocked the front door. Billie brayed a short welcome as they went inside. Carrie snapped on a low lamp and led the way into Shane's room. Quickly she pulled back the sheet and fluffed up his pillow. Zeke complained loudly for a moment from his cage.

"Just lay him down, and I'll take off his shoes and tug off his slacks. No use waking him to put on pajamas."

Shane felt little-boy warm and trusting in his arms. Gently he laid him down and watched as his mother half undressed him. When Brock bent to kiss his soft cheek, Shane's eyes opened sleepily and he smiled at him. "Today was the best ever, Brock. Don't go." Then his eyes fluttered closed.

Brock didn't want to risk looking at Carrie as she covered Shane and tucked him in before kissing him. He turned and walked slowly out of the room. In the semidarkness, he waited for her to join him.

Leaning against the front door frame, he wondered if he'd been showing off today, not something he usually gave in to. Had he hauled out the company plane and taken Shane for a dazzling ride because the boy admired a dead father who used to fly? Or was it the mother he was trying to impress? He looked up as Carrie closed Shane's door and turned to him.

She wore a simple pink dress, belted loosely at the waist. Her hair fell past her shoulders and curled softly around her face. He could see that her eyes were a deep purple as she walked closer. She was quite simply the most beautiful woman he'd ever known. And he wanted her desperately, but he wasn't going to make the first move, even if it killed him. And at the moment he thought it just might.

Carrie stopped close enough to smell a hint of masculine cologne, something expensive, though the brand eluded her. His dark gaze watched her, his expression unreadable.

He was vastly experienced, widely traveled, coolly sophisticated. He was confident, slightly arrogant, yet boyishly appealing. He was rough, he was gentle, he was as sexy as any man she'd ever known. He could, and soon probably would, walk out of her life and perhaps not look back.

She could send him on his way, or she could dive off the cliff into the sea and hope to avoid the treacherous rocks below. She could reach out for life, and not hide out in her hillside home avoiding it. She could take a chance, just one more chance, and pray he wouldn't hurt her. She could offer herself, and he could laugh and turn her down.

Tilting her head up at him, Carrie's expression was solemn.

"Don't go," she whispered. "Please stay with me."

Chapter Eight

The ticking of the clock on the fireplace mantle echoed loudly through the silent house as Carrie stood waiting for Brock's answer. But he continued standing there, searching her eyes. She could stand it no longer. Bending, she turned the lamp one notch higher and tried to ignore her trembling hands.

"Would you like some coffee?" she asked as she headed for the kitchen. It was a mistake, asking him to stay, she told herself, the heat of humiliation spreading up her neck and pinkening her face. This very minute, he was trying to think of a way to refuse without causing a scene.

Behind her, Brock turned off the living room lamp, then came into the kitchen and snapped off the overhead light. He walked to the counter where she was filling the coffeepot at the sink. Moonlight poured in through the window, reflecting the anxiety written on her face in the darkened window. He shut off the water, took her by the shoulders and turned her to face him.

"I don't want coffee." He waited, but she wouldn't look up.

"A drink, then. I still have that wine..."

"Not a drink, either. Look at me." Hesitantly she raised her eyes to meet his as he moved his hands to frame her face. "You. I want only you. I want you so badly I'm shaking. I leave you and go home to close my eyes, and I see you. I sit at my desk and look out my window, and I see you. You're everywhere I go, everywhere I am. How did you do this to me?" He saw some of the doubt leave her as she gave him a nervous smile.

"I didn't mean to do anything. I didn't want to get involved with you, or anyone. But you're everywhere I look, too. I wouldn't be surprised if your face isn't somehow drawn into the cloud formations in my latest painting." She let out a sigh as he pulled her into his arms.

"Are you sure you want me to stay?"

With her cheek resting on his chest so she didn't have to look into his probing gaze, she was better able to tell him how she felt. "I've guarded myself so long, Brock. It's so hard for me to let go. I haven't been with a man since Rusty, and he was the only one—and I was so very young. I want you, but I don't know if I can do this."

"Eight years is a long time to live without loving." He spoke into her hair as he gently stroked her back. He would have to go slowly with her, to somehow erase her doubts about herself and her fears about men. He badly wanted to show her how it could be.

Carrie shrugged within the circle of his arms, hoping she was coming across as nonchalant. "Women aren't as interested in sex as men."

"Is that a fact?"

"Despite what you may have heard to the contrary."

"I think I have spoken with a few women who might disagree with you." He eased back from her and forced her to look at him again. "And, besides, I'm not talking about sex, I'm talking about loving. There's a big difference."

She'd always thought so, in her romantic dreams. But, though Rusty had been insatiably interested in sex, she'd never felt very loved, during or after. She'd thought the lack hers, the tendency toward romanticizing everything her mistake. Now here was a man who seemed aware of the difference. She wanted to know if he meant what he said.

Carrie took a deep, calming breath. "Show me." She saw his eyes change as he acknowledged the challenge and accept it with a soft smile.

"Do you have a bedroom, or do you want to use the kitchen floor?"

Her heart pounding, she took his hand and led him down the hallway past her sleeping son's room. She swallowed the pang of conscience at doing something she'd never done before, take a man to her bed in this house. It was frightening and terribly exciting at the same time.

Now that she'd said yes, Brock was in no hurry. He looked around her room. It was softly feminine yet wisely practical, like the woman who stood beside the brass bed and turned to him with a nervous smile.

She'd shown him her aloof side when he'd first met her. She was a sharp lady making it alone in a tough world. She'd been reluctant to allow him to glimpse her vulnerabilities, but he'd been persistent. He'd held her in his arms last weekend atop a mountain and watched her sleep, watched her finally let go and trust him to just hold her, though she'd regretted even that in the morning. The unfamiliar urge to protect, to cherish and to romance her surprised him with its intensity as he moved closer to her. He reached to turn on the low lamp at her bedside and saw the protest leap into her eyes.

"No," Carrie said. "I like the dark."

"The moonlight isn't enough. I want to see you, and I want you to see me."

She brushed a strand of hair from her cheek, reluctantly giving in to his request. She would close her eyes. She wished he'd hurry. This was taking too long. Maybe she could still change her mind and . . .

Brock touched the warm, smooth skin of her face. "Have I ever told you how very lovely you are?"

She shook her head. "I'm not."

"Stop! You're beautiful. Your cheekbones give you a kind of mysterious Indian look and your eyes are the most fascinating I've ever seen. I could look into them all day." He ran his hand down her throat and low along the scooped neckline of her dress and felt her shudder. "Your skin is so soft." He dipped his head and moved his face into her neck. "And your scent is something that keeps me awake nights. How is it that you always smell so good?"

Shifting, he saw confusion and uncertainty in her gaze. This slow, heady romancing was new to her, and it was making her dreamy, yet unsure. He lowered his mouth to hers and kissed her softly, gently, with the tenderness, the quiet affection she evoked in him so easily.

Her legs were unsteady, her heartbeat erratic and her skin beginning to warm. Carrie took a step backward toward the bed and felt him ease her onto the mattress, then follow her, his mouth never leaving hers. His lips were patient as they moved over hers, his hands lightly stroking her bare arms, his body near but not pressing her. He trailed a path of light kisses along her face, kissing her eyes closed. His touch was soothing, caressing. Gradually she felt the tension in her body leave, yet her senses had never been more alive.

Carrie felt pleasure move through her like the first sip of a rich, potent wine. His scent, his nearness, his taste was drugging her, yet her mind felt free to absorb each separate sensation. The sheet she clutched in her restless hands was soft, smooth and familiar. The aroma of their mingled breath was intoxicating. The texture of his day's beard brushing against her cheek was infinitely arousing. The rustle of the leaves on the tree outside her bedroom window was a gentle summer backdrop to the thundering of her heart. She felt weightless, warm and restive with awakening needs.

Brock sensed the change in her, yet he had no desire to rush. He couldn't take away the hurtful memories of her past encounters, but he could give her this. This slow loving that her fragile beauty demanded, yet somehow she'd never experienced. As he touched his mouth to the pulse pounding in her throat, he heard her sigh his name, and the sound filled him. His name.

He moved back to her mouth, cradling her in his arms, taking her deeper and then deeper still.

Floating. Carrie was floating in a world she'd never known, a world of sensation she'd dreamed existed but had lost hope of ever finding. Mists of delight flooded her being. She had no strength left, for Brock was in total command of her responses. For the first time in her life, she gave over her body to someone else's care, handing him the gift of her trust. It had been a very long time coming.

In the soft glow of the lamp, her skin was a pale rose, velvetlike and delicate, like the flower. He began to undress her, needing to see more. Her eyes opened, but there was no fear in them now, only a watchful curiosity. She shifted to help him unzip her dress, then again as he eased it from her. Her silken teddy fascinated him and he couldn't prevent himself from touching her through the satin softness. Hardening peaks thrust toward his fingers and beckoned his mouth. He lowered his head, put his lips to her and heard the moan she couldn't prevent as her hands buried themselves in his hair.

Nothing she'd ever known had come close to this, Carrie thought as the answering response deep inside her had her hips moving restlessly. He lifted from her then, and waited until she opened her eyes. The look on his face told her that she must be pleasing him. But how could she be, when she'd done nothing but let him kiss and look and touch? Yet his gaze was filled with tenderness as he eased the rest of her clothes from her. He moved slowly, pausing to taste the delicate inside of her elbow, to trail his fingers along the quivering muscles of her stomach, to touch along the inside of her thighs. And she was lost, lost to this man with eyes that told her she was beautiful, gentle hands that knew where and how to touch and his thrilling mouth that fascinated her so.

She took deep breaths, trying to regain some measure of control as he stood and stripped off his shirt and slacks, then bent to kick away the rest. It was the only time he'd moved quickly since he'd walked in the door. Perhaps he was growing impatient and would now take her roughly, and in moments it would all be over. But no.

Carrie felt a small jolt as he lay down close alongside her and flesh touched flesh. His hands were not hurrying, but gently exploring her damp skin. His lips were not rushing, but slowly tasting her breasts, the warm space between and the sheen of her belly as he moved lower.

The wild fragrance of her was tearing at his control. He forced himself to slow the pace even more. He moved his face to within inches of hers as his hand crept down and found her. She gasped, and her eyes flew open; but when she saw him quietly watching her, she gentled, relaxed, and let him start the rhythm. He saw her try to hold still, try to keep her gaze locked with his, but she lost the battle as she thrust her hips upward against his hand. Her eyelids fluttered shut as a soft sound escaped from her and a rosy blush stole over her skin. In another moment she opened her eyes slowly, the look on her face one of astonished pleasure.

She had dreamed, deeply and often, because it was all she'd had for eight long years. But not even in the best of them had her dreams approached the reality of lying with this man, of allowing him to pleasure her, of seeing the tender victory in his eyes. Without shame. Dear God, she'd often been so filled with shame after one of her bouts with Rusty. And now there was only shared passion, an acceptance of a sexuality she hadn't known she possessed, a loving experience she had been ill prepared for. Yet she gratefully reached out to accept it.

Carrie turned to him now and touched his cheek. "I want you to feel as good as I do," she whispered, her eyes on his mouth.

Her words made him ache for all she had never known. "I do. Looking at you makes me feel good. Touching you makes me feel wonderful. Loving you makes me ten feet tall. And there's more."

He shifted to whisper softly into her ear, words of endearment, loving words that let her know how desirable she was to him. Her fingers tentatively explored his back, the need to know him overcoming her shyness. He eased back and drew her hands between them, urging her to learn his body as he was learning hers. At last she did, tentatively at first, touching the coarse hair on his chest, progressing down to his lean stomach. Then more boldly she closed her fingers around him, and he felt her pulse beat wildly in her excitement, matching his own.

The blood was pounding in his head as his mouth found hers, his kiss filled with purpose now. Her lips were avid under his, seeking, losing patience. He realized he'd wanted to give her everything, to show her all there was, yet that wasn't possible all at once. There was so much more, but it would have to wait for another time. His control was nearly gone.

Carrie felt him shift, then slip inside her as if he'd been there before. And he had, but only in her dreams. She felt him move within her, patient and giving, letting the pleasure intensify slowly. She saw him watching her, holding himself in check, and the sweetness of the moment overwhelmed her, bringing tears to her eyes. Never had anyone thought only of her first, never had a man made her feel so much, never had she really been loved till now.

He watched her climb, her cheeks flushed with arousal, and he was flooded with feelings. The ache for release roared in his ears, but he held on. When at last she arched and shuddered and cried out his name, he felt a smile form, and the warmth of it spread. It was all right to let go now, and he did, in an explosion that rocked him. Clinging to her, Brock surrendered to an emotion he couldn't put a name to, and joined her in a new world they'd created together.

He didn't know how much later, two minutes or two hours, he opened his eyes to see hers filled with a dreamy softness that made him smile. "Was...?"

"Shh," she whispered, placing a finger on his lips. "If you ask me how that was for me, I'm going to sock you just as soon as I have the strength to make a fist."

His smile widened. "Is that a question you were used to hearing?"

She sobered quickly and gave a quick shake to her head. "The man I was used to didn't spend much time worrying about how I felt."

He braced his weight on his elbows but was reluctant to withdraw from her. "Is that why you thought you didn't care much for sex?"

"Sex as I knew it was an utter waste of time, and it left me restless and moody." She ran her hands over the strong muscles of his back, resting them on his shoulders. "Making love with you has a decidedly opposite effect."

"Feel like you ate the bear tonight?"

She smiled. "Definitely."

Brock kissed her slowly, lingeringly, then slid his arms around her and rolled onto his back, taking her with him, their bodies still fused. He closed his eyes as she snuggled onto his chest. Something was bothering him, and he was reluctant to put the thought into words.

He hadn't taken her to bed out of lustful curiosity or on an impetuous whim. He'd had no thoughts of a one-night stand nor a quick affair. He hadn't made love with her just once so he could get her out of his system and off his mind, as he'd told himself he would. Already, lying perfectly still just holding her, he could feel fresh desire stirring. The word love came hurtling out of the deep recesses of his brain. He shoved it back.

No, he couldn't let himself fall in love with Carrie Weston. It would screw up all his carefully laid plans for his future, plans that were only now beginning to fall into place. No, this wasn't happening. Good sex sometimes made you mellow, that was all. Mellow and a little crazy.

From the next bedroom, Carrie heard Shane sneeze, and she lifted her head. Only once. Good, he probably wasn't catching a cold. She squinted at the bedside clock. Nearly four. She ran a hand through her hair and eased up on one elbow.

"You'd better get going," she said. "It'll be light outside soon."

He should have known this was coming. Swallowing his disappointment, he locked into her gaze. "Where am I going?" Brock asked quietly.

"Home. You...you can't stay. My son's in the next room."

"I didn't plan to invite him in here with us. There's a lock on your bedroom door. As for tomorrow morning, if he hasn't seen a man acting in a loving way toward his mother, then it's high time he did."

"No!" Her response was low but firm. "I won't have Shane go through what I lived through."

She made as if to roll off of him, but he stopped her. "Your mother brought men to your home?"

Carrie shivered, nodding as she looked away. Maybe if she told him, he'd understand and leave. "She couldn't be without a man in her life. I lost track of the number and of their names. They'd be drinking, and I could hear them through our connecting wall." She shook her head, trying to shake loose the memory. "I won't expose Shane to that."

Another piece of the complicated puzzle known as Carrie Weston slipped into place. He touched her cheek, forcing her to face him. "Is that the reason you've locked yourself away up on this mountain?"

"It's one of two reasons."

"And the other is?"

"I never met anyone I wanted to share my bed with—until you." She felt his hold on her tighten, felt him grow inside her and fill her again. "I don't regret this, Brock. But we have to be discreet."

He fought down an angry surge. "I'm not a back alley lover, and I won't sneak around as if I am."

"I didn't mean that." She was handling this badly. With a start, she realized she was rolling her hips against him and wondered when she'd given her body permission to act on its own. The heat was building rapidly. She tried to calculate if they had enough time to make love again before the sun came up, but his hands had moved to her buttocks and were gently caressing, urging her closer. "Look, I can't think when you do that..."

"I know. That's one reason I do it. You think too damn much. The other reason is it feels good. Carrie, it's all right to feel good. You deserve good things. We all do. Let yourself go."

She shook her head, but her eyes were clouding and her concentration slipping. "No, I can't forget Shane..."

"Shane's only seven, not a teenager like you were, and he's a sound sleeper. And I'm not a string of men. I'm one man, a man who cares a great deal about you, and your son."

Her voice was a husky whisper. "What about tomorrow?"

The big question. Brock didn't want to consider it right now. "We'll think about tomorrow, tomorrow." His hand on the back of her neck brought her lips to his.

His mouth was hard this time, ravenous, evoking a wildness in her that had her pressing her hips against his as she thrust her hands into the thickness of his hair. Carrie found herself filled with cravings she couldn't understand and wishes she knew would never come true. Desire had only been snoozing and now roared to a wakeful state as he moved within her, possessive and demanding.

This was a new Brock who unleashed his power and let her know his needs. Passion flared out of control as her mouth drank from his and her senses tangled with his. His taste was dark, exciting and very male.

She trembled as he drove her, his racing hands setting her skin aflame. And she gave as good as she got.

His mouth crushed hers, hungry for the taste of her. This is how he'd imagined her as he'd lain in his single bed in his rented house. This is what he'd wanted, to release the wildness he'd sensed in her from the first. This is how he'd pictured her—hot, wet and weak for him alone.

He opened his eyes as she pulled back and rose above him, her skin gleaming with passion in the soft lamplight. Her breasts heaved against his chest, her breathing heavy. From a great distance, he heard the swish of the wind against the screen and the forlorn call of a night bird.

Carrie felt the air cool against her overheated skin and saw Brock's dark eyes still on hers. They were filled with desire for her, and with something else.

She sensed something else, only she couldn't think further because the whirlwind took her then and sent her spiraling out of control. She closed her eyes just as Brock's arms tightened about her in a fierce embrace and she heard him sigh her name.

Carrie tried valiantly to ignore the sounds coming from outside her window that intruded on her peaceful sleep. Her foggy mind could barely distinguish them. In the next room, Zeke was demanding his breakfast and freedom from his cage. Outside, the rattle of a noisy truck was coming closer, and Billie was bleating a morning welcome to their visitor. She snuggled into her pillow, but the clamor only grew louder. When she heard the truck door slam and Sonya's husky voice call out, her eyes flew open.

She darted a concerned look at Brock. He was stretched out beside her, quite nude and most unconcerned, the sheet tangled about his feet, and a lazy smile on his face.

"Good morning," he said. "Do you always have people drop in at eight on a Saturday morning?"

Before she could answer, she heard Shane thunder out onto the porch and dash outside to greet Sonya. "Oh, Lord, I'd forgotten," she moaned. "Sonya's taking Shane for the weekend so I can finish the painting." She swung her legs over the side of the bed, then realized she, too, was wearing nothing. She felt the heat rise into her face. Praying Brock wouldn't say a word and Shane would stay outside, she ran to the closet and yanked out a pair of jeans.

"I'll come help you," Brock said as he stretched sleepily.

"No!" She struggled into her jeans. "I don't want them to know you're here." She grabbed a cotton top and pulled it over her head, then shook out her hair. "Please, just stay put, and I'll send them off."

Fighting a grin, Brock lay back with his hands under his head. "All right, but we did forget to hide my car last night."

"Damn," Carrie muttered under her breath. She glanced at her image in the dresser mirror and could have groaned. If anyone alive could see that well-loved look, that warm glow, that swollen mouth and not know what it meant, she'd bet it wasn't Sonya. Sighing, she grabbed her brush and ran it through her hair.

"You look beautiful," Brock said serenely.

She turned to him. She wasn't sure of the proper etiquette between first-time lovers. She felt vulnerable, as if her fragile feelings and the intensity of her response to their lovemaking were somehow stamped on her forehead. Swallowing, she gave him a shaky smile. "You do, too. I'll be back in a minute."

Racing to the door, she slowed as she neared the porch and gulped in a deep breath, hoping it would calm her. It didn't. She stepped out into the bright sunshine where Sonya was standing, listening to Shane rattle on about their plane ride and the diving boys. With a fervent prayer that she could distract Sonya before he spilled all the beans, Carrie arranged her face into a smile and walked toward them.

"Hi," she ventured. Great start, she told herself.

Sonya's wise blue eyes looked her over carefully. "Hi, yourself. I hear you had quite a time yesterday."

She nodded. "Yes. Shane's first airplane ride." She touched her son's shoulder. "How about some breakfast before you two take off?" Eyes on his dark curls, she hoped that Shane's eagerness to be off would take precedence over his appetite.

"I thought we'd indulge ourselves with a sinfully delicious, cholesterol-laden Egg McMuffin breakfast, if that's all right with you." Sonya took a long draw on her ever-present cigarette.

Carrie longed to grab the cigarette from her hand and inhale deeply. Quickly she nodded. "Sure, fine. I packed his clothes yesterday. Shane, run inside and get your bag." She watched the boy run off, then decided she couldn't postpone the inevitable. Raising her eyes to Sonya's, she waited.

"So Shane had a first yesterday with his plane ride." She glanced pointedly toward Brock's red car sitting next to Carrie's Volkswagen. "Did you have a first, too?"

Only from Sonya would she take this kind of probing. Carrie knew her friend had only her best interests at heart. She was the one person who'd been supportive through the turmoil of her relationship with Rusty. But it still wasn't easy. She studied her bare foot as it poked at a clump of grass. "Yes," she answered.

"I see." Sonya blew smoke into the still morning air. "Are you sure you're doing the right thing, honey?"

Carrie turned her back to the window and shoved her hands into the pockets of her jeans. "I'm not sure of anything, Sonya."

"Do you love him?"

"Least of all am I sure of that." Her gaze rose to the sky as she tried to find answers in the wispy cloud formations. "He's everything Rusty wasn't—responsible, successful, loving. And so many things he was— charming, charismatic, with a touch of wanderlust." She shook her head, her eyes filling. "He makes me *feel* so much and it's been so long."

Sonya threw down the cigarette, stepped on it and pulled Carrie into a rough embrace. "I know, honey."

Carrie absorbed her comfort for a long moment. "He makes me feel like a desirable woman, Sonya. I've never known anyone like him."

"Looks like my astrologer friend was right. A big change in your life this year." Sonya drew back, her eyes worried. "Just go slowly, honey. Don't rush into anything."

She gave her friend a quick hug as she heard Shane let the porch door slam shut and come running to the truck. "I won't. Thanks."

"Hey, Mom. Brock says next week he might start me on diving lessons. I won't dive between rocks like those other boys do, but learning to dive would be fun, right, Mom?'' Shane's eager little face looked up at her.

Carrie experienced a momentary pang of fear. She'd left Brock nude in her bed. ''Where is Brock, Shane?''

''In the kitchen. We had some juice together. Can I let him teach me to dive, Mom?''

She let out a relieved sigh as she touched her son's soft cheek. ''We'll see.'' She bent to kiss him. ''You have fun and listen to Sonya.''

Sonya was already behind the wheel of the ancient four-wheel drive she loved to go tooling around in more than her big Caddie. ''We'll be fine,'' she yelled through the open window. ''*You* be careful.''

Nodding, Carrie watched as her son climbed in beside Sonya and her friend turned the chugging vehicle around. Both of them waved as the truck disappeared down the hill. With a relieved sigh, Carrie went into the kitchen and poured herself a big glass of orange juice. She drank most of it, then put on a pot of coffee. Her conscience had given her a bad moment there. She should have realized that Brock would use good judgment. Memories of the best night of her life danced through her mind, and possibilities teased at her, causing her to smile. She really should get to work on the painting. But . . .

She drained her juice and hurried to the bedroom. In the doorway, she stopped. Her heart began to thud in the double time she'd almost begun to get used to as she looked at him. He was nude again, his jeans carelessly flung across the foot of the bed, a lazy smile on his face. He was beautiful—strong and virile and hers for the time being. She walked slowly to the bed.

''Come here,'' he invited.

''I am here. I've put on some coffee. Want some?''

His arm shot out and pulled her down into a sitting position beside him. He cradled her onto his chest. "No, I want you."

Carrie stared into his eyes, wishing for solutions to problems that might never be solved. She smiled at him. He was right. For now, they had today, an endless today that stretched in front of them, filled with glorious possibilities.

She stood, whipped off her shirt and yanked off her jeans. Acting more out of character than she ever had, she climbed atop him and scooted up until their lips were a breath apart. "And I want you, mister. More than I've ever wanted before." Hungrily she pressed her open mouth to his, trying not to think just yet about tomorrow.

Chapter Nine

The painting was almost finished. Carrie wiped her hands on a paint-spattered rag as she sat back and regarded her work. Not bad, if she said so herself. Another couple of hours tomorrow and it should be completed. She sighed. This was an important painting, the first one her father would see up close.

Thoughtfully she cleaned her brushes and placed them upright in their jar. Her father would be arriving in a few days for the grand opening of the McKamey Building. Brock had broadly hinted that he thought she should be there to meet with Mac. But he had also stuck to his promise not to tell anyone until she was ready. The question was, was she ready? Would she ever be?

She had to admit to a certain curiosity. Her early memories of Mac were of a warm and loving man. Brock and Rhoda clearly felt he still was that. Yet she hadn't imagined the scene indelibly etched in her mind of the day he'd ordered her mother and her from his home, telling them to never return. She hadn't invented the facts, that she'd never heard from him since that day, despite her many letters. She'd expected Natalie to be bitter, and she had been, speaking against her ex-husband every chance she'd found. But that alone hadn't colored Carrie's feelings. His silence had.

She went to stand at the wide window of her small studio and gazed out at the late afternoon sun already sliding toward the horizon of the blue sea. If in fact Brock was telling the truth and Mac wouldn't know she was in Carmel until he arrived and she gave permission to tell him, what would his reaction be after all these years? Would he have explanations for his neglect of her, explanations she could somehow accept and live with? A part of her yearned to believe, for Shane's sake.

They weren't exactly overburdened with relatives. Natalie was dead, and she hadn't seen nor heard from Rusty's parents since his funeral. Evidently the Westons weren't interested in developing a relationship with their grandson. Or perhaps they'd avoided her and her son, thinking Carrie would be a financial burden on them if they made any overtures. The very thought made her cringe.

Shane had only his mother and Sonya, a surrogate aunt, but a loving one. Many made do with less, but did she have the right to deny her son the friendship of his grandfather? Perhaps it was time for her to swallow her pride and at least meet with Mac, hear what he had to say. Besides, it would please Brock.

Brock. Carrie slid the window open wider and let the ocean breezes caress her face. She wrapped her arms around herself and closed her eyes, letting the memories of the morning roll across her mind. At twenty-eight she'd lived, married and been widowed, and she hadn't known until last night how it could be between a man and a woman. For years she'd put her romantic dreams aside and suddenly, someone had come into her life who'd made some of them come true. But not all.

Despite her artistic nature, Carrie knew she was a realist. And she knew that, though they'd shared something very special, Brock had no intention of remaining with her. She knew how easily men slipped in and out of women's lives when work or pleasure or fame called them. Brock had spoken many times of how hard he'd worked to get where he was, and that he liked traveling, living in one place for several months, perhaps a year or two, then moving on. The corporate life was demanding, intense, filled with excitement for some. And she wanted that for him if that was his lifelong dream. But Carrie doubted that she'd be comfortable in that life.

She sat on the window ledge and watched a sandpiper circle the backyard, obviously a little confused having wandered so far inland. She knew how the tiny bird felt. She felt a little lost herself and definitely out of her element. She'd seen something in Brock's eyes last night that worried her. She'd finally accepted his friendship, then the desire she could no longer fight. But for a flicker of a moment, she thought she'd seen more. The hesitant beginnings of love.

Love could hurt, she knew from experience. When a man loved a woman, he wanted control, to make the major decisions, to call the shots. Brock would want to take her and her son with him wherever he chose to go. And she, who had been dragged too many places by Natalie, didn't want that life for Shane, or herself again. She'd given Brock her thoughts and confidences, she'd given him her affection, and she'd given him her body. But she couldn't give him her heart. She couldn't risk letting him damage it the way several others had. She knew she wouldn't easily recover from this one. No, loving was too risky, too dangerous. But a caring relationship that involved a physical expression of deep feelings was something else again. Though she had no illusions that his stay here was only temporary, she would enjoy him while she could.

Carrie glanced at the clock on the bookshelf and realized Brock would be returning soon. They'd spent nearly the whole morning in bed, then in the shower laughing and loving until the water had run cold. They'd shared a long, leisurely breakfast, and then he'd left her to get changed and check in with his office while she worked on her painting. Rhoda would be in today, catching up on paperwork, and he'd needed to confer with her since he'd left early yesterday. Then he was returning to spend the evening with Carrie.

Smiling as she left her studio to go change, she acknowledged that she could hardly wait to see him again—and they'd been apart a mere five hours. Smitten, She was definitely smitten with the man. And it felt wonderful.

Brock signed the last of the letters and handed the stack to Rhoda. "Anything else?"

He saw his secretary survey his striped rugby shirt worn over white pants. She raised a brow. "Going to a beach party, boss?"

He grinned at her, something he'd been doing a lot this afternoon, with no apparent reason. Well, he knew the reason for his lighthearted mood, but Rhoda didn't. "Yeah. Try not to have an emergency until at least Monday."

Rhoda straightened the letters unnecessarily as she sat on the edge of the chair across from him. "I've known you for nearly fifteen years, Brock, and I don't believe I've ever seen you quite so eager to be off. Got to be a woman."

Rising, he winked at her. "You should try out for game shows, Rhoda. You're pretty good." Sobering suddenly, he eased a hip onto the edge of his desk. He'd never been close to a woman, with the exception of the one sitting before him. Perhaps it was because he'd known her so long, perhaps because she was a good listener, or perhaps because he knew she regarded him with the fondness usually reserved for a younger brother. At any rate, he trusted her and felt genuine affection for her. Though he hadn't for a while, today he felt a need to run a few thoughts by her.

"You've been divorced for years, Rhoda, been alone a long time. Ever fall in love since that first marriage?"

Crossing her still shapely legs, Rhoda chuckled. "I've tried not to. I'm not real good at it." She gazed out the window. "There was someone, about five years ago. We seemed quite compatible, in many ways. But he had a teenage daughter, and I'd never coped with a child. And he wanted me to quit my job and stay home." She shrugged. "I think committing to someone involves a lot of compromise, and neither of us was willing to do that."

Brock considered her last statement. "I'm not sure I'm good at compromising, either."

"Let me guess. The artist with the beautiful eyes, Carrie Weston, right? She's the one who's got you thinking so hard?"

He nodded. "What do you think of her?"

"Mmm, I only spent half an hour with her. I think she's obviously talented, very lovely, a little standoffish. I also think she's quick and bright and ... and a shade defensive. Perhaps it's a protective device." She looked up. "Am I on target?"

"Close enough. She had an unhappy first marriage and she's got a seven-year-old son."

"How do you feel about instant fatherhood?"

Brock shrugged. "He's a super kid." He shook his head, hardly able to believe they were having this discussion. "I'm the guy who had his whole life planned out, and I sure wasn't going to be stupid enough to let some fleeting, silly emotion like love mess up my plans. If I thought of marriage at all, I thought I'd work out a practical arrangement with someone like Francine who'd understand my work and my ambitions, the way I want to live."

Rhoda looked understanding. "I believe Francine sees herself as part of your future. Has Carrie changed your plans?"

Brock ran a hand through his hair. "Hell, I don't know. Francine knows the score. There's no great love match between us. If we were to get together, it would be a blending of two similar people with similar goals."

"That has all the appeal of a spoiled fish dinner."

"Maybe so, but you know me, Rhoda. I'm a practical guy. I've never believed much in love and romance, until . . ."

"Until recently. Until Carrie." She smiled knowingly. "I hear tell it happens like that."

He rubbed his chin thoughtfully. "I didn't go looking for this. And it's all happened so damn fast. She's got me questioning what I want out of life. How the hell did that happen?"

Rhoda was used to playing devil's advocate. "How does Carrie feel about you?"

Brock thought a moment, not wanting to give away Carrie's background or hint of her relationship to Mac. And there was another question: how would Mac react if he told him that he'd just met his daughter and she'd gotten under his skin? Of course, much depended on how Carrie and Mac hit it off, if and when she would agree to meet with her father. So damn many questions. If only he could sort out his feelings and get on track. This ambivalence was new to him, and he didn't much care for it.

He returned his gaze to Rhoda. "Carrie's a person who guards her feelings. We haven't really talked much about our relationship."

"Do you think Carrie would fit into your life as well as Francine?"

Brock sighed. "A good question. She could if she wanted to. She's an artist, a little bohemian and very private. But she'd fit in anywhere if she had her heart in it." The problem was, though he knew she was beginning to care for him and fighting it all the way, he didn't know if she'd ever trust again, let herself love again. And did he even want that?

"I see. Would she be willing to travel around, to live in foreign locations while you set up branches, or possibly move to Chicago as a home base?"

He hadn't thought about all that. But he couldn't see why not. He could picture showing her London, then maybe Paris, walking along the Seine arm in arm. Shane would love traveling. But Carrie was stubborn, unpredictable and introverted. She might not be easily convinced. "I honestly don't know."

"So you haven't discussed any of this with her?"

"No. I've only started thinking about these things myself."

Rhoda looked skeptical, but she gave him an encouraging smile nonetheless. "Maybe you should."

"Yeah, maybe you're right." He stood. "Tell me, is it natural to feel so damn scared?"

Rising, Rhoda laughed. "Falling in love can be very scary."

"I didn't say I loved her."

"Didn't you?" She kissed his cheek. "I wish you luck, whatever you decide. Frankly I like Francine, but I've never thought she had enough...fire for you. Maybe Carrie does."

"Maybe." Brock hugged her warmly. "Thanks, for listening." He picked up his keys. "Have a good weekend. See you Monday."

"You, too, boss."

Wearing a pensive frown, Brock walked out the door.

Brock offered his hand to Carrie to assist her down the wooden steps that led to the beach. Carrying a large shaggy blanket, she followed him as he juggled a picnic hamper in his free hand. It was twilight, his favorite time of evening, and he saw as they stepped onto the warm sand that this stretch of beach was deserted. He couldn't have planned it better.

"Perfect," he said as he walked her to a spot nicely protected by natural rock formations that formed a semicircle. "I'll bet the view of the sunset from here is spectacular."

Carrie spread out their blanket. "It is. Shane and I cook hot dogs over a fire once in a while down here."

Brock watched the wind playfully pick up strands of her hair and whip it about her face. She hadn't slept much last night, he knew, yet she looked young and carefree tonight. Had he caused some of that glow? "Just the two of you?"

She anchored a corner of the blanket with the basket and the other with her shoes before she looked up at him. "Still fishing? I've told you, you're the only man I've been with in eight years. Isn't that enough for you?"

He dropped down close beside her. "I'm sorry. I seem to have developed a jealous streak in the last few weeks. I never felt that way before meeting you."

Carrie frowned as she pulled a chilled bottle of wine from the hamper. She'd experienced jealousy when she'd been married to Rusty and had seen the way women at the air shows looked at him, hot and hungry. "Better give it up," she told him. "Jealousy can rip you apart. Besides, there's no need."

"Maybe I just wanted to hear you say that."

"Here's something else you might like to hear. I've come to a decision today."

He took the bottle from her and reached for the corkscrew. "What's that?"

"I'd like to meet with my father, preferably before the grand opening."

Brock smiled at her. It was what he'd been hoping to hear. "I don't think you'll regret it." He sighed as he wound the corkscrew. "You've each told me different versions of how you recall the past, but I think somewhere there's been a misunderstanding. You're both good, decent people. I know you'll be able to work things out. Mac is going to be thrilled."

"I want to go slowly, Brock. Could you maybe arrange a meeting at my house? I want to see how things go between us before he meets Shane."

"Sure." He tossed the cork into the basket and waited while she held out the glasses, then poured some into each. He clinked his glass to hers. "Here's to the reunion. May it be all that you wish it to be." Brock sipped, appreciating the chilled fruity flavor. "There was a message from Francine back at the office. I believe you met Mac's assistant. They'll be arriving day after tomorrow."

That soon? Carrie felt a flicker of anxiety, then pushed it to the back of her mind. "Yes, I met Francine. She's very lovely and, from what I gathered, very fond of you."

He raised a brow at her. "Now who's jealous?"

"Not jealous. Curious."

"I haven't exactly been celibate for eight years, but, for the record, Francine and I have been business associates, friends, but never lovers." Carefully he took the glasses from her hand and set both of them on the hamper lid. Easing her onto her back on the blanket, he leaned over her and stared into deep violet eyes. "Since meeting you, I find myself rethinking things

I'd always been pretty sure of. I'm not crazy about making changes.''

She could feel his breath warm on her cheek, her pulse leap in anticipation. He was voicing her thoughts exactly. ''None of us are.''

''Against my will, you're dragging me under.''

''Don't talk yourself into something that isn't there. I haven't asked anything of you.''

''Maybe that's what makes me want to give to you. Damned if I know what it is. I only know it's stronger than anything I've known.'' The need to show her whipped through him. He pulled her to him almost roughly and pressed his lips to hers. She tasted warm from the lowering sun, pungent from the wine, sweet from within. He'd intended to prove his point, yet he was instantly drawn in as his hard body sang a welcome to her softness. As if from a distance, he heard the waves of the sea crash to the shore with more intensity, more volume, as she wrapped herself around him and gave to him. And again, he was lost.

Carrie's mind whirled away as her senses clouded with the taste and feel of him. Hunger rose so quickly it staggered her, and she moaned into his mouth. How could this happen each time, more quickly, more powerfully? Would it go away one day, or just keep growing until there was nothing left of her will to resist him? Her restless hands moved on his back, clutching, kneading, racing across hard muscles. At last he pulled back and gazed at her, looking as shaken as she felt.

Passion, barely controlled, darkened his eyes. ''You want me?'' he asked, his voice rough with emotion.

"You know I do." She whispered the words, trying to draw him closer, her body already moving against his.

"Say it."

"I want you."

"Good, because I want you, too. And it scares the hell out of me."

Fear skittered up her spine, dampening her desire. Her hands dropped from his shirt to the blanket where they shifted restively. "It scares me, too," she admitted. She moved her body against his, wanting to distract him. She didn't want to talk. Talking would only make them more aware of things best left unsaid. She wanted to feel, to forget. She reached to pull his head to hers, but he stopped just short of the kiss.

"What are we going to do about it?"

"Nothing. We're going to enjoy each other while we can. And then you're going off to build buildings, and I'm staying here to paint more seascapes."

"Is that what you want?"

She closed her eyes briefly on a long sigh. "I asked you before not to make me want too much. I reached out once for what I thought I wanted, and I took a big fall. It took me years to put myself back together again. I can't risk that kind of fall again."

His hand played with a lock of her hair. "I want you to know when I came to Carmel I was perfectly contented with my life."

"Good, because I'm very contented with mine." The statement had a few flaws in it, but she wasn't going to think about that just now.

"But things shifted for me. Carrie, you're really messing up my head."

"Don't let me. We're just a man and a woman grabbing a moment, holding each other for a short time against things that go bump in the night, remember?" She believed what she said. Why, then, did she suddenly feel like crying?

"Don't you . . . care at all?"

He sounded so hurt. Damn the man! Carrie twisted beneath him. "Of course I care. But you want too much, Brock. If it's love you're looking for, you've got the wrong woman. Every time I've said those three little words, except to Shane, they've been tossed back into my face. I won't chance it again. It took me eight years—eight long, frustrated, lonely years—to come this far. If it isn't enough for you, let me up and let me go."

He didn't honestly know what he was after. Love? He hadn't thought so, certainly not consciously. But let her go? The very thought had his arms tightening about her.

His mouth crushed down on hers, making further words impossible, taking the steam from her anger. A gull swooped overhead, but Brock didn't see it, didn't hear it. He heard only Carrie's ragged breathing as she fought with herself not to respond to him. So he thrust his tongue into her mouth and engaged hers in a wild duel that had them both practically panting. Only when he felt her arms slide around him again, felt the force of her answering kiss, was he able to loosen his grip on her.

Too fast, he was moving her past reason. Too far, he wanted to take her with him wherever he would lead. Too soon, for her to know her own mind, yet he would rush her. Carrie felt his hands pull the hem of her blouse from the band of her shorts, and his fingers tug at the buttons. A small measure of sanity still remained, and she tried to stop him with her hands.

"What are you doing? This is a public beach." She knew people rarely walked down this far, yet her sense of propriety was making her uneasy.

He lifted his head and glanced both ways. "It's nearly dark, and there's no one coming from either direction." He had her shirt open and his mouth moving to touch her already quivering flesh. "I can't wait. If someone comes from way down the beach, we'll be finished by the time they get here."

Carrie sought to lighten the mood, which had gotten too intense. "Am I going to experience what is widely known as a quickie?"

He raised his eyes and looked at her. "I guarantee you, it'll be worth your while however long it takes." Lowering his head, he closed his lips around a hardening peak as a soft sound escaped from her.

Carrie shut her eyes and gave herself up to the moment, wondering who had won and who had lost, wondering why there had to be a winner and a loser.

Victor McKamey hadn't gotten to be the head of one of the country's most successful and prestigious architectural firms by not having a poker face in his dealings with people. But as Brock sat across the desk from him on Tuesday morning and quietly told him the story of having located the daughter he hadn't seen in eighteen years, Mac was definitely nonplussed.

Brock watched as the older man sat back in his deep leather chair and took his time unwrapping one of the two cigars he allowed himself every day. His hands were steady enough, but his ruddy complexion had paled a shade or two. Silently Brock waited for the questions he knew would be forthcoming.

Mac put the flame of a gold lighter to his cigar and took several short puffs before raising his blue eyes to Brock. "Tell me everything."

And so he did, about how he'd tracked her down through the gallery that represented her work, how he'd sought her out at her painting site on the beach, how he'd commissioned her to do the canvas for their entryway and how she'd discovered who owned the building.

"And she was angry at first?"

"Not so much angry as annoyed at being tricked by me and adamant about not meeting you." He wasn't going to sugarcoat the truth, Brock told himself.

"I see. So how'd you talk her into it?"

"I didn't. I just kept thinking up excuses to see her, telling her more about you every chance I got until she decided on her own that she wanted to see you."

"Did a sell job on her, did you?" The hint of humor was back.

Brock crossed his legs as he searched for the right words. "She'd been brainwashed against you, probably by her mother. I tried to correct some of her misconceptions, as I know them to be. I'm not sure how far I got with her. She can be stubborn."

Mac took another short puff and allowed himself a small smile. "So I recall, even as a child. A chip off the old block, would you say?"

"In some ways." There seemed so much to tell. "Your ex-wife died five years ago."

Mac sobered. "That's about the time I got the notice from the post office box I sent my letters to that Natalie no longer used their facilities. Funny, I'd thought she'd left the area. She'd written that she hated California."

They'd come to the hard part. "About those letters. Carrie claims she never received them."

Setting his cigar in the big glass ashtray, Mac frowned. "What do you mean, never received them?"

"Just that. Not one. No letters, no money, no gifts and no tuition."

"That's a lot of bull, and you know it." Mac never raised his voice but the strength, the quick anger was nonetheless evident. "You mailed many of those letters for me for years when you first came to work with me, didn't you?"

"Yes, I did. I told her as much. She stuck to her story. She told me she'd written you many times, sent you an invitation to her graduation and asked you to walk her down the aisle at her wedding. And she never heard from you."

Mac swiveled about in his chair, his mouth a hard line. "Had to be Natalie. She must have kept my letters from Carolyn." He swiveled back. "She calls herself Carrie now?"

"Yes. What do you suppose happened to the money you sent?"

He gave a short, bitter laugh. "Money always stuck to Natalie's fingers." He shook his head. "I remember one year she wrote that Carolyn—Carrie—needed ten thousand for tuition to this special art school. I sent a check immediately, two years in a row."

"Made out to Carrie?"

"Made out to Carolyn McKamey, and the bank returned them endorsed that way." Mac ran his hand over his thinning, sandy-colored hair.

"I suppose Natalie could have forged her daughter's name. You really didn't know what Carrie's handwriting would look like since she'd left when she was only ten."

"I should have sent them directly to the school or demanded that I talk with the child. I should have...done more. But you know, Natalie kept threatening to take the child away, telling me I'd never hear from her again if I didn't do exactly as she asked. I knew she was capable of that. I figured at least I could see to it that Carrie would have a good education."

Something had been bothering Brock and it was time to ask. "But you're her father. What could Natalie have done if you'd have hired someone, found them both and gone to see your daughter?"

Mac picked up the cigar and drew on it, sending gray smoke into the air. "Natalie was a difficult woman who seldom listened to reason."

Not much of an answer. For the first time, Brock caught a hint of evasion in Mac's tone, but he didn't feel he had the right to press further.

"What's her husband like, the aerial stuntman?"

"Rusty Weston was killed in an air crash eighteen months after they were married."

Mac's eyes registered sympathy. "So Carrie's been alone all this time?"

"Not exactly. She has a son. His name is Shane, and he's seven now."

This news was almost more startling to Mac than the fact that Brock had located his daughter. Carefully he set down the cigar. "A grandson."

"Yes, and he looks just like his mother." Brock leaned forward, glad to be able to tell the man some good things after the hurtful story of the lost letters. "He's got dark, curly hair and Carrie's violet eyes, and he's quick and bright and just a great kid."

"Has she told him about me?"

"I don't think so. She wants to meet with you alone first, probably see how you hit it off, maybe get a few answers. Mac, she may be a little hostile at first."

"I know." He gazed into the smoke cover, lost in his thoughts for a long moment. "So she wrote me lots of letters, eh? Wonder what the hell happened to them?" His gaze drifted to Brock. "What's she like?"

He chose his words carefully. "She's beautiful. She's a terrific mother. I take it her marriage to Rusty wasn't made in heaven, yet she hasn't colored Shane's opinion of his father. She's enormously talented, loves animals and the sea. She rents this sprawling house in Big Sur, up a secluded mountain road, drives a dilapidated Volkswagen and is in debt up to her ears."

"What? I thought you said she gets paid well for her work?"

"She does, but that's recent. She's paying off some debts Rusty had run up before he died."

"Why'd she marry a loser like that?"

"To get away from Natalie, and because she was nineteen and thought she was in love. She's no longer that wide-eyed romantic young woman. She's become a realist, maybe too much so."

Mac's eyes narrowed thoughtfully. "You say you found her about three weeks ago. How well did you get to know her?"

Somehow he'd known they'd get to this. "Pretty well."

"I see." Mac continued to study him through the wispy smoke. But he was shrewd enough not to probe too deeply. "Does she like you?"

Brock kept his gaze steady. "Well enough. I get the impression that she doesn't trust very readily. According to her, you ordered her from your house. Natalie was a drinker, irresponsible, parading a string of men through their home. And Rusty was a spoiled womanizer who put her in debt. Not a good basis for trust."

Sadness filled Mac's eyes. "Poor kid. She has every right to feel as she does. She doesn't trust you, either?"

"I don't think she trusts anyone, except maybe Sonya Nichols, the woman who owns the art gallery that represents her."

"Well, well. You've certainly given me a lot to think about." Mac leaned back in his chair.

"So, do you want to meet with her?"

"Damn right. Set it up as soon as she'll agree." He swiveled to face his friend. "And Brock . . . thanks."

With a smile Brock stood. "You're going to love her."

Mac's blue eyes were a little brighter than usual. "I never stopped," he said softly.

Chapter Ten

I can't believe, after two years on the market, that you've finally got an offer on Natalie's house." Carrie's voice was enthusiastic as she listened to her realtor friend, Phil Hebert, chuckle on the other end of the line. "Tell me about it."

"I knew you'd be surprised. And you've got another shock coming when I tell you how much they're offering." Phil had been in real estate in Carmel for thirty years and liked to drag out the good news.

"Go ahead. I'm sitting down." When he did, she gasped. "Oh, Phil. That old shack's not worth half that. Seventy-five thousand, and I distinctly remember Natalie saying she paid twenty for it, and then there was all the fire damage."

"Sure, but you fixed it up after the fire, little by little. And the renters you had in it for over four years kept the place in good shape." He puffed quietly on his pipe. "I sold that cottage to your mama the year you enrolled in that fancy art school. And you're right about the price, twenty grand. Don't you know how much property's escalated in Carmel since then?"

"I guess not." Seventy-five thousand. She hadn't dreamed the old house was worth that kind of money. If she had, she'd have pushed Phil to sell it much earlier. With that money, and the commission for the new painting, she could actually pay off her loan. Carrie tried to keep calm. "Are you sure, Phil, that there's no catch? Do these people really want the house *as is*?"

"You bet. I think they plan to do a little cosmetic surgery and then rent it out. They asked only that you have the carpeting cleaned and take the stuff that's left in the basement out of there. Think you can handle that, missy?"

She smiled. Phil was as close to an old family friend as she had, someone she and Natalie had met when they'd first arrived in California and were looking for a place to live. Phil had tried to help her mother with her drinking problem and had kept a kindly eye on both of them through the years. He and Sonya had been there for her through the ordeal of Rusty's funeral and subsequently of Shane's birth. She had a genuine affection for Phil and had often wished he'd gotten together with Sonya. Unfortunately, Sonya hadn't complied with her matchmaking attempts.

"Yes, I can certainly handle that. I'll arrange the carpet cleaning right away, and I'll get the basement cleaned out by the weekend. Would that be all right?" She could hear Phil tapping his pipe in his ashtray.

"Sure, sure. Just come on by my office, today or tomorrow, and sign these purchase agreements. Then I'll get the ball rolling."

Old habits died hard, and Carrie felt a pang of doubt. "Phil, you don't think anything will go wrong then? These buyers will really go through with the sale?"

"Lord, missy, I never met a pessimist like you. Never, no sir. Stop worrying. It's a cash sale, and I've got their deposit. You ever know me to lie to you?"

"No, of course not." Still balancing the phone on her lap, she found herself smiling from ear to ear. "Phil, I can't thank you enough. This *truly* makes my day."

"I'm glad, honey. You take care."

Carrie replaced the receiver in its cradle. Freedom from debt was around the corner. Could this be happening to her? That was wonderful news, and her career was also in high gear. Now if only she could make it through Brock's imminent departure, for Chicago or wherever his job took him next, then she might survive. And if only he wouldn't break Shane's heart before leaving. Her own was also experiencing several severe cracks.

Carrie glanced at the clock and put away the last of her brushes, realizing that she'd have to hurry to get cleaned up before Brock and her father arrived. She'd taken Shane to stay overnight with Sonya again, giving her curious friend only a perfunctory explanation. She needed to think her own troubled thoughts through before she discussed them with anyone. Then she'd spent the rest of the afternoon putting finishing touches on the painting, until Phil's phone call.

Pulling off her damp clothes, she jumped into the shower and turned on the spray. What did a twenty-eight-year old daughter who hadn't seen her father since she was ten wear for the occasion? she wondered. It was a hot night with the sea breezes slow in reaching her mountainside house. Something cool and gauzy, soft and sweet? Oh damn! she thought sticking her head under the nozzle to rinse out the shampoo. What difference did it make? Mac wasn't coming to see her wardrobe.

Why was he coming?

Curiosity. Conscience maybe. Perhaps for information. And she could give him plenty. But she needed some answers from him, as well. Carrie turned off the water and reached for a large towel. Wrapping it around her head, she grabbed another and began rubbing herself dry. She couldn't help wondering what Brock had told Mac about her, how much, vaguely or in detail? Surely he hadn't told him that she... that they... no! He would have no reason to share something that personal with her father.

Dry, finally, she went to the bedroom and slipped into the white shirtwaist dress she'd been saving for an occasion. Tonight certainly qualified. And the dress, with the wide belt and full skirt, was perfect. She set it on the bed, then went to blow-dry her hair.

Her thoughts returned to last night, to making love on the beach, and brought a heated response to her cheeks even now. She, who even as a married woman had never allowed the lights on in the bedroom, had actually made love on a public beach. Never mind that not a soul had come by nor probably could have seen them in their secluded alcove if they had, it was to Carrie indicative of the things Brock could get her to do—with just a touch, a look, a word. He'd changed her already, and appeared to want more changes.

They'd eaten then, both ravenously hungry. Cold chicken, ripe cheese, hard rolls, fresh fruit and more wine. And they'd talked. Or rather Brock had talked, about his youth in the small town he hated, about painstakingly getting through the days and nights, always dreaming of moving on. He'd told her he'd always had a restless nature he'd had to put on hold until the time and circumstances were right. He wanted freedom like she did, the freedom to do work he enjoyed, to have enough money not to have to answer to anyone. But there their dreams took different paths.

Brock had spent the first twenty years of his life imprisoned on his aunt and uncle's farm, beholden to them financially and feeling obligated that they'd raised him. After leaving and getting his education, he desperately wanted to see the world, to travel, to taste life. He was finally getting the chance, he'd explained to her, with Mac seriously considering setting up offices in distant places. Yet oddly, he'd told her this with a hint of sadness rather than the excitement she'd expected. And he'd kept watching her, as if waiting for her to say something. But not knowing what he wanted to hear, she'd kept silent.

He'd be leaving soon, she knew. The grand opening was tomorrow, and after it, his work here was finished. He hadn't asked her to go with him, of course. Both of them had stubbornly avoided speaking of feelings deep enough to bind them together. Yet if he had invited her to share his future, she knew what her answer would have to be.

All her life, she'd struggled to have roots, to have a solid home, and now it was within reach. Sonya had told her that when she was able and if she wanted it, she could buy the house she'd thus far been renting. If she didn't want this place, she could soon afford another for her and Shane. A place of their own, where no one could make them leave, where no outsiders could come in unless she wanted them to be there.

Brock wouldn't understand. From age ten when they'd left Illinois to age nineteen when she'd married Rusty, she and Natalie had lived in fourteen different places. Carrie had kept track. Each had been shabbier than the last, smelling of other people, tired old houses with sagging porches and no character. Sometimes they'd skipped out on the rent they owed, sneaking away late at night. Never again, she'd vowed, would she live like a gypsy or leave a debt unpaid. Not even if she loved Brock, would she go with him. And, of course, she didn't love him. It would be stupid to mistake infatuation for love. Carrie couldn't afford to be stupid a second time.

Finished with her hair, she slipped the dress on and stepped into white sandals. Yes, the outfit set off her tan nicely. She moved to the dresser for a light touch of makeup. She'd seen early pictures of her mother, before alcohol and a desperate life-style had stolen her looks, and knew she resembled Natalie a great deal. Would that bring back memories to her father? Well, he'd have to cope. She had a few painful memories to struggle through, also.

And what would Brock be like tonight? Carrie wondered as she walked through the house turning on lamps and checking each room for neatness, placing the pets in Shane's room out of the way. Brock had seemed to want this meeting more than she. Well, now the debt to his benefactor would be paid. He'd found the prodigal daughter. She prayed she'd get through the evening without embarrassing herself.

She'd resorted to fluffing up pillows by the time she heard the sound of Brock's mighty Ferrari engine and

Billie's bleat of cautious welcome from behind the fence. Taking a deep breath, she made herself walk out onto the porch and wait for them.

He was, of course, older looking than the picture in her memory. He was as tall as she remembered, tall and straight, and he had not even the suggestion of a paunch. His sandy hair was thinner, his complexion sort of weathered, but his blue eyes were as kind as she recalled, with a hint of uneasiness in them she could well understand. Brock came up behind him. Wordlessly Carrie swung open the screen door.

"Hello, Carrie," Mac said, offering his hand.

Carrie hesitated only a moment before placing her hand in his. He still exuded that warm strength that was so comforting. "Hello." She took back her hand and held wide the door. "Come in, please." Her father walked past her as she raised her eyes to Brock. He touched her arm and squeezed it lightly as he followed Mac into the living room.

"I've made lemonade," she offered, indicating the pitcher and glasses on the low table in front of the fireplace.

"None for me, thank you," Mac answered, looking around.

She glanced at Brock, who nodded, giving her an encouraging smile. Taking a deep breath, she poured two glasses and handed him one.

Nervous. She was really nervous, Brock thought. He wished he could help her and Mac get through this. But it was a mine field they'd have to make their way through on their own. He was more than a little curious how they'd go about it. Taking the lemonade, he sat down in the easy chair and watched Mac examining a large watercolor hanging over the mantle.

"Did you do this?" he asked Carrie.

"Yes." It was one of her earlier paintings, done in soft pastels, before she'd experimented with the vibrancy of deep colors. She sipped as she watched him study her work. It didn't matter what he thought, she'd told herself. But she knew it did.

"I think I recognize the area. Where did you paint this?"

She walked closer, looking up at the familiar scene. "Outside Monterey. There's a little fishing village just off the coastal highway. I spent a lot of time there one summer." The summer she'd been pregnant with Shane.

"Yes, I know the place. You have a great feel for color and a good eye for detail." He turned to face her. "I'm sure you've been told quite often how very fine an artist you are."

"It's always nice to hear." Her hands were none too steady so she set down her glass and took the chair opposite Brock, leaving the couch for Mac. But he wasn't interested in sitting. His searching gaze seemed to be memorizing the room. Suddenly he spotted Shane's picture. Carrie turned to Brock.

"The painting's finished."

"I'll send the workmen for it first thing in the morning. Do you want to be there to direct the hanging?"

"No, I've already discussed it with Rhoda."

"Fine. She'll be in early." He leaned forward as Mac brought over Shane's picture and sat down on the couch to examine it further. "He's a good-looking boy, isn't he?"

"Yes, he is. Looks a great deal like his mother did at this age." His eyes met Carrie's violet ones, wary and watchful. "You were such a beautiful child, and you've grown into a lovely woman."

"Thank you."

Mac set the picture down with a sigh. "I know this is awkward, for both of us. Tell me about your mother, was she happy?"

And so it begins. Carrie took a deep breath. "I don't think so. She seemed to be searching for something she could never quite find. But everyone thought her very beautiful." At least until the last few years of her life. Carrie watched her fingers fold and refold a section of her skirt, wondering how much he wanted to know.

"Tell me how she died."

Carrie frowned. "Badly. Evidently, she'd been smoking in bed, fallen asleep and the house had caught on fire. She died of smoke inhalation before the fire trucks arrived."

He shook his head, his look compassionate. "You know, I was always trying to get her to quit smoking. What about you, were you there?"

"No, that was five years ago. I had her house repaired, rented it out, and I'm just in the process of selling it. It's in Pacific Grove. Is that where you...where you sent the letters?"

He leaned forward, resting his elbows on his knees, looking a little weary, the line around his eyes deep. "No. Through the Monterey Post Office. Box 229. I sent so many of them, Carrie, one every couple of weeks. Brock here often mailed them for me. I hope you believe me."

She wanted to, she realized. "I sent you lots, too. I mailed you my report cards from school. I invited you to my graduation and...and to my wedding. I..." She swallowed hard, trying not to let the tears take over. "I don't know what happened."

Mac ran a shaky hand over his face. "Natalie never forgave me, I'm sure."

"It's hard to forgive a husband who orders you from your home and tells you never to return." She hated the way her voice shook, but some things had to be said.

"You're right, it must be. Natalie and I quarreled that evening, quarreled severely. She said things, about the past, about...well, that doesn't matter now. I lost my temper. I went storming out, and the next day, I was filled with remorse. But you were both gone. I've had eighteen years to regret how I lashed out that night. Natalie and I had our differences, but I never meant to hurt you, Carrie."

"They weren't easy years for me, either."

Mac's look was beseeching. "Carrie, you've been married since then, and you must know. Sometimes a husband and wife quarrel over...over many things. It has nothing to do with the child."

She remembered her fights with Rusty. If Shane had been alive, he'd have had little to do with them. "I suppose."

"Your mother was...difficult. We wanted different things from life."

Carrie could relate to that easily, knowing she and Rusty had wanted different things also. She looked at the man who was her father and saw the sincerity, the pain. If only she could trust him. "Why didn't you come looking for me, try harder to find me?"

Brock saw the anguish on Mac's face but kept silent.

"I didn't have much money yet then, and I hadn't a clue where to start looking. It was a full two years before Natalie finally wrote me and told me that you were doing well. She asked for money, and I sent it. She promised that she'd write an occasional note and even send pictures if I'd agree not to make trouble for her, as she put it. If I came after you, she said she'd take you away again, and this time I'd never hear another word of you again. I knew she was capable of all that and more. So I waited for bits and pieces through the post office box. And in each letter, I sent you money. On your birthday, and holidays, I sent gifts, clothes, toys."

Carrie clutched her hands tightly in her lap. "I never saw a single dollar, nor a single gift."

Mac took a deep breath. "Your mother must have been so angry with me that she threw away my letters to you."

"Why? I was very young. She could have taken the money without my permission. To keep me from knowing that you cared about me would be so . . . so cruel. I know she was unthinking and irresponsible, but I never thought of her as deliberately cruel."

"She knew how very much keeping you from me would hurt me."

"I don't know." With a shaky hand, she picked up her lemonade and took a long swallow. Could Natalie have done that to her own daughter?

Mac stood and walked to her chair. "Carrie, I can't force you to believe that I tried to keep in touch with you, that I wanted to find you. But it would give me great joy if you could believe that I never stopped loving you. We've lost a lot of years. Won't you please let me try to make up for some of them?"

Blinking back the tears, Carrie got to her feet. "I want to believe you," she said sincerely. She saw his eyes move from her face to the gold heart that dangled on a chain around her neck. Slowly he reached over and touched it.

"I gave you this, on your tenth birthday, just before you left."

Her hand moved to cover his. "I wear it always." She saw that his eyes were damp, too.

"Do you have room in your life for me, Carrie? You and Shane?"

Wordlessly she moved into his embrace and closed her eyes as his arms hugged her tightly to him. What difference did it make who had done what eighteen years ago? Her father was back, and she'd never truly stopped caring. At last, Mac let her go as Brock came up to them.

"Wait until you meet Shane, Grandpa," Brock said, clapping him on the back. Quietly his arm slid around Carrie as she swiped at a tear on her cheek. "You all right?"

Carrie nodded, glad for the comfort of his presence.

"I can't wait to meet that boy," Mac said, a smile lighting his face. "Brock tells me he's smart as a whip."

"I'm a little prejudiced, but I think so."

"Is he coming home tonight?"

"No, but I'll bring him to the opening tomorrow. He'll be thrilled."

Mac moved toward the door. "That'll make two of us." His hand on the door frame, he turned back to look at both of them. Brock's arm was still around Carrie. "I can take the car back to the house, Brock.

Why don't you stay on a while? That is, if Carrie will drive you home later?''

The sly old fox. Brock looked down at Carrie. She'd had a very emotional hour. Maybe she could use a little unwinding in his arms. He waited for her answer, a question in his eyes.

"Yes, why don't you stay?" Carrie asked.

Brock handed Mac the keys without a word.

"Fine." Mac held out his hand to his daughter. "One more hug for the road?"

Smiling, she moved into his arms and kissed his cheek. "Thank you for coming."

"No, I thank you. I'll see you tomorrow."

She felt Brock's arms slide around her as Mac went down the front steps and climbed into the Ferrari. With a quick wave, he went sailing down the road and out of sight. She turned to look up at Brock.

"You told him about us?"

"Not a word. He didn't know a thing until he suggested I stay and you agreed." He saw her make a face. "Are you upset that he's also probably guessed that we're lovers?"

She moved her hands up his shoulders and around his neck. "Is that what we are, lovers?"

"Yes, it is. Come inside and let me show you."

"What a good idea." She bumped the door shut with her hip and reached up for his kiss.

In a town that liked to keep a low profile, the opening of a new office building didn't exactly warrant front-page coverage. Nevertheless, Carrie was amazed to note, the publicity department had evidently done their job well, for the press from several area papers were represented at the gala opening of the McKamey

Building. As she parked her Volkswagen in the crowded lot, she turned off the engine with a sigh, bracing herself for the event.

"Come on, Mom," Shane urged, his hand on the door handle, "let's go inside."

She'd had some anxious moments that morning as she'd picked Shane up from Sonya's and sat him down to explain about meeting his grandfather this afternoon. She'd wound up feeling grateful for the resilience of youth as Shane accepted the thought readily and eagerly looked forward to the meeting. Stepping out of the car now and taking his hand, she smiled down at her son looking so grown-up in his yellow shirt and white slacks.

"Hold on, tiger," she said, as the boy all but pulled her along. "It's going to be a long day."

"Brock's going to be here, too, right?"

"Yes. And so are a lot of other people. You stay close beside me, okay?"

"Sure, Mom. Only I don't have to hold your hand like a baby, do I?"

Carrie shook her head. "Not if you stay where I can see you." She led the way through the glass doors into the lobby.

As promised, her painting was the focal point of the large foyer, gently dominating the room. Carrie stood for a moment, seeing it in place for the first time. She'd chosen to depict a calm sea at night with Big Sur as a backdrop, a full moon illuminating the magnificent mountains and the beauty of the still water. The serene colors blended well with the blues and grays of the lobby. Yes, she was pleased.

Shane tugged at her hand, and she looked up. Odd how her eyes naturally found Brock first, even in the mob milling around, sampling champagne, chatting and admiring both the painting and the understated elegance of the decor. It wasn't just because he was taller and better looking than most. What was it then? she asked herself as she saw him turn and smile at her in that intimate way he had, the way that made everyone else in the room disappear. She recognized a special hello meant only for her in his dark blue gaze. Carrie felt a spreading warmth as she returned his smile across the crowded room and saw him heading toward them.

At her side, he touched her cheek for a moment, then turned to Shane. "Hey, sport, what do you think of all this?"

"Sure are a lot of people here," Shane said, looking around. Though he had an outgoing nature, he hadn't spent a lot of time in crowds and looked a bit hesitant.

"They've come to see your mom's painting and your grandpa's building."

"Where is my grandpa?"

Brock raised his eyes to Carrie. "I think it's time you met him. Shall we go to his office?"

Carrie nodded, a shade nervous herself. She found this all a little unnerving, rediscovering a father and learning he'd be an integral part of the community from now on. At least his company would, for she had no idea how much time, if any, Mac would be spending in the Carmel area personally. All things she'd have to find out, she thought as she followed a chattering Shane and Brock down the corridor that led to the private offices.

First Brock showed them his office and introduced Shane to Rhoda whose inquisitive gaze, Carrie thought, lingered longer than usual on both her and her son. She knows, Carrie decided, and she's not quite sure if she approves. She felt like taking the woman aside and telling her not to worry, that she'd only borrowed Brock for a few weeks and that, very soon now, she and Mac and the company would have him back full-time. Feeling a pang of depression taking over, Carrie plastered on a smile and went on to her father's office.

The meeting went better than she'd dared hope as the effusive young boy and the gentle man whose face was alight with pleasure got acquainted.

"What happened to your front teeth?" Mac asked, smiling at Shane who'd scooted up into one of the leather chairs facing his big desk.

"They fell out, but new ones are coming in. I rode in this big plane. Brock says it's yours. Is it really?"

"Yes, it is. Did you have a good time?"

"Yeah. My dad was a pilot. Could we go again some time?"

"We certainly can. Where would you like to go?"

"Australia. That's where Crocodile Dundee lives. Have you ever been there?"

Mac chuckled. "No, and I'd like to scc it, too."

Sitting in the chair alongside her son, Carrie thought things had gone far enough. She had no intention of allowing her father to do what Brock was so good at, making future plans that business obligations would keep him from carrying out. "Shane, Australia's very far away, and your grandfather's a busy man."

Mac stood and moved alongside Brock who was leaning against the desk. "Not *that* busy." He touched

Shane's dark curls as the boy's big eyes watched him. "Maybe one day we can arrange a trip together."

Carrie felt a flash of annoyance. "Shane has a tendency to take statements like that at face value. Please don't promise him grandiose things that likely won't ever occur."

Mac looked genuinely taken aback. "I think he *should* take my statements at face value. And I assure you I won't make a single promise to him or you, grandiose or otherwise, that I won't follow through on. What made you think otherwise?"

She stood her ground. "I don't want him disappointed. You won't be here for long."

"On the contrary. I've changed my plans. I'm staying on for a while." He smiled warmly down at Shane. "I have a family to get to know." He glanced over at Brock. "We have a big staff, and they're well equipped to run things. I deserve some time off, as Brock is always trying to tell me."

"That's right," Brock agreed. He saw that Carrie still looked skeptical. Well, he'd warned Mac that she didn't trust easily.

"Does that mean you'll have time to come visit us and meet my pets, Grandpa?" Shane wiggled off the chair. "I've got a goat, and Jonathan just had four kittens. You can have one if you want."

Smiling, Mac took the boy's hand. "Kittens, eh? I'd love to meet your pets. Do you want to come with me so I can introduce you to some people?"

Shane glanced at his mother. "Can I, Mom?"

Carrie saw no graceful way to refuse. "Yes, certainly."

On his way to the door, Mac turned. "Did I tell you, Carrie, that your painting is magnificent and worth every penny?'' He acknowledged her smile with one of his own, then took Shane's hand in his. "I'll keep a careful eye on him,'' he assured her as they left the room.

Brock took Carrie's hand and pulled her up and into a light embrace, placing a kiss in her hair. "That wasn't so difficult, was it?''

"I guess not." She sighed heavily. "I wish I didn't feel as though I've lost control of things.''

"It'll take some getting used to." He leaned back from her, his hands resting on her waist. "Have I told you that you're easily the most beautiful woman in the building, maybe the town?''

She couldn't help but smile at that. "No, I think I probably would have remembered that.'' Looking into his eyes, she couldn't help but think how very much her life had changed since this one man had come on the scene. And how it would change again when he left. But she didn't want to think about that.

"You are, you know." He fingered the lapel of her brown linen suit jacket. "This is nice, but you're far more beautiful when you're wearing nothing at all.''

"Brock, honestly!''

He loved to make her blush. "As soon as this is over, what say we go someplace where I can take this outfit off you, slowly piece by piece and . . .''

The door pushed open noisily. "So, this is the lady who's kept our Brock so busy he doesn't even have time to check in with the home office now and then.'' The tall blonde sauntered closer. "I believe we met several weeks ago, Ms. Weston, you may recall. I'm Francine Thomas.'' Her cool blue eyes shifted to Brock. "Hello, darling. I've missed you.''

Chapter Eleven

She doesn't mean anything by it. She calls everyone darling." Brock sat in the passenger seat of Carrie's Volkswagen, watching the testy way she was driving and trying to talk her out of her sudden anger.

"What a precious habit." Carrie's hands hurt from gripping the wheel. She was usually a careful driver, but she felt her foot press harder on the gas pedal, anxious to get home where she felt comfortable and safe.

Aware of Shane sitting in the backseat, Brock tried to keep his voice level. "You have to take Francine with a grain of salt."

"I don't have to take Francine at all. But you could have warned me that she feels you're her personal property."

"That's absurd, and you know it."

She shot him a cool look. "Is it?"

He shifted his long legs in the cramped quarters. Maybe she had a small point. "We work well together, and I admit that perhaps Francine thought that one day we might wind up together. I never encouraged that, but she probably regards you as a threat to her plans."

"Well, you can march right back there and assure her that I'm not in this race to capture Mr. Brock Logan, and she can relax. Matter of fact, I can turn around and take you back so you can put her mind at ease immediately."

"That won't be necessary." He was getting annoyed. "I want to be with you."

"Lucky me."

"Carrie, stop this! And slow down before we wind up wrapped around a tree."

Carrie tapped on the brakes and told herself to calm down as the radio station slid from a news broadcast to an old fifties tune.

"Why in hell don't you get that fixed?" he asked, giving in to an unreasonable anger. This day that had started out so beautifully was quickly turning into a battleground. Damn Francine!

Carrie gritted her teeth. "Now, let's see, you don't like my radio, the way I let my cat wander about getting pregnant, my overprotective attitude toward my son, my so-called indifference to my father or the way I choose to live secluded on a mountain away from the world. Why on earth are you here?"

"Because I love you." That stopped her. Brock saw her foot dance over the brake pedal and in the silence of the car, the radio station flip-flopped again. He waited.

Her heart pounding, Carrie tried to hang on to her anger. "I hate the way you throw things out like dangling carrots in front of a donkey. Football games, diving lessons, offers of love. And you don't mean, you can't mean..."

"I never meant anything more in my life."

"Mom, I'm hungry," Shane said from the backseat. "There's the golden arches."

Her son had never heard her quarrel with anyone, Carrie realized. The boy wasn't as much hungry as trying to diffuse the sudden tension that frightened him. She took a deep breath and tried to sound natural. "Not today, Shane. I'll make you a sandwich when we get home." She glanced at Brock. "Could we discuss this later?"

"Fine with me."

Carrie drove on, the radio serenading them with Broadway show tunes as her mind churned.

It was still churning after the hot dog lunch around the kitchen table where she'd tried to keep a normal conversation going with Shane so he'd not worry. At last he asked to be excused, and she watched him run outside with a wave of relief. She felt Brock's eyes on her as she rose to clear the dishes and knew the next few minutes were going to be difficult.

"I'm sorry if I overreacted," she began, her back to him as she stood at the sink.

"And I'm sorry if I goaded you on." He rose and turned her to face him. "Leave the dishes. We need to talk."

Here it comes, Carrie thought. The goodbye scene. She'd been expecting it. "Go ahead. I'm listening."

"Did you hear what I said in the car, that I love you?"

Her eyes were riveted on the third button of his shirt. "I heard you."

"Well?"

"Well, what? You don't have to give me a string of pretty words. I've already gone to bed with you, more than once."

He grabbed her shoulders, his own anger building. "Bed? This isn't about bed. I love your son, and I love you, do you understand?"

She met his eyes. "Do you?"

"Yes, I want to marry you."

She shook her head. "And what does marriage mean to you? Does it mean that I pack up my paints and my son and move to Chicago with you? And then the following year to London or wherever you and my father decide to open another branch? Does it mean that you get to call the shots, and I get to say 'yes sir'? Or does it mean you give up your dream and accept me the way I am?"

Brock swallowed his exasperation. "Carrie, I make a lot of money. You won't have to work unless you want to, and you can paint anywhere. I can give Shane the best education possible. You won't have to take in washing, or live in someone else's house. We can live anywhere we want, and we can hire someone to do *your* wash."

"You still don't understand." Her voice was getting shrill, so she took a moment to calm herself. "You don't want to marry me, you want to change me. To make me into a dark-haired Francine. The agreeable, perfect partner who'll follow you to the ends of the earth, live where you want, just for the wonder of your company and the contents of your wallet. You want to take away the independence I've fought so hard for.

Well, I don't need your money or your travel plans. I can provide just fine for Shane. I have thoughts and needs of my own. You're not offering love. You're taking away my freedom."

He was having trouble hanging on to his temper. "I thought you cared about me, that you..."

"I do." Fitfully her hands clutched his shirtsleeves. "But I won't live a vagabond life-style, not even for you. I've had a marriage where the man set the rules and I ran along behind like a worshipful puppy. I'm not playing that scene again. I'm not asking you to change. Why must you ask me?" She waved her hand helplessly. "Why can't we just stay the way we are? You come visit when you can, if you want, and I'll... I'll live the way I please." Was that what she wanted? Dear God, what *did* she want?

Brock's face closed in, turning hard. "Is a quick roll in the hay and a day at the beach enough for you?" He watched the blood drain from her face as her startled eyes jumped to his. But he wasn't going to back down. He was fighting for his life here.

Carrie pushed away from him. "Please leave. Right now."

"I wish you'd listen to reason."

"I've listened to all I'm going to."

At the kitchen doorway, he looked back a last time. "We could have had such a good life together." He hated the bleak look in her eyes, knowing he'd put it there. But she was damn stubborn and terribly wrong. Maybe if he left her alone awhile, she'd reconsider and realize he was right.

"I knew the day you walked into my life that you'd hurt me. I wish I'd have listened to my instincts then."

She was beyond talking to. He turned and made his way to the front door. He was too angry to say good-bye to Shane just now.

Carrie gazed out the back screen and saw that Shane was busy playing with his cars in a sandpile. She wanted to scream, to cry, to lash out. But she didn't. She'd known all along it would end. She just hadn't known how badly. Slowly she sat down at the kitchen table and laid her head on her folded arms. She was too sad to weep. She was too busy mourning.

Carrie stared at the canvas on the easel, fighting a mad urge to rip it off and start over. Nothing seemed to go right lately, including her work. Shane had been pestering her to go camping again, but she simply couldn't face climbing that mountain where far too many memories lay like traps waiting to snare her raw emotions. It had been pouring rain for two days. And she hadn't been able to find a home for any of the kittens who, along with their mother, were all over the house. She felt hot, irritable and bone tired. With a self-pitying sigh she hated, she put aside her brushes and decided to call it a day.

A whole week since Brock had walked away. Damn, why couldn't she stop thinking of him? She was better off. She should have been smart enough not to let herself get involved with a man again. But she'd been coaxed in by his tender manner, his sense of humor, his lean good looks and his strong hands warming parts of her she hadn't even known were cold until his touch.

It was going to be harder this time. With Rusty, she'd wanted out, wanted to forget the humiliation of his other women and his cavalier ways. But Brock had taught her body to respond, and now the nights she lay awake longing for him were twice as long as the days when she couldn't erase his features from the screen of her mind. She had only herself to blame, she realized. A woman could be forgiven a first mistake at loving, but the second marked her a hopeless fool. Carrie wasn't comfortable with the label.

The slam of the front door and the thundering of running feet announced that Shane was on his way to her. Automatically she put on a smile. She simply had to stop brooding for his sake.

"Mom, mom! Guess who's here? Grandpa." He stopped before her. "Come see." She rose as she heard him follow Shane into her studio.

"Hello, Carrie," he said in his quiet voice. "I hope you'll forgive my dropping in this way."

"Certainly. How are you?" She still couldn't make herself call him *dad* and Mac seemed too impersonal.

"Fine, fine." His careful perusal of her face told her he could tell she was less than fine herself. "I'm interrupting your work."

"No, actually I've finished for the day. Would you like some iced tea? It's such a hot day." Always a safe topic, the good old weather.

"That would be nice." Mac slid his arm around Shane's shoulders as they walked to the kitchen. "I was just telling Shane out in the yard that I have to fly to Los Angeles this afternoon to pick up some papers, and I'd sure appreciate some company."

Pouring the tea, Carrie sent him a look she hoped told him that she knew a flimsy excuse when she heard one. "Is that right? Everyone else in the company is so busy the president has to run around picking up papers?'' She handed him the frosty glass and gentled her words with a knowing smile.

He coughed into his fist, acknowledging her astuteness. ''I admit to perhaps a small ulterior motive here.'' He sat down and touched the velvety leaf of the African violet in the center of the table. ''Since you've finished for the day, would you and Shane indulge an old man and come with me? We could have dinner there and be back by Shane's bedtime.''

''Yeah, Mom,'' Shane piped in, kneeling on the chair next to her. ''Doesn't that sound neat?''

''It does, indeed, but I have something I must do this afternoon.''

Mac tried his most persuasive tone. ''Can't it be put off a day?''

''I'm afraid not. My realtor called and insisted I clear out the few things remaining in Natalie's house. The closing is to take place tomorrow, and the buyers are to have immediate possession.''

''I see.'' Mac glanced at the disappointment on Shane's face and shifted gears. ''Then I'd ask you for a favor, Carrie. Please allow me to take Shane alone. I promise I won't take my eyes from him for a moment.''

Carrie let out a heavy breath. No one but Sonya had ever watched Shane. Mac was like a stranger to them yet. But as she looked at her son's eager face, and her father's hopeful eyes, she knew she couldn't say no. She may not know the man Mac had become, but she knew the father who'd treated her like a princess for ten years. She gave them both a smile. ''I don't see why not.''

As Shane gave a jubilant shout, Mac's hand reached out to cover hers. ''Thank you for trusting me. I hope you know I want only to get to know both of you better, to spend time with you. I've got a great deal of love stored up that needs to be distributed.''

She smiled at his wording. It was time to let go of the hurtful memories. She'd lost Brock, but he'd given her her father, and for that she was grateful. "We love you, too, Dad." She saw the quick moisture spring into his eyes and noticed that he didn't bother to hide his emotions.

"I've waited such a long time for this. I'll make everything up to you, Carrie. I swear I will.''

"There's nothing to make up for anymore. Let's let the past be. We have a lot of good years ahead to enjoy each other.''

"Yes, thanks to Brock." Mac took a sip of his tea and watched her over the rim of the glass.

Carrie stiffened and the smile slid from her face as she fought to conceal her reaction. "Shane, why don't you go wash up if you're going with Grandpa? And change into your tan pants and that checkered shirt you like so much, okay?''

"Okay. You can come see the fish tank Brock got me, Grandpa.''

"In a minute, Shane." He watched the boy run off to his room.

Carrie cleared her throat. "How is Brock these days?" If she inquired of him casually, as she would about any friend, then perhaps Mac would let it drop.

Mac crossed his long legs. "He was like a caged lion after the opening. So I sent him to Chicago to clear up a matter there. But he called me yesterday, restless as a cat. He gets like that, you know. Always has. Likes to be on the move. I told him to fly to London and look for a site for a possible branch office there.''

Carrie nodded. "So he's in London. Well, that's where he wanted to be, off scouting new frontiers."

Mac studied her a long moment. "Would I be out of line if I asked if you two have a special relationship?"

"I thought we did."

"Funny, that's what he said when I asked him the same question."

She shrugged as her fingers busily wiped the moisture from her tea glass. "We realized we wanted different things from life. Just like you and Natalie. I made that mistake once, too. I don't want to risk another failure."

"Yes, failures can hurt. Living without someone you love can hurt, too. People who're afraid to risk may not get hurt, but they're only half alive. Being alone isn't much fun. I'm rather an expert on that."

Carrie tilted her chin. "I have Shane. And I have my work. You poured yourself into work, and look how successful you've become. Maybe Brock's leaving was the best thing that could have happened." She almost believed the lie.

"Maybe." Mac drained the glass and stood. "I think I'll go check out Shane's fish tank. You sure you won't change your mind and come with us?"

"Positive, thanks. I don't look forward to it, but I've got to get over to Natalie's place for the last time."

"All right, then, another time."

"Yes, the next time." she watched him walk down the hallway. In his mid-fifties, he was still an attractive man, and she wondered why he'd never remarried. Had he loved Natalie, despite her many shortcomings, so much that no one else would do? She shut her eyes, and Brock's image appeared on her closed eyelids. Yes, she could well imagine her father's inability to forget. Some people fell deeply in love only once, and sometimes it was with the wrong person.

The sound of her steps on the kitchen floor echoed through the silent rooms as Carrie inspected the job the cleaning crew she'd hired had done in Natalie's house. The carpeting looked as good as could be expected after four years of renters. And, though the whole place needed both paint and tender loving care, all in all, she wasn't ashamed to turn it over to the new owners. She was, however, still appalled at the price they'd paid for the small two-bedroom cottage, even though the location was desirable.

She'd never lived in this house really, so the memories weren't too many. Natalie had purchased it somehow the year Carrie had begun art school and moved in to live with Sonya. She'd visited her mother here on occasion, but mostly Natalie preferred meeting her at restaurants for a quick lunch or at Sonya's, where she'd inevitably get invited to dinner. Carrie glanced around at the faded wallpaper and the droopy curtains and shook her head. One last chore, to clean out the basement's back room, and she'd wash her hands of this dismal place.

The basement steps were rickety and the lighting poor, but she noticed that the central area that the tenants had used for storage was neat and tidy. She snapped on the overhead bulb in the back room and saw that it contained only a few pitiful remnants of her mother's life. A bent and scratched old filing cabinet had drawers that were difficult to open and proved to be empty. She moved to the corner where a trunk with a large lock hanging on it sat.

Locked, of course, and no key in sight. Carrie sat back on her haunches, thinking. What in the world would Natalie have kept locked up in an old trunk? Glancing around, she saw no tools left behind, or anything she could use to force off the lock. Oh, nuts! She'd get someone to help her haul it outside for the trash truck to pick up and be done with it. Probably old clothes and nothing more.

Grabbing hold of the two handles, she yanked to see if she could move it closer to the stairs and noticed that the hinges were rusty and loose. Her curiosity aroused, she knelt down and gave it a serious pull. More give. Maybe she wouldn't need to remove the lock to check out the contents. She tugged harder and felt the lid open from the back as the hinges gave way. Peering inside in the dim light, she saw papers and envelopes. She wouldn't be surprised if they turned out to be old bills that Natalie had never gotten around to paying.

Rising, she pulled on the lid and dragged the trunk over to the stairs leading up, where the light was brighter. Bending, she picked an envelope out of one pile. A letter addressed to her in an unfamiliar handwriting. Slowly she moved her eyes to the postmark. Chicago. Carrie sat down heavily on the bottom step.

She picked up another and another. All the same handwriting, all addressed to her at P.O. Box 229, Monterey, California. Her father's lost letters. He hadn't been lying and, dear God, Natalie had kept them all from her. Why?

With shaky fingers, she turned one over and saw it had been slit open. Removing the two pages, she quietly read the letter. He'd chatted on, asking questions about her well-being, hoping school was fun, wondering why she didn't write to him. And telling her to spend the fifty dollars enclosed as she saw fit. But there was no money. Carrie rubbed her forehead with a dusty hand.

Had her mother hated Mac so much that she took this way to punish him for banishing her from their home? Perhaps that was why she drank so much, trying to escape from her own terrible deeds. The poor, sad woman. Carrie's anger was gone, replaced by a wave of pity for a woman who'd never found happiness. She'd robbed her daughter and Mac, not just of the money but of years of knowing one another, yet she hadn't enjoyed her vengeance. Sighing, Carrie moved to the second pile of letters.

Her curiosity turned to shock when she saw they were the letters she'd written to her father, some in her early childish scrawl, all nicely stamped and neatly made out to the Chicago address she had memorized. Natalie had always volunteered to mail her letters for her, telling her she would be including a note of her own to Mac so it would be easier. With no reason to suspect a thing, Carrie had gone along with her mother's request. She had to show these to Mac, so he, too, would understand. Then maybe they could put all of the hurtful past to rest. Eighteen years was long enough to carry such a burden.

Just a few more, she thought as she opened another one at random to read. She'd read half a dozen more when she came across one that contained a receipt made out to Natalie McKamey from Phil Hebert in the amount of ten thousand dollars. Frowning, Carrie quickly skimmed the letter with growing suspicion.

"Oh, no," she groaned aloud as Mac wrote that the enclosed check was for her first year's tuition to art school and that there would be another the following year if she did well. So that was how Natalie had paid for this crummy house, with Carrie's tuition money. Fighting tears, thinking of how long it had taken her working part-time after school, living for next to nothing at Sonya's, scrimping to make it through school, Carrie felt like weeping.

She sat there, shuffling through the letters, feeling empty inside. She and Natalie had never been close, but this seemed to make even the memory of a self-indulgent, neurotic woman more painful to bear. Shaking back her hair, Carrie decided she simply would never understand her mother's motivations or her twisted thinking.

Caught up in the past, she decided she'd read just a few more letters. She shoved her hand to the bottom of the pile and scrounged around, searching for one of the earlier letters her father had mailed her. She noticed they seemed to be heaped chronologically on top of one another, so it would stand to reason that the initial ones were near the bottom. Pulling out an old one, she read with sadness how he'd seen her art award and how proud he was of her. Fishing around some more, she brought another up, checked the date and saw that it had been sent approximately two years after their arrival in California.

It was longer than the others she'd read and addressed to Natalie this time, carrying a plea for understanding. Mac wrote of his loneliness and his love for Carrie. Deeply moved, she read on. She was nearly to the end when she read something startling. Her hands trembling, she stood and held the thin paper closer to the light, reading its shocking message a second time.

No, it couldn't be!

Pocketing the letter, Carrie ran up the stairs and turned off the light, leaving the trunk where she'd dragged it to. She left the house, locking it securely, and jumped into her car, breathing hard. A quick glance at her watch told her it was not yet dinnertime. She had a long wait until Mac and Shane would return. And she had a lot to think about.

The crickets were buzzing in a hazy twilight when Carrie heard Mac pull Brock's Ferrari up next to her Volkswagen. Putting out the cigarette she'd been smoking, she listened to Shane's happy chatter as they walked toward the house and heard Mac's low, rumbling laugh. They'd evidently had a good day together and she was glad. She rose from the chair where she'd been waiting and stretched her stiff muscles.

"Hi, Mom," Shane yelled running to her and hugging her. "You should have been with us. We circled all around the sky and Grandpa showed me where they make movies and we flew over Disneyland. Then we had dinner at this super place way up high in this big building. Fried chicken and chocolate ice cream."

"Sounds like you two had a great time."

"We did," Mac said, "but we missed you."

Carrie kept her smile in place. "I missed you, too." She caught the yawn Shane tried to muffle. "You've had a long day, young man. Time for you to thank Grandpa and hit the sack."

"Aw, Mom, can't I stay up just a little longer?"

"Shane." The warning was accompanied by a frown.

"We'll have more good times, Shane," Mac told him. "Come give me a hug."

Shane rushed over and hugged him tight. "Thanks, Grandpa. It was super."

"I thought so, too."

"I'll be right back," Carrie told Mac as Shane ran to his room. "I just want to see him settled."

"I should run along."

"No, please wait. I...I want to ask you something." Carrie saw a quick, curious expression appear on his face, and he nodded and sat down on the couch. Taking a cigar from his shirt, he toyed with it thoughtfully. She walked after Shane.

She returned in less than ten minutes. "I think he was asleep before his head hit the pillow," she said, taking the chair opposite him. "Thank you for showing him such a good time."

"My pleasure." Mac leaned forward, his eyes alert. "What is it you wanted to ask me?"

Carrie cleared her throat. "I'd like to know why you never told me that you're not my real father."

Chapter Twelve

Mac sat quietly reading the letter Carrie had handed him. He'd visibly paled at her question and asked where she'd heard that, and she'd handed him the damning evidence. She watched him finish, draw in a deep breath of air and sit back as he brought his eyes to hers.

"I'm glad it's out, but I didn't tell you for several reasons. First, I had no contact with you until recently. And when I did, I wasn't about to jeopardize our tenuous reunion with news that might very well shatter our new relationship. I hope you'll try to understand the circumstances."

Carrie wasn't sure how she felt at the moment. She only knew she wanted the truth. "I'm listening."

Mac rubbed a hand over his face, gathering his thoughts. "I've already told you that your mother and I quarreled that last night in Chicago, which you probably remember. It was always about the same thing. Perhaps you heard snatches of our disagreements, perhaps you were too young to understand what you heard, I'm not sure. At any rate, Natalie just couldn't manage to stay at home, with you and me. She was very young when I married her, barely nineteen and very beautiful. And spoiled, terribly spoiled, to which I contributed, at first."

Mac glanced up, and when he saw her clear violet gaze on him, he continued. "I desperately wanted to succeed, and I worked long, long hours to achieve financial security, for all of us. When Natalie told me shortly after we were married that she was pregnant, I was overjoyed. She was not. She hated losing her figure and she was bored staying home. She hated keeping house, and, though I believe, in her own way, she loved you after you were born, she wasn't too keen on caring for a baby, either. So after a while, I brought work home, and she began to go out nearly every night. Do you remember sitting with me in the spare room, you messing around with the paints at the easel I made for you and me at my design table?"

"Yes, I remember a lot of evenings like that."

He nodded. "Well, long after I'd tucked you in, Natalie would come home, often drunk, occasionally bragging of parties she'd attended, men she'd met who really appreciated her, anything to taunt me."

"How long did she do this?"

"Oh, even before you were born. I'd often work late at the office in those days, and she became restless being alone so much."

Carrie's heart went out to him as she waited for him to continue.

"That particular night, she came home with her lipstick smeared, and she'd been drinking heavily. I'd about had it. I sent you to your room and I told her I was through putting up with her boozing and running around. I said I wanted a divorce, that I was taking you away from her, and that I'd have no trouble getting custody with her history. That's when she let me have it, told me that you weren't my daughter and that she'd been two months pregnant when we were married."

Carrie let out an almost audible gasp.

"You were so small, not even six pounds. It was easy to believe that you were premature. But something told me Natalie was speaking the truth that night. So I lost my temper and ordered her from the house. You probably overheard that, or she told you later. Please believe me, I was devastated. I didn't mean what I said."

"I . . . I understand," Carrie murmured, desperately trying to.

Looking suddenly older, Mac leaned back as if worn out. "I stormed out and spent the night walking around, cursing the fates and wondering what to do. But I couldn't escape one fact: I loved you. Carrie, please believe me. Fathering is more than biology. I'd loved you from the moment you were placed in my arms in the hospital, and I'd tried to be a good father every day you were with me."

She wanted to let him know she understood. She got up to sit beside him on the couch and reached over to touch his hand. "I remember. You were everything I could have wanted in a father."

Mac seemed to take heart in hearing her words. "I went back to our small apartment, not really knowing what I would do about Natalie, but absolutely certain about you. I intended to fight for you. Only you were both gone. It was two long years before I heard the first word from her. Now you know what she had over me, why I couldn't come to California and search you out after Natalie divorced me. I was legally your father, but I desperately didn't want you to learn that I wasn't biologically your father. I didn't think you'd understand. Perhaps I was wrong. At least, by sending money, I felt I was supporting you."

"Who knows if at that age I would have understood. I like to think I would have." She swiped at a tear that had trailed down her cheek. "I found all the letters you mailed. She'd saved them in this old trunk in her basement. All slit open and the money gone."

Mac shook his head. "How she must have hated me, laughing at my pleas to allow me to visit you, taking the money I'd intended for you."

"She was a bitterly unhappy woman, Dad. Something else. I want you to see the other letters in the trunk. The rest of yours and the ones I wrote to you. She never mailed them for me as I'd thought she had."

"I'd figured as much."

"Why do you suppose she saved all those letters?"

Mac shook his head. "I don't know. I can only guess at some point she wanted you to know the truth. Or at least some of it." He touched her cheek with a none-too-steady hand. "What a lot of wasted years."

"Yes. Oh, and the tuition money. She used it to buy a house. I found the receipt from the realtor. For years I'd wondered how she'd managed to purchase that house, when she seldom had more than beer in the refrigerator. I'd assumed one of her men friends had come up with the cash."

Mac took a deep, fortifying breath. "If you don't consider me your father after what you've learned, I'll try to understand."

Carrie didn't hesitate. She leaned closer and embraced him. "You're the only father I've ever known. I've never stopped loving you, and I want you to be a part of my life and Shane's."

Fighting a wave of emotion, Mac bent his head and kissed her hair. "I can't tell you what it means to hear you say that." After a moment, he eased back from her. "Could you find it in your heart to let this be our little secret? I'd like Shane to believe I'm his real grandfather."

"You *are* his real grandfather, the only one he's ever known. There is one other person I'd like to share this with. Brock. He kept telling me there had to be a solution, that somewhere there'd been a misunderstanding and that we were both good people and could work things out."

He leaned back to study her. "You're in love with him, aren't you?"

Carrie shifted her gaze out the window where the moonlight bounced off the hood of Brock's Ferrari. She'd faced the fact of her mother's deception and faced the return of her father. It was time to face her feelings about Brock. She'd been so afraid to let herself love again, but this week without Brock, she'd felt like a part of her was missing. If she didn't fight to get him back into her life, what would she have? A safe but lonely life, raising her son, putting aside her own needs. Then one day, Shane would leave her, as he must. And what would she be left with?

Only this afternoon, her father had admitted that failing hurt, but that living without love could hurt, too. He'd said that people who were afraid of the risk of loving may never get hurt, but they were only half alive. That's how she'd felt this past week, half alive, incomplete.

She turned back to Mac, considering her words carefully. "Yes, I love him. But we differ on one fundamental issue. He wants to change me, to take me and Shane from here to wherever he feels the urge to be. Chicago, London, some other place he fancies. I don't want that."

"You want him here with you?"

"Yes, but that will never happen. Brock wants to be on the move, to live in exotic locations, to be a mover and a shaker."

"Does he?" Mac sat back with a confident smile. "We'll see. I've known Brock a long while, and in some ways I think I know him better than he knows himself. I sent him to London for a reason, and I made sure he'd be all alone. You see, Carrie, London or Paris or Rome, wherever. They're all beautiful, romantic cities. But when you love someone and they're not with you, each one is the loneliest place on earth. Believe me, I've been there, and I know. But I couldn't *tell* that to Brock. He has to see it for himself. I knew exactly what his sudden restlessness was all about. He loves you, but he's too damn stubborn to admit he needs to compromise. Brock's a smart man. You wait and see. He'll be back. Unless I miss my guess, he simply won't find any beauty, any joy without you with him. Trust me on this."

"You really think he'll come back?"

"Yes, I do. But when he does, are you willing to do some compromising? Perhaps have California as your home base, but do *some* traveling? It wouldn't be like it was when you were a child, having to relocate with your mother. When you go with the one you love, there's an added dimension. Everything looks different. And it would be wonderful for Shane, seeing the world with two parents who love him.''

"I think I could live with that." Carrie smiled, the first genuine smile in a week. "How did you get to be so clever?"

Mac returned the smile. "A lot of living and a lot of pain." He stood, digging for his keys.

"I wish you'd have found someone who could make you happy."

Mac shrugged, dismissing the thought. "Some things aren't in the cards." He took her hand as she stood. "Now that I've found you and Shane, and the truth is finally out and you still accept me, I am happy. That's all I need."

Carrie moved closer to hug him, needing the physical contact. "I hope you're right about Brock."

"I am, you'll see." He cocked his head at her. "Do you remember my telling you a story a long while ago about the bear?"

Carrie nodded. "Yes. I shared that with Brock."

"Well, after this wonderful day spent with Shane and talking this way with you, I want you to know that today I ate the bear."

"I'm glad."

"Good night, Carrie."

"Good night, Dad." She stood watching him leave, leaning her head on the door frame. Would she ever again feel as if she, too, had eaten the bear? she wondered.

It was a perfect June night. Brock looked up at the myriad stars in the clear evening sky as he strolled along the bank of the Thames River. There was a lingering dampness in the air from an earlier rain shower, but the clouds had disappeared for now. He was relieved, for he was getting a little tired of daily downpours.

A young couple ambled past him, arm in arm, absorbed in each other and hardly aware of his presence. Shifting his eyes from them, Brock kept going. He had plenty of reason to feel satisfied for he'd accomplished what he'd set out to do and in a short two weeks. Mac would be pleased.

Brock felt certain Mac hadn't figured he'd find a possible site for a London branch of McKamey and Associates so quickly. The building was in a good location near Leicester Square, not far from Piccadilly. The traffic flow was excellent, the structure itself roomy, with the possibility of expansion present, and the price was right. He'd put down a deposit on a year's rent, lease negotiable, contingent upon Mac's approval within the next thirty days. Yes, all in all, a job well done. Then where, he wondered, was the accompanying elation?

He passed a white-haired woman selling violets from a pushcart and, on impulse, bought a small bouquet. His larger-than-necessary tip earned him a gap-toothed smile from the vendor. Inhaling their gentle fragrance, he walked on. Perhaps his melancholy could be traced to the weather, never too cheery or sunny in this part of the world. Or perhaps it was that he didn't know a soul in town. Of course, if he lived here a while setting up the branch, he'd get acquainted, make friends.

Thinking he owed himself a small celebration, he'd stopped tonight at a wonderful pub in Charing Cross, sampled their ale and enjoyed a filling, if somewhat bland, boiled beef dinner. He'd left his rented car in Trafalgar Square and decided to walk off his heavy meal, following Northumberland Avenue to the Thames. The river flowed silently by as he strolled north on Victoria Embankment.

The Embankment Gardens were just up ahead, carefully illuminated with strategic lighting. Brock stood at the entrance, thinking the scene would make a wonderful painting. Only the artist that came to mind usually painted seascapes. Maybe she could learn to do flowers.

Stuffing his hands in his pants pockets, he walked on. Why was Carrie so damn stubborn? Why couldn't she give it a try, come with him, taste life a little? Why would she want to hide out on a secluded mountain when she could have all he could give her? Why couldn't she bend a little?

He stopped to gaze into the dark waters, and his words echoed back at him. He hadn't exactly demonstrated to her that he was willing to bend even a little, he had to admit. He remembered a conversation he'd had with Rhoda not long ago where she'd told him that committing to someone involved a great deal of compromise. Had he been as stubborn as Carrie about compromising? Rhoda had lost a second chance at love because neither she nor the man she'd mentioned were willing to change, to give, to compromise. He'd thought that terribly sad, at the time. And now he had his own sad plight to consider, and for the very same reasons.

Two giggly teenage girls in short, tight skirts and high heels passed him, hurrying toward the bright lights of the city he'd just left behind. The trouble was that whether he was in the heart of that exciting city, or eating at the cozy pub, or walking along the Thames, nothing seemed right. Nothing pleased him or made him happy. Something was missing. More correctly, someone. Carrie.

Damn it, he loved her. Simple fact. Not so simple a solution to winning her. She was stubborn, determined and maddeningly independent. And from the day he'd found her, he could think of no one else. Now, gone from her for two weeks, he burned for her, his insides constantly churning, his concentration destroyed. Perhaps that was why he was surprised he'd been able to locate a building, for he had little interest in work, something that had never happened to him before.

Compromise. He stopped at a lamppost and stared up at the winking stars. All right, he would learn to compromise somehow. He'd never liked Chicago, anyway; perhaps he could convince Mac to let him move to California. Then maybe together, he and Carrie could build a house, on a mountain if she wanted, or along the seashore, where she could paint happily and there would be a large yard for Shane. And for other children. Brock tightened at the unbidden thought. Yes, he wanted Carrie to have his child, a sister for Shane, a little girl who'd look just like her mother.

Whoa, buddy! he warned himself. Would she marry him if he was willing to do all that? And would she compromise and go with him now and then? Could he make her see that if he gave her her dream, she needed to share his also? He'd patiently shown her the richness of physical love between a man and a woman. Could she also learn to trust him with her future?

Brock ran a hand through his hair, his mouth forming into a determined line. She would, by God. He'd *make* her see. Because he needed her. And he, who never thought he could, would bend for her.

A line from a song he'd heard that afternoon on the car radio came back to him—"I'd rather live in 'her' world than live without 'her' in mine." It played sweetly through his head and his heart as he came to a decision. Yes, they had lived in different worlds up to now. But having found Carrie, having loved her, he acknowledged that being without her wasn't living at all. With a satisfied smile, he turned and headed back in the direction he'd come.

A young girl of six or so was strolling toward him, her fingers clasped tightly in her bearded father's hand. With a silly bow, Brock presented her with the bouquet of violets, noting her shy smile of pleasure. Suddenly in a hurry, he picked up his pace on the way back to his car. As he rushed along, he wondered when the next flight to the States would be leaving.

The sand squished up through his bare toes as Brock walked along the Pacific shoreline. He'd parked on a side street and wound his way along a narrow access to the beach side, choosing to come up on Carrie's house from the back. Perhaps he wanted to give himself a little time. Perhaps he was just a little scared.

He'd arrived in the wee hours of the morning after an overnight flight, during which he'd scarcely closed his eyes. And when he had, scenario after scenario played across his mind as he wondered how best to approach Carrie. When he'd finally reached the house he'd been renting and found Mac having his morning coffee on the terrace, he'd blurted out his tale to his friend. It must have been jet lag, Brock decided, as confidences of a personal nature were not usual with him.

A low-flying gull swooped down and cawed at him before circling back to the sea. He inhaled the salty breeze and found it much more to his liking than the misty rain of London. His unexpected return hadn't come as a shock to Mac at all. Either the man knew him awfully well or he'd done so much living that surprises were indeed few and far between. His advice hadn't been complicated. Rather simple, really. *If you love her, go to her, tell her, make her see. And never make promises you don't intend to keep.* Sounded simple. Could he do that? Brock wondered. He could surely try. And he badly wanted to have the chance.

As he neared the bluff that jutted out from her backyard, he saw Shane sitting on a rock down near the shore, his hair blowing in the breeze, a fishing line dangling in the shallow water. On his shoulder sat Zeke, his mynah bird. He smiled at the picture the kid made in his white shorts, bare-chested and barefoot, his skin a golden tan. His son, maybe soon. If he played his cards right. Brock cleared his throat noisily.

Shane heard and turned his head. With a whoop, he dropped the pole in the sand, leapt from the rock and ran to him as Zeke fluttered off and squawked his own brand of welcome. Shane never simply walked anywhere. Brock stood still, grinning and waiting for the boy to reach him. In moments, he'd hurled himself into Brock's arms for a huge hug. Pleasure raced through him at the feel of the small, energetic body in his arms, filling him with an unexpected surge of love. Early on, the boy had wormed his way into his heart.

"Hey, sport. How you been?"

"Good. Grandpa took me up in his plane for hours and hours, and last week we went for a boat ride and fished off the bow. That's what they call the front of the boat. We didn't catch anything, but it was fun, anyhow."

Brock plopped himself down in the dry sand, and Shane followed suit as Zeke took up his post alongside him. "I'm glad to hear you've been having fun."

"Yeah." The boy's hands dug around in the sand until he found a small stone. Taking careful aim, he threw it out into the rolling waves. "Did you have fun, too?"

"Sort of. Not as much fun as I have here with you."

"Then why'd you go?"

The honesty of children. Brock met his questioning eyes. "I had a job to do. I did it, and I came back."

"I told Mom you'd come back."

His heart skipped a beat. "You and your Mom talked about me?"

"Yeah, a little."

"She told you I wasn't coming back?"

"No. She looked kind of sad, but she didn't want to talk much. So I asked Grandpa if he knew what was wrong. He said she missed you. So I told Mom not to worry, that I knew you'd come back. Grandpa said you would."

Brock found himself smiling. "He did, eh? Seems like Grandpa knows quite a bit."

"Sure does." Shane shifted sand through his fingers and watched the motion. "I like him a lot, but you know what?"

"What?"

He raised his blue-violet eyes to Brock's. "I still missed you."

Sliding an arm about him, Brock pulled him close. "I missed you, too, sport. And I need to ask you for a little advice."

Shane sat up taller, realizing the importance of such a request. "Sure. What?"

"I guess you know I'm pretty crazy about your mom."

"I saw you kissing her in the kitchen once. I never saw Mom kiss anyone else."

"Well, that's only part of it. I want to be with her, and you. I want to marry her."

"You mean stay with us forever?"

"Yes. I need to know how you feel about that, because I don't want to do anything that would make you unhappy."

Shane sat thinking a minute. "Would that mean you'd be my dad?"

"It sure would."

"You wouldn't leave us, you wouldn't make Mom cry?"

"I'd certainly try not to."

With all his accumulated seven-year-old wisdom, Shane nodded. "Then it's okay with me."

"Thanks, Shane." Brock looked out to sea. "The thing is, the last time I was here, I said some things I didn't mean to her, you know? She may still be mad at me, and I'm not sure how to approach her. You got any suggestions?"

Shane brought up his knees and dangled his arms on them. "Mom always tells me when you do something wrong you have to tell the person you hurt that you're sorry and that you'll try to do better from now on."

He looked down at the boy. "Think that's all there is to it?"

"One more thing. You got to hug her. A hug means you love someone even if you make mistakes."

Out of the mouths of babes. Nodding, Brock got to his feet and brushed off the seat of his jeans. "Okay, I'm going to try it. She's up at the house, right?"

"Yeah, she's painting, I think."

He ruffled Shane's hair. "Thanks, sport, for your help."

"Sure. Mom's always fair. She'll listen."

Brock walked toward the steps leading up to the yard. "I certainly hope you're right."

The climb up took forever, or did it just seem like that? Billie was bleating at the fence, evidently having forgotten him during his two-week absence. The more he tried to shush him, the more the damn goat brayed. Squeezing through the gate, Brock made his way to the door with Billie's horns giving short little unfriendly pushes on his rear pockets every step of the way. He hurried onto the porch as quickly and quietly as possible, shutting the screen door behind him. Taking a deep breath, he turned around.

She was standing in the doorway.

She looked more beautiful than he'd remembered, but her eyes were as wary as the first day he'd met her. She wasn't smiling, but she wasn't frowning, either. She simply waited.

He shuffled his feet uneasily, the idea of being at a loss for words because of one small woman unnerving him. "I...I was just talking to Shane, down on the beach." He watched her carefully, but she said nothing. "I came to see him because I needed his advice."

Carrie raised an eyebrow and crossed her arms over her chest. "Is that a fact?"

"Yeah. I told him I'd said and done some stupid things, and I didn't mean most of them. I told him I thought I'd hurt you, and I didn't know how to apologize. I've never been real good at that."

Her hands were damp so she blotted them on her cotton skirt, hoping he couldn't see. Her pulse beat double time as a tiny sliver of hope began to form. She'd come out to check on Shane minutes ago and had seen Brock sitting with her son, chatting man-to-man. Since then, heart in her throat, she'd stood waiting. Now it was showdown time. "No, I don't imagine you have. What did Shane advise you to do?"

He noticed the trembling of her lower lip. Feeling a small surge of confidence, he took two steps closer. "He told me to start by hugging you, because hugging means you love someone even if you make mistakes." Taking the biggest step of his life, Brock closed the short distance between them and put his arms around her.

She waited a heartbeat, then with a soft sigh, she brought her arms up to embrace him, moving her face into his throat. She heard his moan of welcome and choked back a sob of her own.

"I've been a damn, unbending fool, Carrie," he said into her hair. "I know it, and I admit it. I wanted you to do all the compromising. I'm sorry. I love you. Give me another chance, please."

She leaned back to look at him, her eyes bright with unshed tears. "I took too hard a stand, so afraid you'd take me off somewhere and . . . and grow tired of me and leave me."

He hadn't figured that one. Rusty had left her and turned to other women. He should have realized she'd be thinking along those lines. "Never. I've been so unhappy without you."

"Me, too. I hated realizing I needed you, but I do."

He kissed her then, his mouth hard on hers, his hands molding her to him, reassuring himself that she was really there locked in his arms. When he raised his lips from hers, he saw the smoky desire she didn't bother to hide and knew there'd never be another woman for him.

"I can't promise you I'll be perfect, but I'm sure as hell going to try to make you and Shane happy. I've talked to Mac about moving to California. Maybe you and I could draw up plans, build a house together, make it into a home. I've never had a real home, Carrie. I never thought I wanted one until I found you."

"Am I hearing right?" She pressed her seeking fingers into his hair. "Am I dreaming this?"

"I hope not. Would you agree to do some traveling, just now and then, when I have to go on company business, if it's not too often?"

"Yes. I need to compromise, too. I realized that after you left, with Dad's help."

Gently he framed her lovely face in his hands. "Carrie, I've never loved a woman before you. When the feeling began, I didn't recognize it, and when I did, I denied it. I'm new at this, and I have absolutely no experience at being a husband or a father. You'll have to teach me. But I'd like to try, if you'll take a chance on me."

"Yes, oh, yes." And she reached up for his kiss.

She hadn't known one could tell so much from one kiss. The homecoming, the promise, the joy of reunion. She let his mouth tell him what her heart already knew, that this time, it was for keeps. Today she'd truly eaten the bear.

At last, Brock eased back from her and was tucking a strand of hair behind her ear when they heard a noise at the porch steps. He glanced up as Carrie looked over her shoulder.

"Hey, you two," Shane called, "are you going to stand around kissing all day, or can we have some lunch?"

From his perch on the boy's shoulder, Zeke had to have the last word. "Hot damn!"

The shared laughter of the small family rang out and echoed down the bluff the sound of happiness.

* * * * *

Silhouette Romance®

LONG, TALL TEXANS

Diana Palmer brings you the second Award of Excellence title
SUTTON'S WAY

In Diana Palmer's bestselling Long, Tall Texans trilogy, you had a mesmerizing glimpse of Quinn Sutton—a mean, lean Wyoming wildcat of a man, with a disposition to match.

Now, in September, Quinn's back with a story of his own. Set in the Wyoming wilderness, he learns a few things about women from snowbound beauty Amanda Callaway—and a lot more about love.

He's a Texan at heart . . . who soon has a Wyoming wedding in mind!

The Award of Excellence is given to one specially selected title per month. Spend September discovering *Sutton's Way* #670 . . . only in Silhouette Romance.

RS670-1R

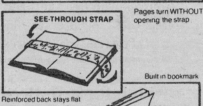

COMING SOON...

Indulge a Little
Give a Lot

An irresistible opportunity to pamper
yourself with free* gifts and help a
great cause, Big Brothers/Big Sisters
Programs and Services.

*With proofs-of-purchase plus postage and handling.

Watch for it in October!

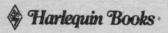

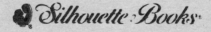

IND